SHE THIEF

DANIEL FINN

FEIWEL AND FRIENDS
New York

I would really like to thank Laura Cecil for
all her good and friendly advice, and the editorial
team at Macmillan, who've been brilliant.

A FEIWEL AND FRIENDS BOOK
An Imprint of Macmillan

SHE THIEF. Copyright © 2009 by Daniel Finn. All rights reserved.
Distributed in Canada by H.B. Fenn and Company, Ltd.
Printed in March 2010 in the United States of America by R. R.
Donnelley & Sons Company, Harrisonburg, Virginia. For information,
address Feiwel and Friends, 175 Fifth Avenue, New York, N.Y. 10010.

A CIP catalogue record for this book is available
from the British Library.

ISBN: 978-0-312-56330-1

Originally published as *Two Good Thieves* by Macmillan
Children's Books, a division of Macmillan Publishers Limited

First published in the United States by Feiwel and Friends,
an imprint of Macmillan

Feiwel and Friends logo designed by Filomena Tuosto

First U.S. Edition: 2010

1 3 5 7 9 10 8 6 4 2
www.feiwelandfriends.com

This is for Tom and Georgia because their shadows step through all the stories I tell.

Chapter One

THE CITY'S BURNING.

The city is always burning.

The big river is baked to a trickle of brown water. One time the docks were busy, now the ghosts of ships moor here, hulks rusting on the mud; and though the sea's just a few miles away only the rich go there, only the rich can go anywhere: down to the white beaches, up to their ranches or away to foreign lands; but when they are in the city they stay cool, in their cool offices behind tinted windows, in their cool gardens that hiss with water, in their cool shops with marble floors and air that streams cool as silk against their smooth faces.

The city is burning.

But the uptown streets are still full of people pushing through the heat and cars crawling slow and policemen—the hard men, in white hats and white gloves and black sunglasses—watching the cars and the people, watching for trouble, watching for scuffed-up children who should stick to their own quarter, not be hanging round up here, near the fancy shops.

They don't see her though because she's too smart to get noticed. She knows how to dress and where to stand. She knows how to drift up through the sweating crowds, maybe sticking close to this woman who could be her mother, to that man who could be her father. She knows how to keep her face blank so it doesn't seem as if she's noticing that woman's fat little purse or that man's thick wallet bulging inside his jacket. She knows how to look serious and sensible, like a good child.

She is a good child, maybe.

She could be twelve, doesn't know exactly how old she is,

doesn't know her real name either, or where she came from. Her skin's dark, flat brown, not like real city people—some of them are so pale they're almost white. They say she must come from upcountry, but there's no way of finding out for sure since she hasn't got any family.

It was Demi who found her sleeping out on the street when she wasn't any bigger than a bag of sweet potato, or so he says; found her down in Basquat, where the small-time farmers have their markets. That's how she got her name. Fay gave her the name. She said, "You gotta have a name, child. How am I gonna tell you things if you running round with no name? You want to make it through to the next meal, you gotta come when I call." So she and Demi called her Basquat for a while. Then Demi said she couldn't have a name that was longer than she was and so she became Baz.

She has no family, unless Fay and Demi are family. Demi is like a brother, and Fay like a big sister, maybe. Fay is the smart one, the one who fixes them up, tells them where to go and what to look for. They've been together for seven years now, seven years since Demi found her and Fay named her. Seven years of watching out for each other.

Baz is watching out for Demi now. She's the eyes looking for trouble while he does the work, moving through the sea of slow people like an eel. He is so neat, so fast, so quick. See him now, close up to this man, that man, to that lady with the big bag swinging on her skinny hip, and he's nothing more than a shadow. Blink and he's gone. Like a playing card: You look at it and it's got a face that looks right back at you, but you twist that card and it's got no side, slip it through a crack in the door and it's gone. That's Demi. Sometimes she thinks he must be a wisp of smoke, not a boy.

There! Done it. So neat you don't see a tear, you don't see a stitch. Nobody sees Demi but Baz. Makes her heart skip a little just to see him do it: one minute he's gliding along, seem like two paces between him and this lady; she pauses to look in a window full of dainty shoes, looks right in, and snap your fingers, he's at her shoulder. Then he's strolling on, passing Baz, slipping her a sweet little purse, a fat little egg. The woman steps into the shop. It could be half an hour before she finds today's a no-shoe day for her.

Baz dreams of being as good as Demi. He puffs up when she asks him how he does it. "You could be as good as me, maybe," he says. "If monkeys could talk and fish could fly, you could be just as good as me." When he teases like this she tries to kick him, kicking air because he moves so fast she can never touch him; and he dances round her, chanting singsong like that talking monkey; but she never stays cross, because she and Demi are two sides of one coin, that's what Fay tells them, and Baz reckons that Demi's maybe better looking than any kind of monkey that she's seen a picture of.

He's got short black spiky hair like most boys in the city, skin the color of those pale olives and brown eyes that make him look like a lost puppy dog. If some kind woman thinks he's a lost child that needs looking after, the next minute she's the one who's lost something, her purse mostly. "Women like that," says Demi, "when they lose their money just get more from the money-pig; women like that, money-pig for us. Don't feel nothing for her, Baz; she don't feel nothing for us. That's how it is. We take her purse and she still rich; we take her money and we stay poor—stay poor till we make it big-time, Baz. That's how it is."

Demi loves the city, every little corner of it. He knows its twists and blind alleys, fat streets and safe, shady squares where you can still find clean water running even in this high heat, even when the city's burning. Demi doesn't want to be any place else. It's different for Baz; she wonders about where they say she came from: upcountry, where it's all green and wide and there's hardly any streets, hardly any houses.

"What kind of place is that, Baz? Just some old dream-place! You foolin me you want to go that place. How we live without people? People just the same as the river, Baz, and we gotta swim in that river."

She doesn't give him much time when he talks fancy: "Then how come this water got pockets that you go putting your hand in all the time?" she says flatly. "I seen no water like that."

"That's cos you the most ignorant girl in the city. Sweet Maria," he says, rolling his eyes up like he's praying, "it's a lucky thing this rag of a girl got me to look after her."

Fay pets him, calls him "my private investment." Says he's going to look after her when she gets old. Fay isn't even half old, maybe late twenties, maybe a bit more. Baz thinks she could be nice-looking. She has a mess of red hair that she won't let Baz comb for her, and her skin is pure white when she bothers to wash, but mostly she doesn't bother, not till she gets real gritty and sour. One time Baz asked her why she didn't let herself be pretty. She said, "I been there, Bazzie, and I'm better like this."

She makes Baz keep her hair short so it's nothing but soft stubble when she runs her hands through it, and when she looks at herself in a shopwindow she sees this boy looking back at her. Sometimes Baz wishes she could let her hair grow and wear a skirt, but she listens to Fay, and she and Demi are always clean, shiny faces, new jeans, clean T-shirts. Smart. "Got to be smart all the time in this city," Fay tells them. "Be smart or the hard man catch you and take you away. He take you away to prison and you don't come back."

Demi says, "Me and Baz run faster than any old policeman. What we got these good sneakers for anyway but to run?" But he listens all the same, even irons his jeans. He and Baz have both seen kids, so young their noses are still running, slung right into the back of the policeman's van. They know kids disappear all the time unless they're smart.

Still, Demi likes to look sharp now. He likes to strut a little, be the man. Baz tells him he looks like one of the dirt chickens you see scuffing about down in the Barrio, where she, Demi and Fay live in an old building that hangs over the dried-out river. But Baz has seen rich ladies giving him a look sometimes, as if he was something they might like to buy, like a funny bag or a soft pair of shoes. Who knows what rich ladies really think? They hide their eyes behind cool black shades; and you can't tell what a person's thinking unless you see their eyes, and even then you can't be sure because eyes don't always tell the truth. That's what Baz reckons.

When he's in the strutting mood he tells Baz that when she's grown-up he might marry her someday, if she's lucky. He says the same thing to Fay, but she just slaps him round the head and tells him not to bother her, but she smiles all the same, even though she doesn't have so much time for Baz and Demi now. She's got other children who come her way, children looking for a place to stay, who've got no home, looking for food. She teaches them how to work on the streets, maybe shoeshine, teaches them some of the tricks she taught Demi and Baz, if they show any talent. The children stay awhile—that's if they can earn their keep. "I ain't a charity," Fay tells them. "Charity ain't no word round here. They got their lives, we got ours," Fay says, and that's it.

Señor Moro is the king of the Barrio; nobody crosses him, not even the police. Fay says Moro has pockets so big he can even fit the captain of police in them. For a long time Baz thought Señor Moro must be a giant to have such big pockets. She knows what kind of a man he is now. Demi showed her a place in the Barrio called Moro's Wall. A nothing place. Once it must have been the end wall of a big building. There's nothing left of the building now, just the wall and a pile of rubble and rubbish around it. The time Demi showed her, there was a small crowd standing around and a dead body on the ground. "Señor Moro have him killed," Demi told her. When she had asked why, he had shrugged. "That's what he do."

Baz now knows better than to pry about Señor Moro or the business he has with Fay, and so back at Fay's place, the den, she keeps a piece of herself locked up, doesn't get too friendly with the small children. If they cry, they cry. Everybody has to cry sometimes. Crying doesn't get you one little thing when you are on the street. She doesn't stop wondering though. Some thoughts come into her head even when she tries to keep them shut out, wondering what happens to the children when they go. Some stay long enough that she thinks Fay is going to let them stay, boys that begin to copy Demi a little, get his swagger, strut a little, get his grin, get too comfortable. She wonders if Raoul is too comfortable.

After Baz—and Demi, of course—Raoul has been with Fay the longest, more than two years. He is good, fast on the street, and everybody likes Raoul. He has a big smile and Baz thinks he has a big heart too; he'll help anyone in the gang, even the littlest child that Fay brings in. But he has a mouth that loves to talk, and Fay's sometimes sharp with him, cuts him down when he speaks out of turn.

Baz moves over to the shady side of the street and buys herself a Coke, feels the purse Demi slipped her, tucked into the top of her jeans. Good leather, but Fay says only bring back the money. "Once you got it, the money yours; purse always belongs to someone. They find it on you, don't come running to me for help." She steps into a quiet side street and in two seconds has emptied the purse—paper money tucked in her shoe, change in her pocket—and is back with the people passing by her.

She sees Demi over by a newsstand, looking at the magazines. The newsstand man is watching him; they watch any kid standing by their stalls whether that kid looks smart or not. People who've got stalls on the street think every child is a thief. Probably right too. She sees one other person who seems to be watching Demi, a pale-looking young man with fair curly hair. Rich maybe, she thinks; she catches the flash of silver at his wrist. He's not doing anything, just smoking a cigarette. Maybe waiting.

Demi catches her eye, and Baz knows that he wants to head right up to the center, so she takes a sip from her Coke and then drops it in a trash bin, right under the nose of a policeman; he's got a face carved out of stone, eyes hidden behind dark glasses. Turning her back on the policeman, she starts to drift up the street, barely glancing across at Demi, but shadowing him all the time.

Just as she has been taught, she studies the people around her, all the time keeping an eye out for the wide-open shopping bag, or the thick wallet just begging to be pulled out of a loose pocket. Her fingers get itchy when she sees a man with a whole roll of notes in his hand, peeling one off to buy himself a cigar and slipping the fat roll back in his hip pocket. A fat, waddling man, with big sweat stains down under his cotton jacket. Easy, she thinks, but she doesn't go near him. Today she is the watcher; her job is to keep the thief safe. Demi would rage if she'd been picking pockets on the side instead of looking out for him. He wouldn't hit her though, never has, not like Fay. She says, you get hit, you learn quick.

All their lives, she and Demi learned quick. She knows Fay wouldn't have kept them otherwise. No mistakes. Never. "You make a mistake," she says, "and I the one who gets taken. If that happen, nobody safe. Everybody I know," and she doesn't just mean the children—Baz reckons she means all those shady men she does business with too, "everybody's name gets told and everybody goes inside. End their time in the Castle." The Castle is where nobody wants to go. The Castle is the city's prison.

Baz remembers little dark snatches of that first time she was on her own. There was noise all the time and it was night-time, lights flashing by, cars maybe, colored lights too. Someone tugging her hand all the time, and her legs so tired she could hardly keep up. She can't picture the person holding her hand. She thinks it was a woman, but doesn't know if it was her mother. She remembers walking and walking till the noise got less but the dark got thicker so she couldn't even see her feet, and she was crying, wanting to be picked up, but the person holding her hand wouldn't pick her up, just kept tugging her along, wanting her to keep going.

Baz remembers pulling her hand away because she just didn't want to go any farther. Maybe the woman stopped and said something to her, maybe not. She remembers this dark shape walking away from her, hunched up a little, like perhaps she was carrying something. Baz wonders sometimes if it was a little baby this person was carrying in her other arm and that was why she wouldn't pick Baz up; or maybe she was sick, or maybe she just didn't want a child hanging on her hand, bawling all the time; maybe she felt it was a better thing to let Baz go and not see what happened to her. Leave her in the darkness.

Baz tries not to think about this woman, but she wonders about her all the same and imagines that if she met her she would ask her why she let go her hand. Baz believes that if a person is lucky enough to have family, real family, you don't let go of the hand holding on to yours. Any fool knows that family is the most precious thing.

It was that next morning that Demi found her on a piece of wasteland near the market, all curled up and fast asleep. A dog right next to her growled, he said, when he came up. She always liked that bit of the story. Seemed like that dog reckoned she was its pup, he said, but he shooed it away all the same. Baz thinks about that dog a lot—how maybe she'll find it one day, though she knows it'd be an old dog now. But she dreams how she would look after it, give it bread softened in milk because it might not have teeth anymore.

She remembers waking and and seeing Demi looking down at her, the sun shining right behind him, and asking him his name.

"Demi," he said. "You got a name of your own?"

She remembers that hollow feeling in the pit of her stomach, hunger, and panic because she didn't know anything, and she might have cried again except this shadowy face above her laughed, and his laughter made her think of sunlight and that had made her feel better. "Why you called Demi?" she had asked him.

"Don't you know nothing?" he said. "Means half, cos I'm half grown. Going to be like a giant when I'm big." She remembers him saying that, and her believing him because he was so much bigger than her then; now she has caught up with him some—even with his strutting and big talk she doesn't reckon that Demi will ever make giant.

He took her back to where he and Fay lived, a shack with a roof and dirt floor. It was a long walk but he talked all the way, and there was Fay right at the door and she picked Baz up in her arms and hugged her like she'd been missing her all her life and wiped her face and gave her her name right there and then, and she had food, and they sat on the floor and ate together, and that is how they became a family, kind of. Fay looked a lot younger and prettier, seemed softer too. Men came and took her out places, and she taught the two children how to take things out of pockets without anyone noticing.

Soon after that Demi and Baz began working together, not thieving on smart streets, but small stuff: bit of shoeshine, going to the market and lifting a little fruit from the stalls maybe, looking lost so that someone gave them a piece of money. Then they began picking pockets. Had to learn to run then.

Now their legs are a little longer and they run a lot faster. They're a good team; know what each other are going to do before it happens, almost. She knows where he's heading now, up to the street where the shops are so cool you can walk past the door and the door swings open like magic and it makes you shiver because the air that comes out is cold as witch breath. That's the truth. And they have more jewels in those shops than you could ever imagine, but unless you look like you've got money swelling out of your pockets, you can't hardly look in the window without a guard breathing down your shoulder.

Demi is standing on the corner. She crosses over to his side of the road but stops about twenty paces away from him, right at the mouth of a little slip of an alley. She knows he's hoping he can strike lucky, maybe get a little parcel with a silver ring all wrapped up in it.

The two of them wait.

Sometimes taxis pull up and rich men and women get in, parcels hanging off them like strange fruit.

They wait.

Five minutes. She's edgy. It's too long. She's seen a police car drive by real slow. She steps back in the shadow, but she's sure he is going to get noticed—even looking good, he's out of place up here. Children don't come to this part of town, not on their own.

Then it happens.

Chapter Two

THE MOMENT SHE SEES the woman with the big yellow hat, clingy skirt and gold bangles on her wrist come teetering out of the shop Baz knows that she's the one that Demi is going to choose. She has fancy shopping bags in one hand, and a little box in the palm of the other. Trailing behind her is a cute girl with cute yellow hair, sucking on an ice pop, and she's chattering to the woman, but the woman is looking at the box. Diamond, thinks Baz. Maybe pearl.

If Demi is going to make a move it has to be now, in the few seconds between the shop door and the curb.

She sees the yellow-hat woman slip the little box into a shoulder bag that she tucks tight under her arm, wave to a taxi and now, with the taxi door swung open and the woman all in a tangle with her little girl and parcels and people passing by, Demi moves in, scooping up a dropped parcel, handing it back, then twisting out of the way as the woman gets in and closing the door for her. As he steps back Baz sees the little box in his right hand. Blind magic, she thinks.

But the little girl isn't blind. Her face is up against the window and she's shouting something and pointing, but Demi is already moving fast, weaving his way through the crowds on the pavement. By the time the woman is out of the taxi, waving her arms frantically and screaming for the police, and the security man from the shop has come running out, Demi has already passed the alley and Baz has the little box. He doesn't look back to see if she's OK, just sprints across the road and swings up onto the back of a moving tram. That's the way they work. That's the way Fay taught them.

But the little girl has keen eyes. She spotted the way Demi was running and saw him swerve by the alley and maybe she saw Baz too, because Baz feels that that whole part of the street is looking her way and there's the razor sound of police whistles cutting the air and she doesn't wait to find out any more but turns on her heels and heads down that long thin alley just as fast as she can, the little box clutched tight in her hand. She wishes she had a pocket or bag she could hide it in, but she hasn't. It doesn't even occur to her to throw it away. Not this. Something like this that might be the most precious thing she and Demi ever got.

"Hey! You! Stop!"

Baz has no intention of stopping; she's programmed to run like a rat, jumping rubbish and bottles and cans, her feet slapping the ground so light and quick that the men lumbering down after her think she's half flying.

She bursts out into the light of a new street like a cork from a bottle and runs smack into the belly of a policeman, who grabs her tight, expecting her to wriggle and scream, but she instantly goes limp as a rag doll. He grunts with surprise and loosens his grip, and Baz kicks, swinging her foot hard and high, snatching her arm free; and he grunts again, more of an "oomph!" because she caught him in a good place and she's off down the street, snaking through the snarled-up traffic. Dodging and weaving. A siren's going, but it's not getting closer because of the jam. And she's jumping bumpers and banging on hoods, and people are yelling and blaring their horns but that could be as much because they're raging about being stuck in traffic as they are about this running girl.

She's got the luck. And she knows it. No sign of a motorcycle or a white police van and there's no police helicopter, what she and Demi call "dirt flies," buzzing overhead. There's just her running and there's no pain or ache in her chest because she loves to run. She and Demi run all the time, part practice, part because they just like to race and Demi's barely got the edge on her anymore because she is fast.

She keeps to side roads, hooks round a square where all the trams seem to roost up in one corner and keeps on going, the little box stuck to the palm of her hand like glue; and that's the prize, the lucky prize. Life is like this. Good luck. Bad luck. And if it's good luck that comes her way she knows she has to grab it, think so quick you hardly think at all and run like the wind. Except there is no wind, only thick sticky air that she cuts through like a knife.

She slows to a lope. Sees a tram heading for the Barrio and swings up on the back like Demi taught her and hangs there with one hand, looking back for the first time and seeing nothing but cars and buses and people moving, going their own way, not minding this girl that looks like a boy hanging out from the back of the tram like some kids do.

Somewhere there is a rich woman kicking up a storm about thieving, no-good children who should be locked up and worse, but Baz doesn't think about her. She thinks about the cute little girl though, and hopes that one time she come across that girl and if she does she's going to rub her cute face right down in the dirt. "Make that hard man snatch me up is what you done, girl. 'Cept I's too quick for him. No one gonna slap me in the Castle!"

Demi took Baz to the Castle one time just to show her. It's out in the third quarter and it's where some people say that hell comes into the city. Baz doesn't believe that sort of talk but she didn't like its tall gray walls and its mean door. Demi told her that at night you could hear the Castle moaning. She went there at night, on her own, just to see if he was telling the truth. She didn't hear moaning but she sensed the place was so full of pain it made her shiver. She never told anyone she'd been back there.

Then she relaxes and smiles. She's free, swinging on the back rail of the tram. Why feel cross about some spoiled girl? She didn't take anything from Baz. Not like in the Barrio—there everybody tries to take what you've got.

Before the tram squeals into Agua, the stop nearest the Barrio, Baz drops off and heads for a row of market stalls. Casually she pauses, bends down as if to redo her laces and pulls out a note from her sneaker. Then she buys a couple of plain T-shirts, one for her and one for Demi, and slips the jeweler's box, now crushed and sweaty, into the paper bag the stallholder gave her for the shirts. Fay isn't going to mind her using some of the money, not when she sees what they have brought her. She picks up some tomatoes and a couple of apples and stuffs them into the top of the bag and then wanders slowly down into Agua.

It's a wide dusty square with nothing much in it except traffic and a few shabby shops selling cheap suitcases. Over in the far corner is a fountain that sometimes runs and sometimes doesn't; this is where Baz thought Demi might wait for her. But there's no sign of him. She's not bothered though; if he's not here he'll be in the Barrio at Mama Bali's, kicking his heels and sipping Coke, wondering what prize is in the box.

He can wait a little; she did the hard work this time. It's not every day you get snatched up like that and then have to run half across the city. She puts the bag carefully on the ledge of the fountain's pool and then scoops away the scummy surface and dips both her hands in up to the wrists. Despite the heat, the water's cool and feels good against her skin. There's another reason for taking her time. The little alleyways running off Agua on this side wriggle down into the heart of the Barrio, with people coming and going all the time. And everybody has eyes here; they see you hurrying along with a grin on your face, they're going to want to know why. Better to go easy, go slow, like the day is the same as any other, burning with heat and not much else. This time, though, there is something else so she thinks about that box nestling down under the tomatoes, and she lets herself imagine a little band of gold, or maybe earrings or a fine chain with a silken pearl, the color of a ghost, or maybe a green stone, emerald . . . Whatever it is, it's going to be so fine, she just knows it is, so fine that Fay will smile and laugh and hug them. And she hasn't done that for a long, long time.

Refreshed, she stands, picks up the bag, takes out an apple to eat and then, glancing back over her shoulder to make sure no one is following, she enters the Barrio. There are no street or alley names here, no map to find your way; if you don't belong, you don't go near the place. Why would you? It's a warren of twists and turns through stinking rubbish, open drains, darkness, broken houses divided up and divided up so that every part, even the stairways, is used by some family. There are stalls and cages stacked up, one on top of another, with people living in them like animals in a zoo, except in a zoo the animals get some space, usually. Not here; space has been squeezed out of the Barrio. There are shacks perched on top of flat roofs, little bridges made from old metal and scrap poking out from one top floor right across to another; and there's wire mesh too, stretched over the alleys, and the rubbish gets caught in it. The funny thing is when the sun filters through the mesh it gets broken into drops of light and looks pretty.

Sometimes Baz thinks that some giant came into the city and took one whole quarter that he didn't like, maybe because it was so poor that he couldn't find anything to eat there, and threw it all up in the air, and when it came tumbling down, all messed and muddled, it became the Barrio. But mostly it feels like there is not enough air to breathe or light to see. The place is a trap; people move into the Barrio from outside, but nobody moves out.

She remembers when they moved from that first place, a dirt-shack settlement on the edge of the city. It was rough there; both she and Demi got into fights, but neither of them ever got hurt as bad as Fay. She came back one morning and she was so beaten she could hardly walk. Baz was frightened that she was going to die, but Demi took charge, washed her face, cleared off the blood and dirt. Her mouth was swollen and her chin was like one big ball. Between the two of them they managed to take her dress off. She had bruises all over her body. When she recovered, the three of them moved away from that place and down into the Barrio. The neighbors, women with hard faces, and their men standing in the shadowy door of their own shacks, just watched them go, said nothing, and Fay stared straight ahead, walked with her chin up, Demi and Baz walking behind. Fay told them they would get protection in the Barrio. She'd met this man, Señor Moro; all they would have to do was to give him some of their money and no one would touch them. Baz reckons everyone in the city probably has to pay money to Señor Moro.

She moves quickly through the warren until she gets to Mama Bali's, a corner shack half taken up by Mama Bali herself, who's as fat as a pumpkin. Baz reckons she can't ever get out of her place, not unless she squeezes herself down to half size; she would just get stuck otherwise. No one is going to rescue you if you get stuck in the Barrio, not too many kind-hearted citizens, though Mama Bali is good to them. She'll give the children a drink of this and that and won't try to charge them as if they were millionaires and won't give them trouble of any kind either.

She said she was a dancer once. Demi told her that if she was a dancer then he was president of the United States. She said that if he was as smart as he kept telling her he was then maybe he would end up president, president of big talk and not much else. Demi said that was fine by him; he didn't want to go any place: the Barrio was his country. Mama Bali didn't bother to reply to that, but the look on her face showed that she didn't think that was so smart.

She has pictures of dancers up on her walls—some men, some women—and Demi is right about one thing: none of them are fat like Mama Bali. They have their arms stretched out like wings and their bodies curved like they're riding air. Nobody dances in the Barrio—not enough room to spin a cat; no time either, no time for anything that doesn't put food in your belly or money in your pocket. Baz dreams that some day the river will run again and they will slip away to upcountry where they have all that open space and then maybe she will try to dance like the people in the pictures.

When Baz comes in Demi is sitting at one of the shack's two tables, Mama Bali is cooking in the back room, singing away in her croaky voice and tossing out comments to Demi. He pushes back a chair for Baz. She senses his excitement, but like her he shows nothing. "You been runnin?" he says, his voice so low it could almost crawl along the floor.

"The uniform man near get me, Demi. Half that street come bustin after me. Know why? Girl seen you give me the box."

He frowns and shrugs at the same time, like it's nothing to do with him, but she knows he doesn't like to hear this. He reckons he's too neat, too slippy to be seen by some small girl. It makes Baz smile, him being so vain like this. "You slowin down in your old age, Demi."

"Me slowin down nothing. Maybe you step out too much, make her see you. You always too rushing."

"Tch. You think I like to go for run, have that man snatch me up and slap me in the Castle? No one see me, you know that. Boy, you just gettin clumsy, is all."

He pushes across his half-drunk can of Coke and lets her tell him how she got free from the policeman—he liked that—and the way she ran through the traffic, "flea-hoppin" she called it.

She breaks off her description when a man that Baz knows by sight, one of Señor Moro's men, comes swaggering in like the place is his, banging on the counter to make Mama Bali come out right away. And she does, bustling out from her back room, giving him coffee, quietening him down, and then Baz sees her pass over a couple of twenties. Mama Bali is frightened of nobody but she still has to pay Señor Moro to keep in business. Everybody has to pay him, even Fay.

With the twenties tucked between his first and second fingers, the man swings round on his stool and looks at the children. Demi sips his Coke. Baz wants to say something, act natural, but she can feel this man's eyes as if they are burning into the back of her neck.

"How's business, Demi?" says the man.

"Got no business."

"Got enough to buy you'self a drink."

"Find me a dollar," says Demi. "Got me lucky one time, is all."

The man laughs. "'Find me a dollar,'" he mimics. "Thief like you find dollar all the time, I reckon. Maybe it's time you start paying the shady man."

"Anything we got go to Fay. She the one do business."

The man ignores this. "And this little girl-boy—what she got in her bag? She get lucky one time too?"

He doesn't know what she has; he's just playing, but Baz feels danger tighten around her. If he decides to take the bag, that's it, all their good luck blown away, all their chances gone. The man slips off the stool and comes over to the table. "So what you been shoppin for, girl-boy?" He knows her name well enough, just wants to needle a little. A man like him is bored unless he's folding money or causing someone pain.

Without looking up Baz holds out the bag to him. "You want the apple? I been saving it," she says; her voice is even, her hand steady.

"Apple," he says. "Eve give Adam one of them and the whole world come tumbling down." He accepts the fruit and takes a juicy bite. "And who give a damn," he says, and laughs and bangs out of the door and into the alley. Baz sees him take another bite and then toss it down into the dirt.

Baz lets out her breath. Demi looks at her, his eyes steady. "You got it still?"

"Course. My sticky fingers let go nothing."

His face suddenly breaks into a big smile, like there had been a dam holding it back. "What you think, Baz? That woman look rich, yeah?"

"She never buy trash."

"Fay don't expect big time, Baz. You think that maybe what we got?"

They're playing a game almost, teasing themselves, like

buying the lottery tickets from the street seller and for the moments before you know you've got nothing again you think about how rich you are and what dream house you're going to be living in in no time at all.

"Fay going to love you, Demi."

"Yeah, maybe. Let's go, Baz. Let's go see."

They get up to leave and Demi puts his head round the doorway to Mama's kitchen, where she's now swabbing the floor with an old floppy mop, sloshing the water round like she has some special supply that the rest of the residents of the Barrio don't have. If Mama's not cooking, she's cleaning. "Hey, I see you been on that diet, Mama. Lookin thinner than a skinny dog," he says.

"My waist is no bigger than your mouth." And she gives him a cuff. Mama Bali likes Demi; most people do, unless they catch him with his hand in their pocket, but then he and Baz never do their business in the Barrio.

*   *   *

They have a secret place close by to Mama Bali's where they go if they want to check something before bringing it back to Fay. Making sure that no one is keeping an eye on them, they cut up a covered way to the right of Mama's kitchen, up some stairs, through a corridor, passing a room packed with men and women gambling with dice and colored sticks, out of a window and then onto what seems almost like an island—a round blue-tiled dome sticking up above a sea of tin roofs. It might have been a church or mosque at some time—not anymore though.

They lean back against the slope and Baz unwraps the little box from the T-shirts she bought and hands it to Demi. He holds it on the palm of his hand. "Are we feeling lucky, Baz?"

"Go on," she says, impatient now.

He slides the top open and delicately fingers out a white gold ring with a stone the size of a butter bean. It catches the sunlight and seems to shiver with the blue of the sky and the deeper blue of the roof tiles.

Baz blinks and stares and Demi puffs out his cheeks. "It some stone, Baz."

For a moment Baz feels as if the stone could draw her into itself, into its world of clean, cool blueness, and then the heat and and thick sweaty smell of the Barrio reasserts itself. "Will it make us rich?" she says, glimpsing that upcountry place she dreams about. "Maybe take us out of here, Demi. What you say? Could it do that?"

"Maybe. Maybe it will. One sure thing: Fay gonna love it, yeah?"

"She love any money thing," Baz says bluntly.

"Raoul gonna be jealous we done so good."

Baz likes Raoul. He's a little younger than Demi but is always trying hard to be better than him. No way he can though; he's still too slow. Too fat, though none of them gets to eat much. "You just fat with words, Raoul," says Fay. "Take care none of your chatter go spillin out into the wrong kind of ears. You best take a tip from Baz. She so quiet, she like the inside of a safe. She keep her secrets locked up tight. You mind the way she is, Raoul, and you'll stay safe." It's true. Baz is quiet around Fay; doesn't talk to anyone much, except maybe Demi. Raoul swears he knows how to keep his mouth shut, but Baz knows that a boy like him has to take extra care; too many people notice a smiling face.

Demi puts away the ring. Then they cut across the Barrio, keeping to the rooftops as much as they can, making toward the river. But when they get close they have to come down to ground level and work their way through alleys that seem to become tighter and tighter, winding around about each other like snakes. They cross a wide, dry ditch humming with flies. Home territory now. That ditch used to run like a stream down to the river, carrying runoff and waste from the warehouses. Now it just stinks and is tangled with weeds and rubbish. When they were smaller Baz and Demi explored all the way along it, squeezing into the drains that led up into the derelict buildings. Can't believe why they did anything so stupid; just a dare maybe. Life's got enough dares for them now, she thinks, without rat-crawling up some old drain.

Beyond the ditch they come to a scuffed-up old warehouse, and that's their home. It's somehow propped up on rotten wooden pylons and leans out over the riverbed at a crazy angle, like it's going to tumble right down at any moment. Baz doesn't give it half a thought; it's looked the same ever since she, Demi and Fay moved there more than six years before.

They tug the warning rope, signaling their arrival, climb stone stairs to the first floor, duck in through a small doorway, up a makeshift ladder and then they are in sticky darkness just outside Fay's den.

But the door is shut.

Baz grips Demi's arm, holding him back from bursting in. They had signaled with the bell so Fay should be at the door or, if she was busy, one of the others.

"What you fussin for, Baz?" His voice a hiss in the darkness.

"She got business, maybe."

"Yeah, well, she got business with us when she see what we bring."

Chapter Three

BUT FOR ONCE Demi doesn't go for the big entrance. He tries the door, finds it unlocked and eases it open. Light flows out into their dark space. A split second later there's a hard crack; someone's being smacked.

"Who you go talkin to? I ask you one time only." Fay's voice, ice-cold angry. The child, Baz can't tell which one, is sniffling.

This is one of the bad times when anything can happen, none of it good. Baz doesn't move, Demi neither. They stand there, hooked half in the dark, half out. They can see a thin slice of the room: the back of a head of red hair, Fay, and a bit of the sniveling child. Baz notices something else: the bitter smell of a cheroot. There's someone else in there other than Fay and the children, someone that maybe is making Fay lash out more than she would do otherwise. She wonders who the child talked to. A policeman maybe.

Another voice—Raoul, of course; only he would be dumb enough to speak out at a time like this. "Fay, he with me most times. I didn't see him talking to no one, except this man. Young and not police. He looked like he come from good family. Smart, you know, good clothes. I thought maybe . . ."

"You don' see nothin half the time!" snaps Fay. Then, curtly, not to Raoul but to the man sitting out of their eyeline, "You want one, you take this one. He been nothin but a mouth to feed. You take him."

What's Fay saying to this man? Baz holds her breath. Now she realizes who's there, saying nothing, smoking a cheroot. She's seen him around—calls himself Uncle Toni, but she doesn't think he's anybody's uncle. He's just a lieutenant to the man who owns everything in the Barrio: Señor Moro. Not that you see Señor Moro making house visits; he sends his shady men. But they never had a man calling to take away a child, not like this, not in front of everyone, like none of them matters to her.

Baz and Demi always reckoned Fay's business with Señor Moro was strictly money. Everyone got to pay the man. There was never talk of the shady men coming round telling her to give up a child. Never.

"Of course"—the man's voice is reasonable, almost like he's doing Fay and the child a favor—"the little one can come with me. What you say? You come with Uncle Toni? Here." Maybe he gives the child something because the sniffling stops.

The smart thing to do would be to slip back to the other end of the floor they're on, scramble out of the window there and climb up to the roof. They can wait there till things quieten and then go in, but before she can grab Demi again, he pushes the door a little wider, just enough to see the man bending down over the boy. She can see who it is now—the boy with the funny name: Pickpack.

That's how Raoul tagged him because when he arrived, hardly more than a few weeks back, he had a parcel done up with string. Wouldn't let anyone touch it; kept picking it up and hugging it. Fay took it away from him one night just to see if it had anything that she ought to be looking after. It had a wood whistle, a worn cloth hat like hill people wear and a couple of photographs. The pictures were of some Indian woman, nothing special, she said. Baz reckoned they were special to Pickpack though, perhaps his mother or a sister. Nobody paid him much attention. Nobody except Raoul. Raoul took him out, tried to teach him things. Now he's going.

"You should teach your boys better manners," says the man, standing. He takes Pickpack's hand in his and then turns and looks toward Baz and Demi, his face expressionless. "Or you think it a good thing them spyin on you from your own doorway?" Baz edges a little closer to Demi.

Fay shrugs. "They ring: I hear 'em. They done right, not comin in." She looks worn out, her face the same color as the dirty old white linen jacket she wears all the time. The rage is all burned out. It happens like that with Fay.

She turns away, shoving her hands in her trouser pockets. "You go," she says to the man. "You got what you came for, ain't nothin more up here you takin away with you. But mind that child don't go sneakin on you. He got a blab mouth."

The man doesn't answer. Demi and Baz stand aside as the shady man and Pickpack leave. Pickpack's eyes are round, like he's staring at something only he can see. Baz knows that what is happening is a bad thing. You don't let go of the hand that you've been holding on to, but then maybe nobody had ever held Pickpack's hand. The man is holding his hand now, but that's different.

Baz looks away. She hardens her heart. She doesn't know that this is what she is doing but it is exacly that. In another life she might have touched Pickpack's arm, wished him good luck, something little like that, but she does none of these things. Instead she copies Demi and saunters into the room after him. One thing Fay taught her and Demi is that you've got to keep living, you got to keep your mind on getting through to the next day.

"Well," she says, "what you two got to show for yourselves?"

She is not eager, nor excited, but Demi doesn't seem to notice.

This is now his time. He swaggers a little. "We got something," he says, pretend-casual.

There are five children scattered around the den and they all look up at Demi when he says this, like his words are a sudden cool breeze. Raoul's at the old table opposite the door; a couple of boys, Javi and Sol, not much older than Baz when Demi found her, are over by the tall skinny window that looks up-river. Javi is sitting on his bedroll on the floor holding his knees, Sol's on the bench under the window. Big Giaccomo and Miguel are by the cold fireplace, where Fay does the cooking. Miguel with his narrow, watchful eyes is tucked back in the shadow, almost out of sight. Giaccomo has his mouth open, staring at Demi and Baz like they have just appeared out of thin air. He's maybe a head taller than any of the others and broad-shouldered too. Demi thinks he's sixteen but that his mind got stuck at ten. He and Miguel are always together. Baz doesn't mind Giaccomo, but Miguel makes her think of a rat. She doesn't like him, but he's a clever thief. There are no girls except for Baz. Seven in the gang now Pickpack's gone.

"Show." Fay has her arms folded, half looking out of the window, out to the dead river.

"You want to see what we got," says Demi, "you gotta say please. I—"

She snaps her fingers impatiently. "Demi! Show what you got."

Silently he hands over the box, but he looks her straight in the eye, like he wants her to know he is a somebody, not like the others, not to be treated like the others.

"Nice box," she says, her voice different slightly. Baz thinks that maybe Pickpack is already slipping out of her mind. Fay has moods like summer storms: after two minutes the clouds roll away and the sun shines. "You got only this? All day and one box?"

Wordlessly Baz slips the folded money from out of her sneakers and hands it over. Fay flips the notes, automatically checking the value. She gives a cursory nod of acknowledgment. "Good," she says. "It gonna help pay the bills—payin out all the time, seems to me." She slips the wad into her pocket. "What's the story on this little box, Demi?"

"It took some work. You know what I'm saying, Fay. Baz an' me had to do the hard-man sprint." Baz keeps quiet, lets Demi do his act, though he only ran a couple of yards before he was nice and easy on a tram. "What you think, Fay? We done this and we give it to you." He throws his hands up in the air like older men do, but it looks funny when he does it because he's still small.

"Where you get it, Demi?"

"Capricia. Fancy jewel store, uptown."

"I know Capricia." She's got both hands round the box, cradling it. She's behaving just like the children did, delaying, squeezing out the pleasure. Her tone sharpens suddenly. "What you do this for, stealin in a shop? How many times I tell you? They got cameras. You a fool if you step inside a shop like that. Your face gonna be on every screen in every police station in the city . . ."

"Hey, Fay, I know this. What you tellin me this ol' stuff for? I clip the lady when she come out the shop. You gonna open the box or you gonna stand there bad-mouthin us for what we bring you?"

"OK. We'll see. Maybe you found some old costume ring. Maybe something pretty I can sell—buy you all a plate of Mama's fat sausages."

But when she lifts the lid she catches her breath. Baz has never seen her react like this. Never, not even over the fattest wallet. She holds up the ring to the light and it glitters, a thousand specks of blue in that one stone. "So pretty," she says. "Look at that," she breathes. "Something, hey." She puts a hand on Demi's shoulder and pulls him a little bit toward her, so he can see what she's seeing. "Like a thimble of blue ice." The only ice Baz has seen is in the inside of a freezer, or in a drink, and it's never been blue.

Demi is not looking at the stone but at Fay as if he is expecting her to bend down and give him a hug, give him a kiss, but Fay only has eyes for the ring.

"Who you take this from?"

"Woman. Uptown."

"Some rich woman," says Fay. "Whoever lose this not gonna be happy. Maybe it gonna stir things up a little. You be careful," she says to Demi, "and you don't breathe about this to no one." She turns to the rest of the gang. "Here, boys, come and see what you can do, when you get as smart as Demi."

They gather round. Raoul tries to hold it but she smacks him, not cross, just a cuff. The young ones look but don't see anything to get excited over. Miguel stares and licks his lips with the tip of his tongue.

"You bring me something half as good as this and then you start earning your keep. But you never, never say anythin about this to no one. You know what happen to a boy who let his mouth run." She doesn't have to say any more than that. The boys look at her, their faces solemn. They know. She smiles. "Here." She pulls a greasy five-dollar bill from the little leather pouch she keeps on a thong round her neck. "Go get a drink at Mama Bali's. You get food when you come back, but you don't say nothin about this. You mind me? Raoul, you listenin? You know what happen to the child who got a fat mouth." She laughs. They don't laugh, but Raoul takes the bill and they jostle their way out of the den. Treats don't happen so often.

"They good boys," she says when they have gone out, "not like that Pickpack. He was gonna bring trouble." She sees Demi is going to say something and raises a finger. "You stop. History is history." Then she holds the ring up again, taking out a little glass that she grips in her eye to look at it more closely. After a moment she says, "I put it in a safe place, OK." It's not really a question; Fay always hides away their takings. "Baz, get some glasses and a little wine. We'll have a drink together, just we three."

"Like old times," says Demi.

She looks back from the door and smiles. "New times, Demi. This gonna keep me in my old age."

"Just you, Fay? What 'bout me 'n Baz—what gonna keep us?"

She doesn't miss a beat. "You too young to think 'bout bein old." She laughs, then says, "We always gonna share—ain't that right, Baz?"

"Course, Fay."

One time, when she was small and Fay was still teaching her and Demi how to thieve, Baz took money out of the pocket of one of the men who came calling. When she showed Fay, Fay beat her so hard she had bruises on her face. "You don't never thief here! Never! Why? Cos they'll come back here when they find their money gone and who they gonna blame? Who?" And she smacked her again. Demi was sitting in the corner and he kept very quiet and very still, hoping the storm wouldn't bother him.

"They gonna find me," Fay shouted, "and they gonna blame me! And they gonna hurt me! You want that to happen?"

"No."

She took the money Baz stole, but Baz doesn't remember her ever giving it back to that man. That was a long time ago, before they moved to the Barrio, but Baz has never forgotten. Now Fay hardly ever gives out money. She says she's got to save all the time.

With Fay out of the room, Demi says, "You know where she hide her things?"

Baz is shocked. "Fay kill anyone who know that!"

"I got eyes."

"Don't you say that! You hear me, Demi. Don't say nothing—you see what happen to Pickpack."

He reaches for the bottle and pours himself a slug of yellowy wine. "Don't mix me with that child. I tell you what I know, Baz, cos what if somethin happen . . . ? Things harder. Don't you feel it? Shady man crawling all over the Barrio, taking this, taking that. Fay harder too. Maybe we on our own one time, maybe just you . . . So listen, she got a place down in the basement . . ."

"That one place I ain't never gonna go."

Demi ignores this. "I sneak down after her one time, Baz. I think maybe she drunk too much because she stumbling all over and muttering but she still keep looking around like all the time she expectin someone come sneaking up behind her."

"Yes, you."

"Yeah." He doesn't smile, but then Baz isn't smiling either. "I see her take out a brick from the old wall and pull out a tin with all her precious things in it. And you know she pick them out one a' time, and look the way she look at that ring, like she love them. She don't look at nothin else like that, not even me nor you, Baz. And you 'n me brought those things, you know." He laughs like he doesn't care. "I thought family share all it got. Sometimes I think all we get to share is trouble."

"Hush that! Fay gonna rage if she hear you talk like this!" Talk like this frightens Baz. Sometimes it is best to keep things close, to think your own thoughts, have your own secrets. She reckons everyone—Fay, Demi too—has their own. Some secrets it's best not to share, even in a family, specially if they are to do with Fay. This is what she thinks.

Demi gives her a funny look. "We gotta look out for ourselves, Baz. Fay good to us, but things change."

"What thing gonna change, Demi?" asks Fay, coming in through the door. Baz reckons she can hear whispering down in the Barrio, if the whispering is about her. She sits beside them and pours a full glass of wine and takes a good long drink, nearly draining the glass. "Mm? You still love me, Demi? I the one?"

Demi shrugs. Only Fay can take the steam out of Demi; most times he could talk his way seven times round the city, if anyone willing to listen.

She pats his cheek. "You gonna get the girls running for you, Demi, when you a man. Maybe you got some sweet girl looking for you right now." She winks at Baz.

"Got no one but you, Fay," he says.

"What? Ugly old thing like me?" She gives a real throaty laugh, half wine and half tobacco. "What you say, Baz? Is this boy cheatin on me?"

"Demi don't cheat," Baz says. Fay's games don't interest her. She's looking out of the window, watching the sun settling down across from the dead river, burning hazy and yellow like it's sickening. In five minutes it will be gone, and then with a click of your fingers it will be dark across the Barrio. "Fay, what we gonna do when we got it made?" she asks.

Fay empties her glass and refills it. "Go upcountry maybe. They got a lake up there, big as the ocean, with a dam longer than the highway, and the land's green, Baz."

Baz's interest quickens. "We could get a farm, maybe have animals."

Fay laughs again. "You think me and Demi would make good farmers? All that diggin and muckin. These hands never done no diggin and ain't intendin that they do. No, maybe we go north, get a smart place, keep our food in a freezer, maybe get fat by a swimmin pool. I seen pictures of places like that." And she begins to picture the life they might lead one day, the three of them, safe out of the Barrio.

Demi relaxes. He loves to hear her talk like this. Maybe he believes her, maybe he doesn't, but the words soothe. They don't do anything for Baz though. She fetches the tin buckets and goes out to collect water for cooking and washing.

Raoul meets her as she is crossing the dry ditch and offers to keep her company down to the well. "Makin plans, hey?"

"What you mean?"

"You, Demi and Fay. We just scadabouts; you got it safe." He's teasing but serious too.

"Don't think anyone that safe, Raoul. Stick around long enough, keep your head down and you work with me and Demi, then Fay treat you same as we."

"If I mind my fat mouth."

"If you mind that, the whole world gonna say thank you."

They laugh and walk slowly past the old men sitting playing dice, then into the closed-in yard where the old well is. Not drinking water. This gives you sweats if you drink it, but it's almost free; good water comes in a bottle and costs nearly as much as the wine Fay keeps.

"Haul that bucket for you, Baz?" A tall spindly figure in a torn vest steps out of the shadow.

"Haul my own bucket, Lucien," she says. Says it each time she comes but it makes no difference, and she knows it.

"Still cost you."

Lucien is a strange one. He lives holed up in a corner of this yard. He must be the poorest person in the Barrio; about the only thing he can call his own are the running sores he's got down both his arms. The only one who looks after him is Mama Bali, which Baz thinks is funny because he's so thin and she's big and fat. He brings her water for her washing and she gives him a meal every day. No one minds Lucien, and most people pay him the two cents he charges for his bad water.

Baz slips him two coins.

"Lost another one, Baz, hey?" he says softly. He's got a funny, hesitant way of talking and his words have a whistle to them as if his teeth are bunched around the wrong way in his mouth.

"What you say?"

Raoul glances at her.

"I seen the man go by with one of your boys, little one with the packet." He watches her drop the bucket down the well. "You take care, Baz. Don't let Fay be givin you away. End up working on the Mountain."

Baz has never seen the Mountain but she just knows it is the worst place there is. It's somewhere outside the city, on the far side of the river, a big hill of stinking rubbish, and anyone working there ends up as rubbish too.

"Fay don't give way nothin," says Baz automatically, jigging the bucket to make it fill. "Pickpack bring trouble on his own head." But she wonders if this is true.

"Whatever you say."

Lucien drifts back to the shadowy corner where he spends his day. Baz slowly hauls the bucket up while Raoul hums, leaning on the rim of the shaft, looking down. "You know that man I said I seen Pickpack talkin to?" he says. "I seen him again, right after we get our drink at Mama Bali's place. He was down the alley a piece. Could've been a college boy maybe, had him a fat watch on him, good clothes, you know. I don't know what he come looking for, but all he gonna find is trouble, coming down here dressed like that. Nearly gone and told him that too."

She looks at him surprised. "But you didn't?"

"No! You think I just some donkey-brain, like Giaccomo?" He grins and then gets serious again. "I wondered if he looking for somethin, Baz, maybe even looking for us. I followed him to see what he was at. And you know where he went then?"

She shakes her head.

"Moro's place—the Slow Bar. Walked right in like he got business there."

"Maybe he did. But I tell you, no one come lookin for us unless they see your fat hand dippin in somebody's pocket." But an unwelcome thought flickers across her mind. It couldn't be that yellow hat. It couldn't be someone already sniffing a trail into the Barrio. Maybe that yellow-hat woman got a big-shot husband, someone big as Señor Moro. And she hopes that the ring that seemed to promise so much isn't going to bring bad luck.

Raoul laughs. A moment later he says, "Where you think

Pickpack get taken? You think Lucien right? Moro get them taken to the Mountain?" He shudders. She doesn't answer. "I seen three go in my time," he says after a pause, watching her while she squats beside the bucket and washes her hands and arms. "No one say nothing 'bout where they go."

Baz stands and looks down the well. The air smells of dirt and damp stone.

"Fay won't talk 'bout it." The truth is neither Demi nor Baz talk about it either, not to each other nor to anyone else.

"I think people should look out for each other. What you think, Baz?"

"Sure." She looks out for Demi all the time.

He helps her hike the bucket over the rim and then she drops the second. Again they hear the hollow splash and faint slooshing gurgle as the bucket fills.

"I mean it, Baz. I swear I never let Fay give you away to one of Señor Moro's men like she give Pickpack. You promise you do the same for me?"

He's smiling because Raoul always smiles, but his eyes look like deep pools of worry, and that surprises her. "I promise," she says.

He laughs again and then together they pick up the buckets and begin the walk back.

*　　*　　*

She keeps to herself in the den, helping Fay get the food ready and clearing up afterward, but then, as the boys sit around talking, watching the beat-up TV they've got hooked up in the corner, she slips away. And for some reason she feels more unsafe than she can ever remember. It was all Raoul's talk about that young man and maybe what Lucien was saying too, suggesting poor little Pickpack was going to end up on the Mountain. Now she keeps thinking of the hand that let her go, leaving her in the dark.

She slips through the Barrio carefully, tucking herself into darkness any time she senses anyone near, wondering if the strange college man Raoul saw is spying on her, and she half wishes Demi had never lifted that ring. Finally she comes down onto the hard mud at the edge of the river, some four hundred yards upstream from the den. Out here there's some light from the starry sky and she can see what she's looking for: an old stubby pilot boat keeled over at a crazy angle and way out on the mud. She takes off her good sneakers and begins to walk along the dead river's edge.

Chapter Four

BAZ LOOKS BACK over her shoulder a couple of times, remembering as she does so Demi's description of the way Fay went so cautiously down to her hiding place. Maybe she's a little bit like Fay, she thinks. Perhaps if you stay with anyone long enough you get to be like that person. She hopes not, but she glances back anyhow. Demi tried to follow her once, but she saw him and gave him the slip. He knows she has a place somewhere along the river, but Fay told him to leave her alone. "A girl need her space. You boys like monkeys, hang your dirty feet all over the place. She need quiet time. That right, Baz?"

Baz hadn't ever really thought why she wanted her own place. She liked being with Demi, with the others too, and the den always felt safe, even when she slept up on the flat roof, but in a secret place you could burrow yourself away and lock out all the bad thoughts that came creeping and threatening.

She'd explored other hulks, but mostly they were easy to get out to and so not safe. They were ruined and rusty, scarred with graffiti, and they stank. Anything that could be unscrewed or levered out with a crowbar had been taken; everything else was smashed and broken. It took her a long time to find a way out to the old pilot boat, but now it's hers—a memory of the time when the river flowed and the city breathed toward the sea.

At first she walks at a gradual angle away from the shore, stepping lightly because in places the mud is soft and you can sink up to your neck. She knows this because the first time she came out she brought an old curtain pole and used it to test the way. Then, where the river curves, she strikes straight out across the mud. Twenty paces later she turns right and makes toward an old iron channel buoy lying on its side. Carefully she goes round this and then cuts back left, making an almost perfect zigzag out to the boat. Fifteen yards from the hull she pauses, and then runs as fast as she can. The mud is soft here, a slip or stumble and she's gone, but she doesn't hesitate; she's made the journey many times and knows what to do. And even as her right foot sinks up to the ankle, she grabs the makeshift ladder she's rigged up from before and with a satisfying sucking sound she pulls her foot clear and scrabbles up to the deck. She cleans her feet with water she brought out in a plastic Coke bottle and then pads along the sloping deck to the gangway that leads down to the saloon.

She's made a nest of soft things on the downside of the sloping floor, where she can lie and look up through the hatch and see the stars and the slow-moving moon till sleep comes. When she dreams it is always the same one: she can hear thunder, far away at first, then it comes closer and closer and she knows it's not real thunder because she can see no lightning ripping across the night sky. She's on deck, gripping the rails, up at the raised bow, staring upstream where a big wave, maybe twenty maybe thirty feet high, is rolling down the dry riverbed, its crest peeling, foaming phosphorescent white. And she knows it'll pour into the Barrio and wash all the mess and filth right out into the ocean, and it will sweep her away with it too; but she is gripping the rails so tightly her hands hurt because maybe the wave will lift the old boat right off the mud and she'll be there like Noah, but with no family and no animals. She always wakes before the wave reaches the boat, wanting to know what will happen.

This is a night when sleep comes slowly, and when she does sleep there are no dreams that she can remember. She wakes in the darkness thinking about the Mountain, and she has an uncomfortable feeling, like a dirty itch right in the middle of her back, that someone's watching her. She knows that's foolish because no one can see her where she is now, unless there's some some magic man with shady eyes standing on the shoreline, staring right through the hull of the boat, but there's no such thing. Baz is practical; survival is all about being practical; fancy make-believe doesn't interest her.

When she wakes again a dirty gray light is falling down the hatchway. She smells the rust and mud and hears the soft sound of the early-morning city mumbling to itself. She climbs up onto the deck. In less than an hour, once the sun has fully risen, the tug will heat up like an oven and the iron deck will burn through her shoes, but this moment is good. There's always a breath of a breeze first thing; it carries the city sound out to her and a faint tang of salt from the faraway sea.

The far side of the river is a foreign land to Baz. There's smoke, and houses, but they are way in the distance, and then, farther away still, a low range of misty hills, and behind them the mountains.

*　　*　　*

She finds herself thinking about Pickpack but like someone who is out of reach. Raoul was really bothered, she could see that, but Demi, after his tiny protest, would now have forgotten him completely. She knows it would be sensible to be like Demi and forget. She pushes Pickpack from her thoughts and busies herself getting ready for the day.

The sun is fully up now, glaring into her eyes so she can no longer see the far shore. She turns away. Time to head back for another day's work. She makes her sliding run across the mud, zigzagging to the shore, and although she sees some silent figures trudging off to their day's labor, she's back at the den before anyone is up. She doesn't ring the warning bell, not at this hour; if the policemen or any kind of hard men raided the den in the morning, they would just get to see children sleeping; there would be no kind of thieving evidence for them to be dragging anyone off to the Castle, that's for sure.

She makes coffee and takes a cup into Fay, who has a little corner room in what is otherwise just an open space. Her red hair all tousled out on the pillow is like a wild halo, not gold though like for the good angels and saints, but fiery. Her face is pale, her eyes open, her lips clamped tight, as if she's in some pain. Baz wonders if she's sickening, but Fay never complains of not feeling well and her expression softens when Baz comes into her room with her morning coffee. Then Baz goes back and pulls out some tomatoes, cheese and yesterday's bread.

This is the routine. The boys wake and yawn and shuffle and scratch. Then Fay comes in. She has already decided what everyone will be doing that day. Sometimes she holds back the younger ones so she can teach them, but mostly she pairs up the boys. She says it's always safer in twos because one can always act as lookout, the way Baz and Demi work, but Baz knows it also means that she gets two accounts of the day and can sniff out if anything is being kept back. Fay can read the boys like a newspaper. They all try to cheat her at some time; she expects it, but she doesn't let them get away with anything and if they don't learn, if they try their luck one too many times, they find themselves moving on. She and Demi used to ask, "Oh, what happen to so and so?" and Fay would just say, "That boy a thief—nobody thief from Fay. He move on." They don't ask anymore. Now Baz reckons that the boys don't just "move on," they get escorted away like Pickpack, maybe end up climbing the Mountain like Raoul said.

She and Demi always bring back everything they get, everything except the small bit of money they might spend on food or at Mama Bali's, and maybe Fay trusts the two of them a little more than the others. Baz thinks that Fay probably doesn't even wholly trust herself. Demi, half admiringly, always says, "You watch what you say all time you round her. I swear that Fay can see round corners and hear a rat squeak way down in the alley, specially if that rat squeakin something 'bout her." Baz reckons Demi needs to listen to his own advice a bit more.

The boys are sent off—Raoul is told that Giaccomo is working with him and they are to keep away from the center of town. The theft of the ring from the woman outside the fancy store will have caused a stir, and all the security guards will be sharp-eyed today.

Fay, Demi and Baz are left sitting round the table. Raoul had stolen a wallet that has nothing but lottery tickets stuffed in it so Fay is checking the numbers against the ones being given out on the TV, scrumpling each one up in turn when the numbers don't match. "Don't know why I bother with that boy; he bring me nothing half the time and he eat more food than anyone," she says. "Time you two went to work. Where you want to go today?"

"Norte," Demi says. He'd been talking to Raoul earlier and had told him that that was where he and Baz would go. It's one of the four railway stations that serve the city. You get good pickings in railway stations: tourists coming and going, people thinking about how to get to where they're going, carrying more than they should maybe. But, like most places, plenty of uniforms watching out for thieves like Demi and Baz.

Fay grunts and then gives a little exclamation of triumph as a couple of her numbers match.

"Why that please you?" says Demi. "What you got? Maybe twenty."

"They say money don't grow on trees," she says, "but sometimes it does," and she laughs. "Then you got to pick, see. Don't you turn your nose up at nothin, you hear. Money is what we need, all the time." Her attention goes back to the tickets and the screen.

"So Raoul pick you something," says Baz, standing up. "He pick you twenty."

Fay reaches for a pack of her thin black cigars, puts one to her lips. "You like him, eh?" she says, and then lights the cigar, eyeing Baz through the drift of smoke.

Baz shrugs.

"More than Demi here?" She's teasing, but Baz doesn't rise to the bait. "You want to work with the fat boy?"

"Raoul's OK," Demi offers. "Slower 'n me, but he's OK."

"He talk too much," Fay says flatly, tossing the last of the tickets on to the floor. "Twenty don't buy much in this world. Now go—I got things need doin."

Demi wanders over to the basin in the corner and washes his face and neck. Baz lingers by the table, waiting. Fay smokes her cigar, scrolling through messages on her cell phone. Baz scoops up the tickets Fay had tossed aside and says, "Fay, what happen the other side of the river? How come we never go there?"

"Why you want to know? Ain't nothin there worth us pickin for."

"If you want to go north," says Demi coming back, rubbing his face with an old T-shirt and grabbing a clean one from his space, "you go right over the bridge, and the road take you all the way up."

"That the road we take when we make enough money?"
Baz asks.

"Enough! What you talkin 'bout? You want to live on
dream, girl? We got nothin."

"What about that ring? That make you happy enough. Me
'n Baz bring you stuff all the time."

"I had enough about ring. That ring buy me nothin till I find
a way to turn it into dollar. You think that's so easy? You go find
some business. I tell you what we need: we need dollar. This
much." She stretches her arms like she's holding a sack as big
and fat as Mama Bali. "Understand? More than you ever dream
'bout."

"Like a mountain," says Baz.

"Now you talkin, girl. Now go on out of here and leave me
some peace. Here"—she pulls out a note from her neck purse—
"you need money for the tram. See? Win twenty on a ticket an'
lose it right away."

Demi takes the note and gets up. Baz gets up too, but at the
door she turns back and says, "Fay, did the shady man go put
Pickpack on the Mountain?"

"Tha's enough! I don't want to hear 'bout any of that from
you. You hear me! You wanna stay safe, you stay quiet, Baz."

"Just askin, Fay."

"Just nothin, Baz." Then she seems to relent. "You take care.
I don't wanna hear some hard man been an' slap you both in the
Castle."

"We comin back, Fay," says Demi, and pulls at Baz's arm
and then turns and slithers down the ladder and Baz follows.
"Why you ask that stuff, Baz? Only gets her in a black mood.
Raoul gonna have to watch his step cos of you."

"You say things too she don't like, 'bout money."

"I think she love money more 'n anythin."

"You think she's sickenin? She don' look so good anymore."

"She fine. You just fuss. Fay's gonna live forever; tougher than anyone in this city. Just love money too much, is all."

Mama Bali is washing the window to her kitchen when the two pass. "I swear I'm gonna take the plug out that dam they got upriver, give the whole place a scrub," she says as she has many times before, and it's probably the reason that Baz has the dream of the flood. "Some young man askin me if I hear any talk 'bout some ring. Offer me money. I wondered if he was lookin for someone with dancing fingers, Demi, someone like you maybe."

"Only people come lookin for me are girls like you, Mama."

Baz keeps her face still. The ring. How come something so pretty bring so much worry with it? It doesn't seem to worry Demi though.

Mama Bali laughs. "Not this time. This man came down here easy as you please, like he don't mind where he is. Uptown boy. I told him get on back where he belong 'fore someone bring him grief." She frowns. "You know what he says? He says he carry his own grief to give anyone who bother him. He may be uptown, but he's not so different to boys round here."

"Like me?"

She laughs again. "You're not no good, Demi, you just plain bad. But I tell you, something happenin round here, cos I got one of Señor Moro's muscle-boy comin askin me thing too, askin what I know 'bout this, 'bout that, 'bout a ring. If you two know somethin, you keep real quiet. You hear me?"

"Hear you all the time, Mama, but me an' Baz just a pair of angels who know nothin 'bout nothin." And he dances away before Mama Bali can cuff him.

She laughs and shakes her head. "You goin make some girl unhappy. Tell you that for nothin. Baz, you watch yourself."

Baz has a feeling that it is the ring that could make them both unhappy.

She and Demi hardly talk at all until they have crossed the city by tram and reached the station. Some days Baz feels the excitement of moving through the crowds, working with Demi, watching his magic, but some days start all awkwardly, like every streetlight turning red, every door shutting in your face. Today's one of those days.

Demi doesn't think so. When he swings down from the tram outside Norte he grins, and for a second Baz thinks he's about to rub his hands in anticipation of a good day with rich pickings.

Some people think that the station is special, like a palace. It's big all right, with broad white steps that take you to the busy concourse, but the station just makes Baz feel small—not handy small so you don't get noticed but ant small, like you've a good chance of getting stood on.

"We gonna do well today, Bazzie." Demi stretches and cracks his fingers. "Gonna show Fay, we bring home nuff to build a whole house."

"Like we done yesterday?"

"Every day a special day with Demi. You peel your eyes, girl, and watch me move."

*　　*　　*

The first thing they do is go and buy platform tickets. It's a small investment but worth it if a policeman starts asking them questions because they can then say they are meeting a relative off a train. Then, sticking close together, they wander out onto the concourse, look at the arrival times so they know what to say if they do get stopped, and then buy themselves a drink each and sit and watch.

Train stations like this one are a bit like the ocean; that's what Fay told them way back: you wait till the tide comes in, the beach gets washed over with people racing to and from the trains and then you move in. You don't get a lot of time to fix your mark; you just get in the crowd and you let it take you this way and that, but your eyes are peeled. You see a purse looking like it needs lifting and you wash by that body and then you're gone; and you don't make another move until the next tide comes in. Fay always made it sound like a day out, and Baz remembers that the first time she came into a station with Demi she was excited, but that excitement didn't last long.

It was the third time they had worked Norte that things went so bad. The two of them had just pulled a new stunt. They thought they had been so clever. Baz pretended to cry. She was littler then and Fay let her wear girl things and she could do the big round eyes to perfection. A man stopped. He had a pointy gray beard but she remembers nothing else about him except that as he was bending over to ask her what the matter was, Demi plucked out his wallet neat as a monkey picking a flea. And just then a boy came running right at them and Baz panicked. It's never happened since, but right then she froze, thought the boy had seen them, was going to tell the police and then she would be bundled up and sent straight to the Castle. She knew she should be running too but she just could not move.

The boy would have slammed right into her but the man with the beard snatched her arm and pulled her back. She'd wailed, thinking that was it, she'd been caught, but the man just let her go and hurried away. But she saw the boy's face close up: mouth open scragging in the air, and she saw the whites of his eyes. He was a street boy, no shoes, raggedy vest all torn and sweat-stained, but he could move all right: head back, arms pumping. He zigzagged a porter pushing a loaded trolley and vaulted straight over the barrier and onto a platform. Maybe he hoped to jump the train that was just leaving. If he did he was too late because it was halfway down the platform and picking up speed.

There were three men on that boy's tail and not one of them was in uniform. It was the first time Baz had seen the plainclothes police in action: the dreaded APA. Back then she hadn't known anything about them apart from their name; now she can spot them a mile away.

Seeing that he wasn't going to make the train, the boy leaped down onto the track. The men didn't hesitate. The first man followed, vaulting the barrier while the other two blocked the way and shooed people away. They didn't want anyone to get too close to the action, but from where she was, Baz could see the first man dropping down onto the track. The boy was perhaps twenty or thirty paces ahead. Not far, but with luck maybe he could outrun his pursuer.

But then she saw that the man had no intention of running: he pulled out a gun from his loose jacket, took aim, shot, and the boy dropped like a mule kicked him in the back, arms flung out as he was thrown facedown onto the track. She could see he was still alive because he was moving still, trying to drag himself along the track. The man didn't hurry. He just walked up to the boy, stood looking down at him for a moment, and then brought the gun up and shot him again. The boy didn't move after that.

She remembered feeling dead inside and Demi pulling her away. "Thief live on borrowed time," Demi said, trying to sound tough, sound like Fay, because that was one of her first lessons to them. "Thief live on borrowed time so you better make use of every second you got, and you be careful, you hear." She always used to end by saying that, and they *were* careful, but they had seen children beaten and they knew that bad things happen, but never anything as bad as this. A boy being shot down, right in broad daylight, with people only a spit away and no one saying anything. Maybe Demi couldn't shake it from his mind either because a little while later, when they were riding the tram back to the Barrio together, he said, just out of the blue, "Like a dog, Baz. That's how they done him— like a dog no single body want."

So now, having seen just about everything Norte has to offer, as they drink their drinks they scan the concourse looking for police, looking for APA men. They're always young, the ones on the street, and lean, like wolves, she thinks. They all have faces shadowed with stubble and like just about every other policeman in the city they wear shades on their eyes. They wear designer jeans, none of the cheap copy stuff from the market stalls, and a loose jacket of one sort or another to cover up the gun they all carry. If you look close, you can see the bulge. The most giveaway thing, though, is that they are never doing anything other than looking, all the time, just watching people, just like her and Demi, she thinks.

Today there's no sign of APA, and that's good. When the next train comes in, they slip from their stools and Demi does his business, and moments later passes a little clip with notes bunched into it to Baz, and then they drift back to a different stall, wait for another train. Do the same. Wait for one more. "Three time lucky," says Demi. Baz thinks luck only runs one time round the track, but she trusts Demi so she follows him out into the swirling crowd, not treading on his heels, giving him space, just keeping his bobbing head in view so she can move when he makes his strike.

She sees him switching to the right, suddenly closing in on a target. Baz glimpses a dumpy-looking woman fumbling in her bag. This is the one, and then suddenly Demi is swerving away, turning back toward her, making a face: "Back off!" She spins on her heel and nearly gets knocked off balance by a family all bunched together, pushing through, talking at the top of their voices. Then she catches up with Demi, who's waiting for her to one side of the ticket barrier.

"You see 'em?" he asks.

"Who?"

"Raoul and Giaccomo. Who told them come up here? Fay know this our place today. I tell you, that boy get right in my way! He do that again I gonna kick him so hard he won't be fat-grinnin for a week."

"Raoul wouldn't come up here unless he been told."

"Well, who tol' him?" he snaps, "I's this close"—he snaps his fingers—"and then *Phoof!* He come steppin right in on me, goin for that bag . . ."

"He get it?"

"Sure. Blind man could've scoop that bag."

Then as Demi is still angrily gesticulating, there's the shrieking of whistles and angry shouting. The crowd on the concourse washes apart and reveals a little tableau that gives Baz a sharp shock, like someone's smacked her on the heart with a stick.

Raoul is on his knees, head bowed forward. A uniformed policeman stands behind him, a stubby blackjack swinging from his right hand. Two other policemen stand to one side, talking to the dumpy woman, who's clutching her bag to her chest as if the police might want to have a go at taking it from her too.

Baz takes a step back and scans the crowd, looking for Giaccomo. He should be on the edge somewhere so he's able to tell Fay exactly what happens to Raoul, but there's no sign of him. Instinctively she moves in closer. Maybe, she thinks, she can find out where they're going to take him. She's aware of Demi at her shoulder. He's not angry now. Whatever will happen to poor Raoul is going to be a hundred times worse than anything Demi might have wished on him.

The few members of the crowd who had paused to watch the arrest have lost interest and moved on. Just another pickpocket. Just another street child. There's no pity for the small, chubby boy, not even when the policeman standing behind him suddenly tightens his grip on the blackjack and thwacks the boy, hard, one, two, three times on his bowed back. Baz flinches. Poor Raoul! A watching man grumbles, "Vermin. They should put them down . . ."

"How you say that!" She can't help herself; a rage takes her as bad as any that bites Fay sometimes. "Maybe he got bad father like you . . . !" Her words come out in a shouted angry jumble. The man's eyes widen; the policemen turns; Demi snatches her arm. Only Raoul doesn't react.

"Sorry. So sorry," says Demi, pulling Baz back. "My sister, she's soft, you know. Don't like nobody getting hurt. Hey, hey. Now come away."

She's not thinking about what she can do; she's not thinking at all. She's so angry and frightened she just wants to tip her head back and scream. It's like a storm raging on the inside of her face. She's never like this. Never. Always so controlled, watchful, thoughtful; not now though, and only Demi's tight grip on her arm and sudden shake jerks her back to herself.

"Girls, eh," says the man.

"Yes, señor, of course. Just a girl. She don't mean nothin."

The man nods. The policemen turn back to their business and Baz drops her head. The storm has stilled and the tension eases out of Demi. He puts his arm round her shoulders and turns her away from Raoul. There's nothing they can do, except leave the station before the police start asking them questions, maybe search them, find the money from the first two little dips Demi's made, money tucked in Baz's shoe.

"You scare me, Baz. You look like you want to bite the man."

"Scare myself." She feels herself tremble.

"At least it the uniform man that catch him, not APA."

Yes, she thinks, at least he will just get beaten, not shot. But after the beating, what then? The Castle maybe . . .

"Demi, what can we do?" She begins to talk rapidly, urgently. "We make distraction, like that time before . . ."

*   *   *

"That thief, he a friend of yours." The words, statement rather than question, are spoken with a lazy uptown drawl. They cut across Baz's planning and startle her: a young man, tall and slim, head and shoulders taller than her and Demi, is blocking their way. But for some reason her first impression is not of his face but of the buttoned cuff of an expensive shirt, of a silver tag looped round a thin wrist, of a hand that's clean and pale with neat trimmed nails, and he's holding a notebook. Baz is stupidly conscious of her bitten nails, her cheap clothes, and then feels a flush of anxiety. Had he heard what they were saying?

"Nothing to me," she says. There's something familiar about this boy, student maybe—something she can't quite place. Soft skin, a bit like Fay, but with hair that frizzes round his head in a tight yellow halo that makes Baz think of the church in the plaza by the Barrio, with all those pictures in its high windows of stiff men and women in bright colors. But this boy doesn't come from any church window. His eyes are sharp and he's staring at Demi like he knows him. He ignores Baz.

"Maybe I can help," he says.

Demi shrugs. "We never see that boy before."

"You sure?"

"Yeah. I know who I know. OK. Let's go," he says to Baz, but Baz doesn't shift, she's looking steadily at the boy. She's seen him before, she knows she has.

"You don't want my help then. You don't care that this boy is going to go to prison."

"Who're you?" says Baz abruptly. "You don't come here to catch train."

He smiles but doesn't answer. There's something creepy about his silence.

"You wanna help that boy, you go ahead," says Demi. "Mean nothin to us. We gotta go."

The boy steps aside, letting Demi and Baz walk on toward the main entrance. "I seen him before," Baz says. "That boy—yesterday when you scoop that ring—at the newsstand, before you move uptown. Remember?"

Demi shakes his head. "Mean nothin to me."

"Raoul say some boy hanging round the Barrio, talk to Pickpack, Mama Bali too. Maybe him?"

"Maybe." Then, "Raoul not gonna be sayin too much o' nothin now."

It's only when they are on the steps leading down from Norte that Baz feels free, feels that the rich young man is no longer watching them. That place is like a trap, she thinks. Snap you up. Outside is better. The street's got space. "We don't work this place again, Demi. It's not good."

"We do OK."

Better than Raoul, she thinks, with his smile and fat words. What's going to happen to him now? Will they take him to the Castle? Will Raoul keep his mouth shut? "Fay gonna rage 'bout all this happenin," she says. "We don't do good enough to stop her ragin." Fay's said it a thousand times: "If one of you's fool enough to get snatched up by the police, then nobody safe. I'm not safe. Don't you let that happen."

"We done what business we can," says Demi sullenly.

But Baz knows she's right and she doesn't look forward to their homecoming.

Chapter Five

THEY RUN FOR A TRAM and jostle their way to free seats near the back and begin the long ride back to the Barrio. They fret and worry about Raoul until there's nothing more to say, and then it's Demi who brings up the subject of the man. "Who that man anyway?" he says. "He got no business steppin in, sayin he can do this, he can do that." He snaps his fingers. "Some big shot—that what he think he is."

"Like he know who we are."

"Nobody know me. Nobody see me." He slaps his palm against the window as if he's smudging a bug, but there's no bug there. "Journalisto," he says suddenly after a moment's silence. He looks happier. "Think that what he is, Baz."

"Make a story just about you."

"Maybe." He puffs out his chest. "I make a good story."

Maybe he would, but if there was ever an article about him—or her—it would be the end. The policeman, he reads a paper, sees their picture and *Bang!* they would be in the Castle in no time at all. "Better for you if you learn how to make somethin useful . . . ," she says.

"Eh?"

"Tortilla."

Demi's never helped make a meal in his life. He makes a dismissive gesture with his hand, not in the mood for her teasing. After a moment he says, "Journalisto got to be older 'n that boy; don't got such fine clothes neither."

She doesn't know. Maybe this is true, maybe not, but it makes her think again. "APA?"

Demi shakes his head. "Too young."

"Too young, yeah. Student maybe."

"What kind of student hang round askin questions like that, pretendin he can help? Why he interested in me an' you? We nothin to people like him."

She doesn't know. She just doesn't like the feeling that anyone might be watching them. The only safe thing to be is anonymous, a shadow in the street—better still, invisible. She stares out at the honking traffic, the fleeting figures in doorways, men and women sauntering arm in arm, people who maybe know nothing about the Barrio, nothing about what she and Demi do so that they can live and be family.

She wonders what Fay will do about what happened today. Rage at her and Demi for letting it happen? That's for sure. Threaten to treat them like she treated Pickpack? Maybe she should. Hadn't Baz promised to look out for Raoul? She had. But there was nothing she could have done.

Demi's bothered too, because out of nowhere he says, "You goin to tell 'bout that . . . ," he hesitates, " 'bout that man?"

She shakes her head. "You think we oughta call 'bout Raoul?" Calling means getting off the tram, finding a pay phone. She and Demi don't carry cell phones. Fay doesn't like them to. She never says why, but Baz has figured it out. If they ever get picked up and they have cell phones, what are the police going to do? Check the numbers they have been calling and there'll only be one number on the list: Fay. Fay is always careful.

He says, "She find out soon enough when we get back."

They change trams three times and reach Agua with the sun high up over the city. They buy some bread and a scoop of black beans and sit on the edge of the fountain, but there's nothing but a trickle coming out of it today. A coach passes by full of schoolchildren in neat white shirts, their faces pressed up against the windows. They make Baz think of prisoners on the way to the Castle. Except prisoners don't get to go in a coach with air-conditioning. Baz has no interest in school. Fay taught her and Demi to read a little and write their names. Demi picks up the paper sometimes, looks at the pictures, reads the captions to the football stories. She can read the street names, find her way around. "We gonna be back real early," says Baz. "Maybe we should stay out a while longer." Neither of them wants to go back. Neither of them really wants to talk about what happened.

Demi shrugs. "We can do something else."

A police car goes slowly by. Like the schoolchildren, the policemen stare out of the windows, no expression. Like sharks, Baz thinks, always circling round the edge of the Barrio, hoping to pick someone up, maybe someone like Baz or Demi. They eat their food and stare right back, kicking their heels against the edge of the fountain. The police never drive into the Barrio—the streets are too small, and even if they could, a nice smart police car wouldn't last long.

The police car pulls up in front of a bar on the other side of the square; the Slow Bar it's called. It belongs to Señor Moro. One of the policemen gets out. He's probably just getting a beer for himself, but Baz keeps watching him; she's carrying more money than any child round this part of town should. "Maybe we move on, Demi."

"Sure." He wipes a thin trickle of bean juice from his chin. Neither of them wants to face Fay right away. "I got something I want to show you. Maybe something gonna make Fay smile."

They drift away from the square, not straight down into the Barrio but a little to the right toward the old docks. There's hardly any business down there anymore, hardly any people either. Most of the warehouses are boarded up or falling down. They pass scraps of rough ground, overgrown with thorny scrub and burnt grass, noisy with the scratching of cicadas.

"Some guy gonna make big money developin all this."

Demi likes to talk about how you can make big money.

"That you?" she says.

"Tha's me. Rich and fat."

A couple of trucks rumble by and haul up in front of one of the few working warehouses. "This the place," he says. The trucks have backed up to a big door, and there's a metal ramp sticking out of the building and running right down into the back of the truck. They hear a loud crack and then a *whoosh*, voices calling and a motor in the background whining on. When they come a little closer, Baz can see that what's sliding down the ramp are great blocks of ice. White, she thinks, like chunks of heaven. "They sell it up at the market. Fish an' meat gotta have ice."

"Hey, I know that stuff. Why you so interested?" And then she remembers what Fay said when he gave her the ring, that it was like a thimble of ice, and she realizes what's been running through his mind: the boy's crazy.

"What you say, Baz? You think we can haul a block back 'fore it go and melt on us?"

She shakes her head. "We got an icebox; don't need more."

He pulls a face. "That ain't the point. Don' you understand nothin? Fay gonna like it."

"Fay gonna call you a fool."

As always, Demi just doesn't hear when Baz says things that he doesn't agree with. "You wanna bet me 'bout takin one back?"

"That old block is almost bigger 'n you are." Then she tilts her head to one side, pretending to study him. "Sure, I bet you five."

He slaps her hand, then runs round the back of the truck and yells to the guys inside. A block comes hooshing down as he's shouting and slams into the truck and he has to lean quickly out of the way not to get smacked. Then a hand comes out of the doorway and he puts a note in it and the next moment a smaller block comes sliding down.

"Gimme a hand."

She makes a face but grips the block against her belly, feeling the cold burning and biting her fingers, while he strips off his shirt so he can wrap the block in it and carry it that way, up on his shoulders. First he sets off walking but then as the ice starts to leak away he breaks into a jog.

"Imagine her face," he says, panting. "She ain't gonna believe it when she sees this." Even with his shirt round the ice, his ear is turning blue.

"Fay gonna be lucky if she see any of that. And you gonna be lucky if your ear don't fall off."

"You just worried 'bout losin your money." And he runs faster; Baz runs alongside him, easily matching his pace, teasing him, both of them letting this game swallow up what happened up at Norte.

By the time they enter the Barrio the block is half its original size. "Good money just melting in your hand."

"Don't say I pay money for this," he pants.

It's hard running in the Barrio, with all its twists and turns. Then some young bucks trip Demi up and the ice goes flying into the dirt. He takes half a second to get his breath back and then he curses so viciously they back off. Baz scoops the block up for him. He grabs it from her and then they are running again, running and running. Over the ditch. Up the stairs, bursting into the den with a shout: "Fay! Look!"

At this time of day light is flooding in through the windows, but the air is still heavy with the heat and the smell of dry mud and rubbish.

There is no sign of Fay.

Demi lets the ice fall onto the table and then slumps down into a chair, his chest heaving. Baz looks at him and thinks it's like his heart has suddenly got heavy. She gets a dish and puts the lump of ice in that. It's about the size of four fists now, nothing so special.

Of course this is when she comes in, shoulders hunched up, hands in her jacket pockets. The air is stifling, but Baz can feel the frost off Fay. Nobody's having a good day in this part of town.

"Why din't you call me?" is the first thing she asks, pulling out *el Jumento*, the city's daily paper, and dropping it on the table.

Baz looks at Demi. Fay already knows about Raoul, she realizes. Demi is looking at the little slab of ice. "Came back, didn't we? Who told you about it anyway?"

"Miguel call me."

"How come Miguel know anything 'bout this set?"

"That boy smart. Find out things," she says.

Smart? Miguel? Baz would never have thought of him as smart; sneaky maybe. Miguel put the finger on Pickpack.

"OK," says Fay. "Now you tell me what happen? Did you see anything?"

Demi gives an account of what they did see, though Baz notices that he leaves out any mention of the young man and his strange offer of help. Idly she pulls the newspaper toward her so she can see the picture, and a face that seems familiar in some way looks out at her.

"Raoul will talk."

"No," Baz says. "You got him wrong, Fay."

Fay looks at her, surprised. "What you say, Baz? You crossing me?"

"Raoul won't say nothing 'bout you, 'bout us. Raoul need this place more than anything."

Demi's surprised now. "He tell you all this?"

"Yeah," she says. "He tol' me."

"And I told him to mind what he say too," says Fay, "told him about a hundred time."

She sits down at the table beside Baz, who's using one finger to trace the headline: "Police Wife Robbed." Fay reads the opening paragraph out loud for her. "'Señora Dolucca, wife of a senior captain in the city police, was robbed while shopping yesterday. The item stolen was a ring—'"

"Demi took that ring."

Fay gives a short laugh. "You chose the wife of a police chief; why not steal from a judge next time, so he put you in prison for a hundred years? You know what else it say here: 'Captain offers a reward for information leading to the return of the ring.'"

Baz looks up and thinks how that ring seems to be building up a storm. Demi never grabbed packets before, always a bag, always a purse.

"How 'bout that?" says Fay. "And this captain also say: 'It's time tougher action was taken against these children who prey on innocent, honest citizens.' How you like that? You been preyin 'bout the city like some wild animal, Demi!"

Demi shrugs. "How do I know who she is? She just a tip-pytap woman with more parcels hangin off her than fruit from a tree."

Baz looks up. "When you seen a fruit tree?"

"I seen pictures."

Fay pushes the paper over to Baz. "You wantin to practice your reading, girl? Maybe get a job? Maybe be a teacher? How 'bout that? First teacher in the Barrio. Better be quick though—it say right there in that paper how everybody in the city want to pull down the Barrio. Got too much thief." She laughs again and then notices the dish with the little melting sugar cube of ice. "What's this?"

"Brought you block of ice."

"Brought me a dish of water is what you done. You losin your mind, Demi? You pay money for this?"

"Pay money for nothin, Fay."

"What else you bring back?"

Baz takes out the dollar bills and gives them to Demi, who passes them to Fay. She flips through them. "This all? You tellin me this all you get? You been spendin"—her eyes narrow—"or you hidin what you get from me?"

Demi is at last stung into an angry response. "When we ever done that? We bring you thing all the time. You know; you say it yourself. So what you sayin now, Fay? What you sayin?"

She pushes the notes away from her. "I got pressure on me you don't know 'bout and I need money more 'n this to see me through safely. You want to keep livin here? You want to keep eatin here? You got to do better than this."

"Who threatening you, Fay?"

The warning bell jangles. Fay sweeps the cash into her pocket and then, moments later, they hear the sound of feet scabbling up the ladder and heavy breathing. Only one person pants like that when he's climbing up here, thinks Baz.

She runs to the door and swings it open.

And there's Raoul. He's not smiling, but he's there, and there's no policeman standing behind him either.

Chapter Six

BAZ ALMOST FLINGS HER ARMS round him, except that's not their way in the den. Outside in the city, she's seen people hugging and holding hands all the time, but Fay never had truck with any of that, except when they were really small. "You keep you' distance and you don't get hurt," she told them, and that's the way it's always been—some teasing at times, that's all. It doesn't stop you liking a person though, and Baz likes Raoul—not like Demi perhaps, but she likes his talk, his "fat words." She likes the way she can see his feelings. No one shows much of anything in the den, except Fay when she's raging.

She touches his arm. "You safe, Raoul! How come?" and she pulls him into the room.

Demi bounces up and jabs Raoul, play punching. "You give the hard man the quick run, you—"

Fay cuts across, snapping: "What you think you do comin here, Raoul, after what happen? What got in your head? Don't you think the policeman goin to follow you? Don't you think 'bout that?"

"Fay, I got nowhere . . . No one follow me . . ."

She ignores him. "Miguel, run see if anyone in this part of the Barrio shouldn't be here. Take this." She tosses him a cell phone. "You see anything, you call me. Go!"

And he's gone.

Fay turns back to Raoul. Her face is tight, her eyes flecked with red, rims red too. She rubs her brow with the back of her hand and then breathes deeply. "OK," she says. "OK." Softening a little. "Here. Come, sit, an' you tell Fay what happen."

Raoul nods, relieved by her change of tone. Maybe everything will be all right. He doesn't try to apologize, no point. He just pulls up a chair to the table and sits down opposite the dish; there's a thin skim of ice no thicker than a fingernail. He pokes at it while Baz goes to look for a drink for him, coming back with a cold Coke. He pulls back the tab, but doesn't drink.

"Well, what you have to say, Raoul? And mind you tell the truth. What you doin goin up to Norte? That's one. Two is where Giaccomo? Didn't he come with you? Or maybe he tucked away in the Castle—is that what you sayin?"

Raoul looks miserable. He twists the can round and round in his hand. Baz has half a mind to take it away from him. Then in a flat voice he tells his story. He knows they weren't meant to go to Norte but he wanted to beat Demi, just one time, bring back more, and he and Giaccomo thought that if Demi and Baz were going to the station then that was the best place to be. He didn't mean any harm by it. He looked for the others, but then there was this chance, the crowd was moving quickly. Just a chance and it looked so easy. It was easy. It was perfect, except he tripped and Giaccomo wasn't there on his heels to pick the bag from him and run with it. Then there were the police and questions and . . .

Fay interrupts. "You never work the station before. Have you heard me telling you how you got to wait, how you got to do this and that?"

"No," he admits, "but I been up there, Fay. I been watching, tryin to learn."

"So how you get away, Raoul? You never been so fast on your feet, not that I seen."

"I . . ." He hesitates and then hurriedly falls into what Baz can tell is a prepared story about how the police had to break up a fight and he managed to slip away and dive under a trolley stacked with mailbags where he hid until he saw a chance to sprint for the entrance. Then he caught the tram. No one was following him. He looks up. His eyes meet Baz's and she turns away. If it's true, then neither she nor Demi saw any of it.

Baz glances at Fay. She's not even looking at Raoul but checking her phone and then sending a text. "Uh-uh," she says. "And that it?" Baz can tell she's made a decision, though she can't tell what it is. She's not angry anymore though.

"Yeah," says Raoul. "Swear to God."

Fay clicks her phone shut. "Miguel seen nothing," she says. "No one follow you then, Raoul. Tha's good. Miguel on the way back with Giaccomo right now." She texts again.

Raoul's shoulders dip a little as he relaxes. He finally takes a swig of the Coke and then stifles a burp. "Giacco, tha's good."

"Finish that down now, Raoul, and then you run me a message." She gets up and goes to her room.

Quickly, while Fay is out of the way, Baz whispers, "What happen, Raoul?"

"Yeah," says Demi, coming up on the other side of Raoul, "Fay don't believe that ol' story you give her."

Raoul looks awkward, shamed, as if he knows he's been stupid. "I know, but she kill me whatever I tell her, cos she not goin to believe it. Listen—some young guy who got money in his pocket, he come right up and pay off the policeman." He shrugs. "I know. Who gonna believe that? But it's truth, Baz. The hard man don't mind those dollars, I tell you. An' all the young guy want to know is if I work in the Barrio for a woman call Fay."

"You say yes?"

"You think I'm crazy? Course I say no, but you know what? That young man just laugh an'—"

"Here," says Fay as she comes back in. "I got a packet got to go to this man. You find him in the Slow Bar down on Agua. You know that place. Don't go losin it, Raoul. This important big-time."

"Sure thing, Fay."

"I trust you, Raoul."

"Sure thing, Fay." He smiles and leaves just as the bell jangles. "Tha's Miguel," says Fay.

Baz follows Raoul out through the door onto the darkened landing space. He smiles at her. "It's OK, see?" And then he scrambles down the ladder. There are voices as the boys pass each other: Miguel's a murmur, Raoul's louder. Then the clatter of the two boys climbing up to the den, first Miguel and then the larger Giaccomo.

"Well," says Fay. "Quite a party."

Giaccomo looks uncomfortable. Miguel nudges him and he shakes him off. "Giaccomo got something to say," says Miguel. "Go on, say it."

"You seen it too."

Fay waits.

It's something to do with Raoul, Baz is sure. She looks at Demi and he looks away. He knows too.

"It's Raoul," says Giaccomo. "We seen him . . ." He corrects himself. "I seen him talkin with the policeman. They tellin him things. I try to hear but I can't get up close, you know, and then one of the policeman get a call on his radio and then I get moved on by the crowd, you know, and the next time I get to look, Raoul's gone." He pauses. "I think they maybe let him go, Fay. Maybe he promise something. I don't know, but you tol' us never say nothin to the uniform and Raoul was sayin things, for sure he was." He sort of stumbled to a finish.

"I seen him too," Miguel says quickly.

"Seem like the whole world come to Norte but we, we get tol' nothin 'bout this," Demi says. "What business you got goin there, Miguel?"

The boy slides a little closer to Fay. "She tol' me to follow Raoul."

"Spying. Tha's nice, Miguel. You spy on just Raoul or maybe you spy on us all one time?"

"I only doin what she tell me."

"Yes," says Fay. "Leave him be, Demi. You an' Baz don't mind nothing 'bout how the boys handlin their business. Miguel smart; he keep an eye for me. Raoul been worrying me; all his talkin goin to bring bad times right down on me. 'Swear to God!' " She laughs. "You hear him? 'Swear to God,' he say, and he tell me nothin but lies. Now"—she turns to Baz—"you got anythin to say 'bout this? You and Demi there. You see him get taken. That right?"

"We told you."

"And you see him talking to the policeman?" Fay looks at her in a way she never has done before, so cold, like Baz could be anyone, some stranger off the street.

Baz looks at Miguel. His eyes are fixed on Fay. It's not just his face that makes her think of those slippy river rats, poking about in the rubbish along the shore, scuttling humpbacked out of her way every time she goes down to the hulk. No. It's something that he's done, and she knows in her bones that he's the one who has betrayed them, not Raoul. Giaccomo does what Miguel tells him, and Fay listens to Miguel. Why does she do that? Why him more than Demi, more than her?

"Got no tongue, Baz?"

She shrugs. "The policeman asks him questions; he gotta make some kind of answer."

"I seen him talkin too," says Demi. "Don't mean much."

"But they let him go. That mean something."

"Phooh! Fay, you hard to please. You get the heebies when we tell you he get taken; you get the heebies when he get away. This day ain't nothin pleasin you."

Giaccomo looks like he wishes he could disappear. Miguel darts a look at Demi and then back at Fay, gauging her reaction.

Fay doesn't react for a moment, then she gives her short, barking laugh. "You said it."

"So what gonna happen with Raoul?" Only Demi could get away with this.

"When Raoul come back, we see what he say."

Baz wonders what she would do if she was Raoul. Would she come back? Wouldn't anywhere be safer than here? After all, Pickpack was taken away, just like that and for the same thing: talking to the man in uniform.

*   *   *

The moment is over. Fay goes out, taking Miguel with her, but she doesn't say where. Sol and Javi come back and pour a handful of change on the table. They've done well, and Demi slaps them on the shoulder and tells them they've got real class and that he's going to have to watch out or they'll be putting him out of business. They grin and puff up a little, copying the way Demi behaves when he's pleased with himself, but then in a little while they drift off to play football, leaving Demi and Baz alone together. "You know," says Demi, "you right about that Miguel—he got rat blood and he poisonin Fay, telling her thing all the time. She take more notice of him than she do me and you."

"Fay been round rats too long to be fooled by this boy," says Baz, but it doesn't convince Demi, who pulls a face and says nothing. Outside the sky finally darkens. The others come back for the shared evening meal of pork strips, onion and black bean, but Raoul still hasn't returned and she knows something is very wrong.

She and Fay make the meal ready, but when Baz asks her about Raoul she shrugs as if he, like Pickpack, is now history. Baz presses her, ignores Demi, who's signaling her to shut up. "You send him down to Señor Moro bar. You never send one of us down there before. Maybe you call him. See if—"

"See what?" Her voice is icy. "A boy can't run a message, he no good to me, so stop your fussing or maybe you want to find someplace else to live. Think about that. No one that important here but me—remember that."

Baz shows nothing on her face. She doesn't even blink, but she turns away and feels a pain as if she's been cut. Fay has never said this to her before. She sees Miguel looking at her and she looks back at him straight until he lowers his eyes. He's the poison maybe, telling Fay things. Baz wonders how many kinds of poison there can be in the world.

She watches the way Fay scoops up the boys' change without a word and pours it into a box she keeps in her room, Sol all the time watching her with his big eyes. "Good," she says finally, when Demi says again how well they've done. "Good"— but it is as if the word's been dragged out of her. Then she serves food for them all but doesn't eat herself, just nurses a bottle of wine at the head of the table. When the warning bell jangles she doesn't even move.

"You think that's Raoul?" asks Baz.

Fay shrugs, unconcerned, and then a moment later says,

"No. Not him." Baz and Demi exchange glances. How does she know?

"You want me to check?" asks Demi.

"We got nothin to hide from this man."

So she is expecting someone. "You want us to go out?" Baz asks.

"No. Why not hear? All of you. Why not?" She shrugs and nods for Demi to pull open the door, which he does, and then he retreats to the far side of the room as if he too senses that whoever is coming in will be a threat and the farther away you are the safer you'll be. It's not true, of course. Baz knows that and stays where she is, a little back and to one side of Fay.

Chapter Seven

NOT ONE BUT THREE PEOPLE enter the room, all men, all shady men, though Baz has seen only one of them before. The one on the right is Toni, Uncle Toni, with a smile that Baz reckons he gets sprayed on every morning, just like the women in the fancy hair salons who get their hair piled up and fixed so it stays looking weird and expensive all day. The one on the left is muscle. He's wearing a black string vest so he can show off his tattoo and the long scar down his right arm. He's one who doesn't care too much about sharp suits and Italian shoes. Baz reckons he's a bad-dream man, someone who is never happy unless he is doing harm.

"Fay!"

It's the man in between the two of them who speaks. Everyone knows his name, though unless you visit his place, the Slow Bar on Agua, you have little chance of seeing him. He's the spider of the Barrio, Señor Moro. He sits in his room and tugs the threads that make everyone else dance. He doesn't make social visits.

They come to a stop in a little V formation. Moro is older than his two shady men, jabs of gray in his black hair, and he's stumpy-looking, like he's half rich man, half rubbish. He's the one wearing the real expensive suit but under his jacket he only has a vest on, white, and grubby white too, like he wants the world to know he can spend money and still be ugly just because he wants to. He has a cigar in his hand, no thin cheroot but a fat smoldering Havana. He wants people to smell him coming.

"Fay," he says again, like she's a long-lost friend, his voice like gravel. "Long time since you come to see me. How are you—you and your children?" He lets the question hang in the air for a moment. "Maybe you want me to sit down, yes? My legs, you know, so bad." He settles himself down with a little performance of sighs and then straightening of his trousers. The children watch from the edges of the room, all of them keeping still, not wanting to be noticed. "No running for me anymore. Maybe you run, Fay. Though you not lookin so good. Maybe you got a fever. You got a fever, Fay?"

"I don't carry no fever, Señor Moro." Baz doesn't remember Fay sounding this polite ever before.

He nods and puffs his cigar. "That's good. And business is good," he says, pulling the newspaper toward him, tapping the front-page picture of the yellow-hat lady. "So many robberies. So much thief in the city." His voice one of mock concern. "A good ring this señora lost. Very good, I hear. Many thousand dollar."

Baz wants to look at Demi, who's standing the other side of Fay. She doesn't though; she keeps her eyes fixed on the spider. The ring that looked like it had swallowed up a little piece of sky—was it just a bad-luck ring?

"I read the story," says Fay. "Just another rich woman making fuss. She probably do a deal with the shop, say that old ring worth more than it is. Insurance. That's the way they are."

"Yes," Moro agrees amicably. "The way they are. Nobody can trust nobody no more. Not even the rich, not even the wife of Dolucca."

Baz holds her breath. Everybody in the room knows what this means, even little Sol. Who's going to be fool enough to steal from the captain of the city police? Demi! she thinks. Demi, why you choose this woman? Stealing from the captain got to be like banging on the door of the Castle, asking the hard man to waste no time, lock you up straight away.

If Fay is surprised she keeps it well hidden. "Who down in the Barrio going to care if the captain wife lose some precious thing?"

Moro lets smoke roll out of his mouth, then tips the ash from his cigar onto the table. "Just say, this captain is a man I know. He do me favor. You understand? Like I do you favor, Fay. You remember, you getting a bad time and you comin into the Barrio and you see me so no one come botherin you and you get you'self a tidy business. Always a question of business. Me and the Captain, we have business, and so it's an unlucky thief who steal from him, you know. Very unlucky."

"What this to me?" asks Fay.

But Baz understands, and she knows Fay understands too; they all do. Demi, face as blank as a frying pan, knows too. He knows he is this close to getting swallowed by the spider. Moro and the Captain dance to their own tune, and if one stops dancing everything is going to tumble down. She keeps her face still but she feels like the whole Barrio is looking at her, looking at Demi, saying they the ones.

Moro gives an elaborate shrug. "Because you got children with busy fingers, Fay, so maybe you have the ring. Maybe that boy"—he jabs the half-smoked cigar toward Demi—"maybe he the one who lift it out of Señora Dolucca's hand. You a good thief, boy?"

Demi lifts his chin. Baz is frightened that he'll strut and show off now, but he doesn't; he keeps his mouth shut. Moro looks at him, then he turns his attention back to Fay. "If you have it, Fay, you should be smart and give it to me, eh."

"If I have it! What you think I keep such a thing?" She waves the idea away with one hand.

"Sure, sure," soothes Moro. "But smart businesswoman like you, Fay, know that something big like that everyone going to be looking for it, everyone hear about it. Ring like that going to be hard to turn into cash. If someone try selling that ring, I going to hear about it. So maybe you keep it hidden. Hold on to it, yes. Investment for you. Maybe you have a place in the Barrio you keep precious things." He takes a deep pull on his cigar and slowly lets the smoke ease out from his mouth. "A secret place," he says, stretching the words softly like the exhaled smoke.

Baz keeps her face still but she's thinking about Fay's hidey-hole with all its treasures, somewhere down in the basement.

"If I got so much thing hidden away, you think I stay here, in a place like this?"

"Maybe. Maybe you like to pretend. Everybody pretend a little. I 'spect you pretend a little to your children."

"They behave themself, they get fair deal from me." Her voice is suddenly sharp.

"Of course, of course . . . we understand, but your boy Raoul been talking, telling my boys things." He laughs. "My boys a little older than yours." And he indicates Toni and the bad-dream man with the tattoos. "He tell them that a ring got given you. Say it look pretty good."

"Raoul got a fat mouth," says Fay bitterly. "I send you that boy cos you askin me for a boy." If Fay sees the look Baz gives her, she ignores it. "You tell me you got a job need doing and you need one of my boys. That's what you tell me. Raoul only child I can spare, and I can spare him cos he talk too much. You can listen to what he say, but don't go expectin fact and truth. Raoul make up things just cos that's what he think you want to know. Isn't that right, Demi?"

"Tha's right, Fay," Demi says. "Raoul all talk." His voice is level, his eyes fixed steady on the spider.

Moro smiles. "Of course, I should know better, shouldn't I, Fay? Know better than listen to some child you got. Maybe same applies to this boy here, this one who tellin me he such a good thief. Maybe I take him too, keep him for you."

"You got Raoul," says Fay. "You keep him. Demi work for me. You want me paying you my dues, then I need him work for me."

Moro's eyes narrow and he stares at her through the drift of brown smoke from his cigar, making up his mind. Baz feels like there's a hand round her throat, choking her. This man got Raoul; if he take Demi, he going to have to take her too. The den is so quiet all she can hear is her own breathing, her heart banging. "All right," says Moro, leaning forward and grinding out the cigar on the table. "Keep him. I keep the other one. The one with the mouth. He can work for me on the Mountain. Boy like that a good worker, strong. That's good for the Mountain."

The Mountain! The Mountain across the river. Baz knows in her heart that Fay's not going to protest. What does Raoul mean to her now? Nothing but trouble. The two years he spent with them, all his jokes and smiles, all gone. Like dust, thinks Baz. Dust to Fay.

Moro looks round at the children in the room as if sizing them up, like so much meat for the butcher's slab. "The Mountain always need quick hands; it don't care what a body says. Nobody listen on the Mountain. So you keep what you got,

Fay"—he takes a long pull on the cigar and exhales—"but this thing about the ring: I don't like this thing about the ring. It seem to me that if I give someone a helping hand, you know what I am saying, a protective arm, and that someone then choose to bite the helping hand, that's not a good thing. That person lose everything." He stands up. "I want the ring, Fay. If you got it, you bring it to me; if you don't have it, then you get busy and you find it. You got two days."

"Of course, Señor Moro. I get them all looking."

"Yes, you do that, because if I don't get that ring, I will take every one of your little family here. Take them all." He snaps a blunt finger and thumb. "Then you just like when you first come to me. Alone, Fay, and worth nothing because now you are getting old, and you don't look so good."

Fay doesn't move. Doesn't react in any way at all, though all the children are looking at her. "Two days, so they better get working, hey, your little family—work hard and find me that ring, then everything is safe again, which is how I like things to be." He turns to go, but at the door he stops as if a new thought has come to him. "Your rent, Fay, it's almost nothing. You got to pay a little more." For some reason he looks directly at Baz this time, and Baz feels his eyes behind his dark glasses and the way he looks makes her imagine his stumpy fingers touching her face. She tries not to shudder. Moro's gaze moves back to Fay.

"I pay you all the time," she says.

"Yeah, you good," he says, "but"—and he lifts his hands up, palm outward—"I'm a businessman too, Fay, so you pay, or I take everything."

Fay nods.

"Good." Moro plucks a piece of paper from his top pocket.

"This what I want," he says, letting it flutter to the floor. He doesn't wait for Fay to pick it up and read the new sum. He signals to his two men and the three walk out.

There is silence in the den, all of them listening to the clump of the men going down the ladder, and then far away the bang of the door closing as they go out into the alley.

Fay stoops to pick up the paper and her shoulders sag. Miguel brings her a glass of her wine and then stands a little behind her, like a shadow.

"How much he askin?" says Demi.

"He want all we got, all I saved."

"You gonna give him that ring I took?"

"No."

"Well, what you gonna do?" asks Demi.

"Me?" Her voice sharpens. "I do the thinkin. You, you goin to be workin double-time. All of you!"

Baz is thinking about Raoul. Raoul with no one. Raoul alone in the dark. What kind of work do you do on the Mountain?

"OK, tha's fine, Fay," Demi's saying. "You get thinkin. We get out of your hair, OK. Give you some peace." He signals Baz and Sol and the others and they head for the door, but Miguel lingers.

As they are going out Baz hears Miguel saying, "I got someone wantin to meet you, Fay. He got money, knows people. Maybe he can help, Fay . . ."

Chapter Eight

THE NEXT MORNING Fay hustled them out to work the market. She wouldn't talk about Moro, she half went into a rage when they asked about Raoul, and when they came back at lunchtime with a roll of grubby dollars slipped from a bag here, a pocket there, she just took the money from them and complained they were getting lazy. "Miguel pulling in more than you, Demi. What happen you get slow all a sudden?"

She sent them straight back out. Told them to work the business quarter. They did. They worked every street, must have walked a hundred miles—that's what it felt like to Baz, and they hardly made enough for the tram ride home.

"You think Señor Moro keep Raoul in the bar, make him work there, run errand for him maybe?" They had avoided talking about him all day.

Demi shrugged and stuck his hands in his pockets and studied the tips of his sneakers like they were something special. "How anyone gonna know 'bout that, 'cept the big man himself?" But when they had swung down at Agua, he'd agreed to stake out the Slow Bar for a little while, see if they catch a sight of Raoul.

They spent so long hanging out by the dead fountain that one of Moro's men saw them and came sauntering over, all greased-back hair and tight vest to show his muscle. "You looking for something? Fay tell you come down here?"

"No, we just waitin on . . . waiting on Sol. He said to meet up for goin in," said Demi, "but maybe somethin happen. Come on, Baz, we better move."

"Yes," said the man, his voice touched up with a little bit of pretend concern. "Maybe something happen."

"Where the boy?" said Baz abruptly.

"The boy?"

"Came with a message from Fay yesterday." She shrugged off Demi's hand. "He workin in the bar?"

The man gave a slow shake of his head. "Well," he said, "that the sort of thing only Señor Moro really know about. You want to come ask him, hey?" He held out his hand, inviting Baz to take it, to come with him, to stroll across to the Slow Bar.

She took a step back and Demi took her arm again, yanked her away. "We got to go."

"Another time," the man said, calling after them as they walked quickly away across the square. "Another time you maybe come callin . . ."

Fay took one look at the sorry wallet Demi laid on the table and sent them out again. "I got business meetin and you two scratchin my nerves. Baz, go buy some food." She peeled a couple of dollars from the wallet and gave them to her. "No meat—just bread and beans will do."

Now Baz and Demi sit out on the front steps, the flat heat of the afternoon pressing in on them. She hugs her knees. Demi's frowning and flipping stones down onto the muddy shoreline. "Why everythin turn sour, Baz? Why Señor Moro digging his hooks in Fay, big-time skunkin into our place, threatenin and blowin his smoke; and we got to do this and we got to do that and I don't know what we got no more?"

"She give him Raoul."

"Maybe she done the right thing. Maybe Raoul say things."

A rat noses out from the rubbish underneath their building and

Demi savagely hurls a stone at it. Hits the rat too, but it doesn't do it no harm, just makes it scuttle back into the shadows. "Not sayin he turn bad on us, Baz, but maybe Moro make him talk; maybe that Uncle Toni twist him up a little. Not Raoul, not you, maybe even not me match for what they do to make a body spill a little more talk 'n they should."

"You don't think she done right! You don't think Raoul ever say thing to cause us trouble! How you think that 'bout Raoul? You know Raoul!"

"How he shake the uniform up at Norte? You seen him taken."

"Somethin happen. Count the time something happen for us and we give policeman the slip."

She watches him flip another stone. After a moment she says, "She smile at him, Demi, and tell him he's all right, and then she give him right over to Señor Moro. You think she do that to us one time?"

"Why you sayin that? You an' me, we all she got."

"She don't care 'bout us, Demi. All she think 'bout is money." She rocks a little as she hugs her knees. "Who she gonna send next time, Demi? You gonna shrug if she send me down the Slow Bar?"

"Fay not sendin you or me anywhere we don't want to go. We like family, Baz."

"Raoul family."

"Almost."

"Raoul family. Raoul family till what she done yesterday. Raoul nothing now 'less we do somethin." She stands. "Raoul been put on the Mountain, Demi. I know by the way that man talk."

He hurls a stone out to the dead river as far as he can,

watches till it hits the mud, sending up a tiny splat. "You think we just go walk out there and take him away. You sayin that? You mad crazy."

"No. You ever talk to Lucien 'bout how he come away from there?"

"No."

"That's what we do," she says firmly. "We get Lucien tell us how bad the Mountain is. Tell us how we get in, how we get out. All we got are stories Fay tell the little ones, give them bad dream, make them do what she want. Same stories she told us. Now we go see the real thing."

He stands. "An' if we do this thing, you gonna stop pickin and givin out your sour face all the time?"

"Only got one face, Demi."

He shakes his head and grins. "You 'bout the most strange thing in the Barrio. They ever make a museum here, they gonna put you in it." He dusts his hands down on his jeans. "So we go find Lucien."

*   *   *

Lucien is where he always is, at the well, helping Mama Bali draw washing water. "Seen you lost another one, Baz," he says in his soft, half-whispering voice.

Mama Bali straightens her back and wipes the sweat from her face. "Mind your business, Lucien, and then no one bother you." But she gives Demi and Baz a keen look. "You got troubles?"

"Everybody got troubles, Mama; we just got questions for Lucien." He glances at Baz and then looks over his shoulder as if he feels Fay's got her eyes on him somehow.

"Raoul been put on the Mountain," she says bluntly.

"Everybody know it one bad place, so you tell us how we get him out o' there. You tell us the way we do it."

Mama blows out her cheeks like she's some giant balloon monkey. "Mountain?" she says. "Show your scars, Lucien."

Reluctantly Lucien pulls up the leg of his tracksuit bottom— his calves and shins are pitted with old cuts and tears. "I got lucky," he says. "I got so sick my mother put me out on the road. She thinking one of the drivers take me back to the city, take me to hospital. Come here instead. Sickness passed." He wipes the back of his hand across his brow and smiles at Baz. "Now Lucien haul buckets, cos that a whole lot better than scratchin dirt like a chicken. Or rat."

"You can get in and out then?"

"That time. That time ten years back. Business run the Mountain now. Señor Moro. They got fence and wire round the place. Guards too. Like a prison now: nobody come off that place. Just work an' die. Don't know how you get in, Baz—cut the wire maybe, but you better not go anywhere near that place."

"He got an honest job," says Mama, hands on broad hips, face gleaming in the heat, "something you two don't know too much 'bout. Here, you help me an' Lucien carry these buckets back to my place."

Demi sticks his hands in his pockets and stuffs out his chest. "My hands too precious for your old buckets."

She smiles. "Ain't nothing precious 'bout you, Demi." And with that she picks up one of the buckets and sets off with Lucien beside her.

"Phooph! Haulin dirty water; she soon get me washin her front step!" But when Baz silently picks up one of the remaining cans he picks up the other and the two of them follow Mama and Lucien back to her place.

She thanks them and gives them icy juice in tall cold glasses and in front of Lucien she puts a plate of cold beans and pork. He eats delicately, not like the boys in the den, who scoff their food like hungry dogs, but then he's older than any of them and he has a gentle way about him that you don't see in the Barrio. But he's still so thin; Baz reckons he'd fade to nothing if Mama Bali didn't give him a meal every day.

"Thank you for telling us 'bout the Mountain, Lucien," she says, and he smiles at her, lifting his hand to hide his crooked and broken teeth. Then lowers his head to his food. "What happen to your family?" she asks after watching him a moment. But he doesn't look up this time and he doesn't smile, just slowly continues to eat his food.

"Maybe you two should think about finding honest work one of these days," says Mama Bali as they're leaving. "Keep out of trouble that way."

"I keep out of trouble just fine, Mama," says Demi, but then as they walk back to the den, he says, "Honest work? What's honest work? Honest work get you working on this Mountain maybe; talking with a fat mouth get you on the Mountain. 'Bout the only thing keep you and me from that place, Baz, is being a good thief." He wriggles his fingers under her nose so she has to tilt her head away. "This gotta be my magic."

"Yeah," she says, "you better use your magic get Raoul out o' that place."

"Tomorrow. Tomorrow we catch a ride over the bridge. No problem. Find him and haul him out of there. It gonna be my first honest thing. You watch me—I gonna be some monkey-man." And he wriggles his fingers again and bounces up and down on his toes until she has to smile. Then he gives a whoop and starts doing jump turns against the wall of the alley, then cheeking this man, making a joke with that man, as they make their way back to the den. Sometimes Demi makes you feel he's king of the world. But Lucien said the Mountain was more like a prison than anything else. To steal Raoul out of a prison they got to be really the best thief in the city.

Chapter Nine

FAY'S ON HER OWN, cooking up the evening meal, when Baz and Demi get back, jacket on the back of the chair, a big black pot simmering with stew: the air is hot and heavy with a rich and meaty smell. She's chopping sweet potato and humming along to a samba that's playing on the radio. Her knife goes *thucka thuck* to the beat. It's as if Moro has never been.

Storm and shine, thinks Baz. Fay and Demi aren't so different from each other. They've got moods that switch on and off like an electric light. Funny thing is Fay is often at her sweetest when she's cooking. Mama Bali is sweet all the time. Maybe, thinks Baz, the smell of food on a hot stove just makes a body feel good.

She washes her hands in the basin by the window and then stands beside Fay. Demi goes over to his corner, where he has a couple of shelves for his clothes and a suitcase with no handle that he keeps stuffed under his cot-bed. Baz doesn't think he's got anything but old magazines and pictures he's pulled out of the papers, mostly to do with his football team. She's noticed how he's taken to checking his things almost every time he comes in the room. Fay's got a rule that there's no borrowing or stealing in the den, but he checks all the same. Just like Fay, Baz thinks, except he doesn't look over his shoulder all the time.

Baz watches Fay a little while to see what she's doing and then, without being asked, begins to help, picking up a small plastic-handled knife and cutting down into the hard sweet potato.

She pushes Raoul into a dark corner of her mind. Raoul and

his fat mouth just have to wait till she and Demi have a clear day, because that is what Lucien said they would need to get out to the Mountain, do what they have to do and come back again. It was possible. He said that though it was fenced and there were guards, they were there to keep the working children from getting out and so there was a chance that it mightn't be so hard breaking in. Nobody talked about how they would get out again.

When she had asked Lucien whether Raoul would be all right working on the Mountain for maybe a few days, maybe longer, he didn't look her in the eye, just kept his head down, slow spooning in Mama's stew. Easiest thing, he said between mouthfuls, fall sick on the Mountain. It just happen, happen all the time . . . but your friend, maybe he get lucky, you know . . .

But maybe they would have to wait longer. If Fay kept them working like she had today they would never get free, because Fay must never know what they planned to do. If she ever thought that they had gone behind her back and then done something that could stir more trouble between her and Señor, she would parcel them up, slide them into the dead river—or give them straight over to the shady man, which would come to about the same thing, the end of her and Demi.

Fay takes the cut sweet potato, shovels it into a baking tin and pours a little oil over. Roast vegetable. Baz can't remember a time Fay took this much trouble over a meal for them.

"You work something out about the big man, about how you going to pay him?" asks Demi, coming back to the table.

"Maybe I do," she says, and smiles.

That's why she seems so easy. Got something figured. Maybe even heard something. Fay has threads running out across the city, tapping into this, into that. Fay knows how to squeeze a little bit of something out of anyone she ever knew but she stays hidden in the middle of the Barrio, waiting for the good things to come to her.

"What you do 'bout that ring, Fay?"

"What ring?" She wipes the back of her hand against her nose and then carries on with her chopping.

Demi grins and leans over the pot. "You want some help with that thing? Mmm, what you got cooking in there, Fay? Smells real special." Another sniff.

She pushes him away. "What you think 'bout going into a new line of work, Demi?" she says.

"What's that?" he says, and sits down, putting his feet up on the table and reaching for the paper, the offer of help slipping quickly from his mind. "Everybody know I got genius at what I do, Fay. What you want me to be now? Some kind o' rocket scientist maybe?"

"Rocket science won't pay my bills." She gathers up the beans and adds them to the stew. "How 'bout this: a big house, marble floors . . ."

"You want me to go buildin!"

"Will you listen one time! This place got garden, swimmin pool, high walls, got fancy things, got a safe too, stacks of dollar bill, got more thing than you dream of."

"You talkin 'bout one of them places up in Reggio."

"Could be."

"And what's some fancy place up in that quarter got to do with me? Got no shops, no busy streets, got nothing but high walls and big gates. That's just rich-man country."

"Slip into one of them houses and you come out a rich boy. You do this thing, Demi, and we all be rich, pay off the man and still some."

Baz keeps bowed over her cutting, clipping red pepper into strips, but she keeps looking up, watching Fay, hearing the way she's playing Demi: a little bit of praise talk, a little pinch of promise, like the way she's cooking. Keeping her voice easy, making this job sound easy too.

And for all his protests, and for all his promises about rescuing Raoul, she can tell Demi will fall into doing whatever Fay has set up. It's the way he is—the way he is with her.

"What!" He pulls a face like she's just told him he's got to jump to the moon. Demi can't say anything or think anything unless he can double its size. "How I get in one of them houses? They got guards and locks and they got dogs, I bet, with teeth just waiting to bite my leg clean off. No thief much good hoppin round on one leg." And he starts to hop, making out like he's trying to pick a pocket and falling all over the place; Baz laughs, loving his clowning. Fay lets him have his play, nodding a little, smiling . . . "OK, OK, Demi."

But he keeps going, getting up from the floor and miming sneaking in through huge gates. "You get by the gate and the guard and the dog," he says all hushed, as if the guard and the dog might be hearing him. Then he claps his hands to his ears. "And wha' do you know? They got an alarm that'll call every uniform in the city to come and haul that stupid thief straight down to the Castle. And you know what? That thief don't deserve any better. Nothin but a fool try his hand in Reggio. Fay, you been sippin wine all day, you come up with ideas like that; sippin wine or listenin to a crazy man." He dusts his hands off against the back of his jeans and sits back down at the table. If it weren't for the clowning, Baz thinks he could be one of those lawyers you see sometimes on the TV programs.

"Suppose you go to this fancy house and there's no alarm,

no lock, whole place sitting wide-open—what you say then? You say that sound too difficult?"

"Sound like you been dreaming. Tell me—who go and buy a place like you say, have all them thing, guard and gate and all, and then leave out a sign sayin: OK, you come an' walk in now, take what you want!"

"Well, I think maybe we got a place just like that." She scratches her arms and then pushes her hair out of her eyes with the back of her hand. "Someone workin on the inside, someone who give us the right time, someone who know all the numbers."

"You know this person?" Demi dumps himself back down in a chair at the table.

"I got more history than you know, Demi. I maybe know this person from way back, before even you come along. Maybe knew him when I was a girl and him just a baby." She half laughs. "Me and a baby. That's something to think about, hey."

"What happen?"

Baz glances at her and senses Fay doesn't want to talk anymore about this baby. Perhaps it was her own child. It's hardly possible to imagine Fay having a child of her own, but Baz remembers her when she first got taken in by Fay and Demi; she was pretty then, softer. Not much softness now. She stays locked most of the time, just like the precious things Demi says she has down in the basement.

"What happen to this baby, Fay?" presses Demi.

"Things happen all the time," she says with a shrug, turning away from them and back to the cooking pot, "most of them bad but sometime you can't tell if a thing bad or if it goin to turn good. There's a family want that baby, a family that can raise it good, give it fine things. So I walk 'cross half the city and give it them." Baz pictures a young Fay holding a baby, maybe its small hand gripping her finger, she then having to unpeel those little fingers so she can give it across to this woman who is going to be the new mother, and then Fay turning and going away down some long street. The picture makes Baz uncomfortable. She concentrates on the next job, chopping garlic.

"They give you money?" asks Demi.

"What is this? Course I get money. How come I feed you all the time; you just walking stomach, talking mouth." She checks the stew, gives it a stir and then turns the heat down a little and puts a blackened lid on the pot.

"Then?"

"Then nothing. What eating you, Demi? You asking so many questions, I can't hardly think straight."

Baz's knife slips and she nicks the tip of her finger.

"Woah! Who the clumsy one here? Give me that." She sweeps the peppers Baz has been chopping over onto her side and her knife flickers over the last two or three. Baz watches the blade, sucking her finger.

"What kind of she-thief you gonna be if you go cutting your fingers?"

"You ever go back and see that child?" asks Demi, tilting back in his chair.

"Why you want to know that, Demi? You got someone wantin to know these things?"

Demi holds up his hands like he wants to ward her off from charging him, but it's sort of teasing. "Hey, Fay, I'm just asking. Thought I was the first, all the time I thought that, so I gotta right to know."

"What right you got? You want be a newspaper man or you

want to be a thief, get rich? You choose, cos if you want to be poking round like a river rat, then you can move on, you hear me. You better off if you be a little more like Baz. She don't bother me some like you."

Baz turns away and carries the knives and chopping board over to the sink in the corner. She tips a little water into the sink and cleans the knives. She doesn't want attention; she wants to know about this first boy too, just as much as it seems Demi does.

"Come on, Fay, you tellin me what I want to know because I'm the one who brings you things; I'm the one you want to go squeezing into some rich folk's house; and you just tellin me I'm safe doing this but you only half tellin me why. So come on—what happen then, this child that come along before me? What happen, hey?"

"Life go on, Demi. That's what happen. That's what happen all the time unless you make some mistake and end up walking right into the Castle." There's the scrape of a match, and when Baz turns round and comes back to join them, Fay is sitting, elbows on the table, one of her bitter black cigars in her mouth. "One good thing though," she says, her voice softening, maybe one of those doors inside her opening a little chink again, "this family get rich; this child grow up. Maybe time come round when this child remember how he got so lucky and bring some o' that luck right back on me. Dream 'bout that sometime but dreamin get you nothin, but you know sometime you do a thing and it come back to you, like investment. Like I put time into you an' Baz, and you bring me thing, hey."

"Bring you thing all the time, Fay," says Demi, and then, "this the one on the inside, Fay? The one goin to help us an' make us rich?"

She nods and smiles. Baz hasn't seen her smile this much; she seems almost a different person. "This child all grown now. He somethin . . ." And then she cuts off as the boys start to drift back in, Miguel with them. Whenever Miguel is in a group, Baz notices, the group always seems quiet, like somehow he slaps a little mud on their souls. But when Fay greets them and they see that she's in a smiling mood, they liven up, rag a little, turn on the TV. Fay lets them be, even though the music she was humming along to gets swallowed up by the jangle of the cartoon they're watching.

Miguel doesn't sit with the others; he comes over to Fay, his eyes flicking toward Demi and Baz, taking them in, then looking up at Fay like he's expecting a pat. Fay doesn't pat and Fay doesn't hug, except when a child's so small she can pick it up.

Baz wonders why Fay tolerates Miguel in a way that she doesn't the others. She favors him. How long has he been with them? Five, six weeks maybe. Not like most of the others, picked up near the bus station, lost and hungry, thinking the city's going to give them a life they didn't have in the country. Miguel was different. He found them, made his own way right down into the Barrio, right to the den. Like Demi, he's a city boy. And she doesn't trust him.

For half a moment Baz has one of those sliding thoughts that slip unbidden into the mind: could he have been Fay's first child, the one she's been telling them about? Of course not, too young, younger than Demi. She favors him though.

Demi nods his head toward Miguel. "He got anything to do with this job you been tellin about?"

"He know the house," says Fay. "And he the go-between for me and this grown child, this young man who gonna bring my luck back; that's what Miguel done. You mind him."

"I mind him, Baz too, so long as he mind us and not go talkin and whisperin us into trouble, like what happen to Raoul."

"Raoul find his own trouble," she says sharply. "Miguel done nothin but help. You listenin, Demi?"

"OK, OK. So when d'we get to meet this wonder-man child you got hidden away?"

Fay looks at Miguel. "Maybe when we done eatin." She smiles, pours a little more wine in her glass and downs it. "Good times, Bazzie. Good times—I promise, eh."

Baz plays the game. "We go north; get a place, like you say."

"Sure. If we rich you think I gonna stay here? You think I some old mad woman, Demi?"

Demi grins. The thought of scooping up some big money always makes Demi happy. "No, Fay. You the one look out for us all."

She smiles, and Miguel, looking up at her, has a little smile on his face too. "Remember that, remember that all the time. Now you an' me got to do some plannin, Demi. Even a walk-in got to be perfect."

"Sure thing."

Everybody got something to smile about, thinks Baz, everybody 'cept Raoul.

Fay bangs her spoon against the pot, calling the boys to eat. Miguel's first in line, bowl ready, but Demi just walks straight past him, and when Fay serves him she nods. He is still number one.

Chapter Ten

IT'S LATE. The den is steamy and sour. The boys, their meal finished, are clustered around the TV, watching the news; Fay's in
her easy chair, smoking her cigarillo. The little ashtray by her
elbow is overflowing with butts. Baz reckons she's spent a
heavy day putting burnt tobacco in her lungs.

Outside there's a crack and the sky lights up. The TV goes
black and the boys groan and then cheer when it flickers back
on again. Thunder rumbles over the Barrio. Dry storm. Electric.
No rain. Never rain. Just noise and heavy air and sweat.

"Hey, Demi," shouts Javi. "Police chief again, Captain Dolucca
he'self. He want to skin you. He say it right now. Say: gonna
skin any one-time bad thief-boy, skin him and then burn down
the Barrio and build a new shiny city right here." They laugh
and jeer. Demi's top dog, the one the boys want to be like, but if
he gets walked into the Castle nobody in the den is going to
mind that much because they all want his place.

"Captain say nobody safe no more cos this city got best
thief in the world." That was Sol. "He gonna say that about me
soon-time."

Javi smacks him on the back of the head. "You only thief
stuff that don't matter."

"Where's Miguel?" Demi's standing easy like nothing's bothering him, one eye half on the TV screen.

"Running errand for Fay," says Sol.

"That right, Fay? Miguel doin some business for you?" says
Demi, glancing across at Baz, who's washing up the last of the
dishes with Giaccomo. Baz shrugs; she hadn't noticed him going
out either. " 'Bout the only thing that boy can do is run errand."

Fay looks ghost white in the flickering light, her eyes open but like she's not seeing anything. Baz wonders whether she even heard Demi's question. She can be like this at times, tucked away inside herself. Baz used to call these her trouble times, and she and Demi would tiptoe round her. "She got troubles," Demi would say. When Baz was a little older she noticed that trouble time often came with a bottle of rum or red wine. There's a bottle of clear rum on the floor by her chair now, half empty, but Baz knows she's not sick with drink right now. It's the boy, she guesses. Maybe she's worrying now that this young man, her one-time child, is going to change his mind about helping her, and then what will she do?

Demi saunters over to the bucket and slaps water on his face. Fay watches him and gives a little shiver. She gets strange fancies sometimes, specially if she's been drinking a little. Baz keeps watching Fay, watching Demi. "What you think about this police chief, Fay?" he asks. "He going to come bothering us down here, you reckon?" He cups his hands and gives his face another splash.

The TV screen shows a black police van pulling up outside the high white walls of the Castle and a line of children shuffling up to the door. Every so often this is what happens: someone sitting behind a big desk calls for a crackdown, and the police scour the streets and lock up any scuffed-up child they find. The camera cuts back to the police chief. He has a fat, waxy black mustache that looks as if it's been stuck onto his face.

"So this captain is Señor Moro's policeman, the one he tell us about, the one he do business with, the one whose wife lost her ring—what you think, Fay?"

Baz holds her breath, waiting for Fay to give Demi a piece

of her mind, tell him not to give her cheek or else she'll give him right away like Pickpack. Easy come, easy go. Time you go, Demi, your mouth got too big—that's what she could say. But Fay just shivers again and her voice is a little thick with drink when she speaks. "Mind what you say 'bout that man, Demi. He gonna hear what you say before you even say it."

"He that good? I just thinkin he Barrio bad man, not the devil he'self."

Outside silent lightning ripples across the sky. The bulb hanging over the table dims and then brightens.

The warning bell jangles and they are all startled into action.

Demi snaps his feet off the table. Baz moves away from the door, goes to the bucket and washes her hands quickly. Then, when the door opens and she sees who this stranger is that Miguel has brought back to the den, she moves a little farther back into the shadows.

Student? No.

Journalisto? No.

Like an angel from that church window, an uptown angel with a blond halo of curls; Fay's grown-up boy-child.

"Hey," says Demi, walking over to stand beside Fay, "look who the rat brought in. We got fancy visitor, Fay."

Miguel darts an angry look at Demi, but the uptown angel ignores them all. His eyes are on Fay.

"I brought him," says Miguel needlessly.

"You're a good boy," says Fay to Miguel. Then she gets up from her chair. "So you come back like we agreed, hey." She holds open her hands like she thinks this young man, her angel-boy, the one she gave away for dollars, is going to come running into her arms, but he doesn't move from the door. He takes his time, looking first at her, then round the den. Baz tries to see the place the way he's seeing it now, their den, their safe place: make-do furnishings scavenged from the flea markets; boxes and buckets and clothes strung on a line; shadows, mess and a ring of faces looking back at him. He nods as if checking them off one by one, Demi last. "Ah," he says, "you're the thief they all talk about. You think you're maybe fast enough to pick my pocket?"

"You got anything worth me takin?" says Demi. While he's talking, Javi has slunk around the wall till he's behind the young man. He's good, Javi, thinks Baz, like a slippy shadow. She sees his hand move out toward the man's pocket.

Quick as a snake, the young man has Javi's wrist and has whipped him round, jerking him off balance. Javi gives a yelp as his arm twists, and then the young man just lets him go so Javi drops to his knees. The young man smiles. "Good," he says, "but not so quick."

Fay claps her hands. "Very good," she says. "Fast. Good to be fast like that when you down in the Barrio." No one else claps. "Come. We talk some business."

Javi gets up and, clutching his arm, creeps back to his place in the corner.

The young man ignores him; his attention is all the time on Demi. "You better than him?" he asks.

Demi shrugs. "You want to see me work, you watch me on the street sometime. I don't work in here. You want a monkey do tricks, you go find a zoo."

"I don't need a zoo," he says, his eyes never leaving Demi's face. "I've seen you work on the street. Saw you take that woman's shopping, steal her precious jewelry." He gives a thin laugh. "Unlucky to choose the wife of the chief of police."

Demi jumps to his feet. "You makin' a threat to me?" The young man's amused expression doesn't change. Demi bobs on his toes like he's ready to throw a punch at him—except he has a table in the way. Fay cuffs him, makes him sit again.

"Mind the way you talk," she snaps. "This man got a business venture; we listen to him."

"'This man'?" says the young man, unruffled, still amused. "'This man'? Don't they know who I am?"

"They know I look after you, find you a good home when you no more than a small child. And look at you now," she says admiringly. "You got good clothes, you speak educated, and I bet you got money in your wallet. Miguel!" she says sharply. "You didn't bring him through no bad place in the Barrio?" Baz notices that she still hasn't used the young man's name and she wonders why not, wonders if there is something special about this family she gave her baby to. She also notices the way Fay can hardly take her eyes off him.

"No one touch him, Fay."

"Good boy. Come and sit. Baz, bring a little wine. Miguel, clear the table."

They sit, the young man on Fay's left and Demi to her right. Baz puts a jug on the table and a small plate of sliced cold spicy sausage. Fay splashes wine into a glass for her son and then for Demi, but not for the others. Demi adds water to his. The young man, watching, does the same. Fay says, "Good to be careful in a new place, yes?"

The young man raises his glass. "I'm always careful . . . Mother," he says, and then sips the watered wine.

For half a moment Fay seems almost taken aback, and then her expression softens into a real smile. She nods and raises her glass in a silent toast to this smart, self-possessed young señor whom she gave away for a clutch of dollars. Around the table though there's silence. Demi looks at Fay and then, challengingly, at the young man. "Fay, 'bout time you tell us—what is this boy? Why, if he so special, he come down to mix in the Barrio? You tell us why we got to trust him."

"Yes," agrees the boy, "why don't you tell them?" And there is just a hint of mockery in his voice when he says, "After all, aren't we family?"

Chapter Eleven

Family.

It's like when someone slaps down a winning card and everyone who's in the game just stares. Javi's eyes are wet and shiny,
not really understanding the significance of what's been said;
Giacco grins and nods like he knows what's going on, but he
understands less than little Javi; Miguel licks his lips and
watches the young man, as does Demi. Only Baz, standing away
from the others, over by the sink, stares at Fay. Fay's smiling,
and she only does that when she's got what she wants. Baz is
wondering whether this hard uptown angel really is her son.
He could be eighteen, could be older. Fay never tells when Baz
asks her age, just laughs and says, "Old, old as I look." She doesn't
look that old to Baz, maybe in her thirties somewhere; she doesn't
know. Maybe late twenties. That would mean she'd have been
around twelve when she'd had a baby, younger than Baz is now.
It happens, Baz knows that. She's seen them in the Barrio, in the
poor quarters, young girls, skinny and drawn, clutching a little
bundled-up baby; and they always look scared and hungry, and
so tired a thin wind would spin them away. It's hard to imagine
Fay like that; she's too strong. Too strong to give away her
blood child. But that's what she said she'd done.

A burst of lightning splashes over the Barrio, brightening
the room for a heartbeat. The young man catches Baz's eye and
holds her in his gaze. She drops her eyes, suddenly shamed. He
makes her think of an angel and he makes her think of a wolf.

"You sayin somethin, Fay?" says Demi. "We got a right to
know about this . . . boy you got. He got a name even?"

Fay, still smiling, pats the young man's arm and says, "He can speak for himself."

"Sure." He lets his left hand rest for a moment on top of Fay's. Mother and son? Brother and sister almost. Both fair-haired, fair-skinned too, compared with the rest of them. "The name they give me is Eduardo Dolucca." The way he speaks is clean and precise, almost shiny, thinks Baz, like an uptown car. "Does that mean anything to you?"

"*The* Dolucca?" Demi tries to keep the surprise and suspicion out of his voice. He doesn't succeed. If this boy is who he says he is, his daddy is the captain of police and the yellow-hat lady is the woman whose ring Demi stole.

"Yes." The boy smiles. "My mother was clever to find me such a family, no?" Baz doesn't believe the smile, doesn't believe he feels cleverness was anything to do with it.

"I wanted you safe," says Fay. She purses her lips and blows out a thin stream of smoke. "I did not think about what happen when the years go by. I was young. I had to live." She taps ash into the bowl. "Maybe we talk of this some other time."

Demi doesn't agree. "We should know why he come here, Fay. Why he watching us all the time; he watching what we do on the street, maybe take pictures. All he got to do is show them to his father." He snaps his fingers. "Hey! He could put us all in the Castle, easy as that. You thought about that, Fay?"

Fay makes a dismissive gesture with her hand. "Demi, grow up. You waste time."

But Demi's in full flow. "And why should he come here? He got the good life. Look at him. Rich boy!" He says the two words like they're a bad taste in his mouth. "You go to college?" Eduardo inclines his head. "You buy things. Look at his watch." They look at it. Eduardo holds it up for them to see:

chunky and silver. It's like wearing a hundred dollars on your wrist, thinks Baz. Not a wise thing to do in the Barrio, but then no one bothered him. To her, he looks like he's half at home already, but there is something in what Demi is saying. This plan he's put on the table to Fay; it's going to mean them robbing his house, stealing from the captain of police when they have already stolen a ring from his wife. Won't that bring everything tumbling down round their heads?

"Why you come to the Barrio?" says Demi. "Fay maybe one time your mother, but you got your family. Why don't you leave us alone? We do OK without you. Fay, tell him."

Fay doesn't tell him.

"I got business," says Eduardo. "You don't like it, you go."

Demi slams back his chair and jumps to his feet. "Me? What you mean, I go? What happen round this place without me?" He slaps his puffed-out chest. "I go, then Fay don't got no business!"

Any moment there is going to be trouble. Baz knows it; she's seen fights breaking out as sudden as the lightning, and then there is nothing but blood and hurt. "Demi!" Baz says sharply, and somehow this warning acts like a splash of ice water. Demi spins on his heels and, muttering crossly, walks over to a corner and throws himself down into an old easy chair.

Eduardo laughs. "Hey! Half-kilo macho man! How about that?"

Fay lights another little cigar and waves out the match. "All right," she says. "Enough." Demi opens his mouth to speak but Fay cuts him off. "Demi, I don't want a word from you. No, not one. You sit and you listen." All softness from the drink has gone. Business brings the world back into focus for Fay. To Eduardo she says, but much more softly, "No one as good as Demi, so stop this, both of you."

Eduardo smiles at Demi. "Sure. I take back what I said. I know you're good, fast. Very fast." He snaps his fingers. "Like that, eh?"

The boys round the table like this. "Yeah, he's good," says big Giaccomo. "Demi quicker than Miguel, and Miguel pretty quick. That right, Miguel? You pretty quick, hey?" But Miguel doesn't join in with this moment of approval. He moves a little closer to Eduardo, his eyes watchful, flicking from Fay to the others, back to Fay, as if he is half expecting some secret word of command. Baz can't take her eyes from Eduardo's hands: pale, with long fingers and clean trimmed nails. Hands a fine lady would have.

"Tell them why you come, Eduardo," says Fay. "Tell them, then we can do business."

"Sure." His voice seems all easy reason, smooth as butter and oil. "But I don't see why you think it necessary. What you got here is a little bit too much equal rights. But what do I know?"

"Yes," says Fay, "you don't know so much 'bout what we got here so do what I ask. This my place, and these boys do good enough. So you give them reason to trust you . . ."

"All right, that's no problem."

Baz brings a fresh jug of water to the table. Eduardo helps himself and then smiles at her. She takes a glass to Demi, sitting coiled up in his chair, an angry shadow in the corner of the room. He takes the drink without thanking her, all his attention on Eduardo, who has started to tell his story.

"The couple Fay sell me to want a boy, so they're happy. They give me this name. Teach me good manners. Captain Dolucca likes good manners. Teach me respect too. Put me through school. I work hard. Do well." He pauses. "But then comes a change: my lovely new mother who couldn't have any children has a baby girl. A big change. I'm ten and suddenly I become invisible because they're so busy with little Niña. Everybody loves little Niña. And she's smart. Has everybody eating out of her hand.

"I get in a little trouble in school. Nothing much. A small thing, but this is when I begin my real education because my father, the Captain, is angry with me, very angry. He beats me and he calls me 'Barrio filth,' and I don't know why he says this to me . . . till he explains very simply, very carefully, so that even though I am only ten I will never forget exactly who I am. And he tells me that my real mother was a street girl, someone he tried to help, and when she had a baby, me, he takes me as a kindness, a charity. This is what he says. Because this woman didn't care too much about the baby so long as she gets money."

Fay smacks the table. "The man is a pig! He doesn't tell the truth."

"The man is a pig," agrees Eduardo smoothly, "but this is what he tells me. And he threatens me, says that unless I am very good he will send me back to where I come from, to the Barrio, back to my birth mother because she is a thief, a thief queen with children she teaches to thieve and steal till they are a plague in the city, and"—he raises his hands apologetically—"he says worse things about my mother, much worse. Then he says is this what I want, to go back to the Barrio and become a thief, because if I do that, he will catch me like he is going to catch my mother and put us both in the Castle." He smiles at Fay.

"I say no, of course, but I become a boy who learns," continues Eduardo. "I watch and I listen and I learn many things. I see that this father of mine is become an important man in the police, but I see something else. I see the way our house always has money, very much money, and he always has a smart car. And always we have visitors who carry briefcases. And these men are not police but what my father calls business colleagues, colleagues who keep bringing him gifts, at the end of every month. After these visits my father always goes into his office and puts all the envelopes they give him into his safe.

"It doesn't take me too long to figure out that my father, this good man, this man who likes respect and good manners, does a little business on the side of being a policeman. I am curious to know what he keeps putting away into the safe in his office. I wait for a long time but then I find a way to open his safe and I see how much money my important policeman father has gathered from all these . . . gifts. And I think that being a po- liceman is not much different to being a thief. In fact I think that being a thief is a better life, more honest." He gives a dry, sarcastic laugh. "I see how he is. I see how he treats his wife sometimes. I don't believe he ever did a good thing in his life. And I wonder more and more about my real mother and what made her give me away to him. So I make a decision: that I will go to college and learn everything I can. That I will find out who is my birth mother. And I will find a way of taking all the good things away from this lying man and give them to her. And so this is what I do. I watch. I learn. I learn everything about the Barrio and, with what he already told me about my mother, I find my way here. This is it; and I show her a way of making good business together."

Fay claps her hands. "How about that!" she says. The boys in the den like the story too. They like the thought of a boy turning his back on the police, on the hard man who is always running them down, moving them on. They gaze at Eduardo like he's already a hero.

Baz thinks that this story is hiding more than it is telling them but she can't say that; she can only listen. She pours out a little more wine and then goes to stand behind Demi's chair. The rest of the boys are sent off because Eduardo wants to go through the plan. It's simple. He holds up one key. "This is to the alarm. My father turns it on every night. I wait till he goes to bed. I turn it off. I open a window. You climb in. You walk into the office." He holds up a card with a house address and a number on it. "This is the number to the safe in my father's study. You take the money. Throw the money out of the window. Turn on the alarm. If you don't, then he's going to think the thief is in the house."

Demi leans back in his chair. "And they'll suspect you?"

He shrugs. "More likely he's going to think it's one of his business partners—coming back to collect some of the 'presents,' you know."

"Maybe he gonna think it Señor Moro," Fay says. "Put him out the picture. Put *him* in the Castle."

Eduardo gives his easy laugh. "So you do this. It's no problem. You switch on the alarm, then you got thirty seconds to get out of the window before the alarm goes off. It will take you less than thirty seconds to drop down to the street. The alarm goes. You get in the car. My father wakes up. By the time he's gone to his office and found he's been robbed, you're halfway home. Easy. And what we take will be enough for us all, I promise you. You walk away with more than you ever dreamed of." He holds out his hand to Fay. "My gift to you, Mother. We get this money and we can become big, big business."

"You think the captain of police is going to do nothing?" asks Demi. "He just gonna let us walk off like that, his money in our pockets?"

"What can he do? How can he say he's been robbed of money he shouldn't have?"

"And you?"

"Me? I told you. I shall be asleep in my bed. I wait a little time and then I join you and we become something special in the Barrio."

"Yes, with that kind of money we special all right. We pay off what we owe to Moro," says Fay. "I tell you, Eduardo, he squeezin me tighter an' tighter."

Like one of them fat snakes they got upcountry, thinks Baz, squeeze a dog till it's dead then swallow it whole.

"I got the boys and Baz working all the time there is, but we in a hard place here: we got the Captain shaking down the streets, and Moro sayin if he don't get what he want, he goin to take them, the boys, maybe one at a time, maybe take them all just like that, and leave me nothin." She grinds out her cigar. "And nothing I can do but pay an' pay. Maybe this mean we get done with that man for good, hey."

"Oh yes," agrees Eduardo quietly. "We deal with the big se-ñor for sure."

"You hear that, Baz? This one move we make gonna set us free." She puts one arm round Eduardo's waist and gives him a hug.

Baz can't remember the last time Fay showed herself so happy. She teases and jokes sometimes, pats a child on the head, sometimes touches Demi on the cheek when she's feeling soft, but mostly Fay doesn't feel soft. She keeps hard like the stone in a ring, hard and sharp, because she's maybe the only woman in the Barrio doing what she does, and doing it without the police knowing about her. She's not put an arm round Baz since she was little, before they came into the Barrio.

"Demi," says Fay, "what you think? You quit your foolish raging and ready to make some good money?"

Demi says, "If this what you want, OK. Sure. Don't sound like you need real skill, like what we do on the street every day, more like cash an' carry to me, but you want me to do this thing, sure I can do it. But I don't see why you don't tell Miguel to do this job—he can climb through a window, or Sol, or any of them." His voice is neutral. This is business. "Why you got to have me?"

Eduardo doesn't hesitate. "My mother says you're the best. Got the most experience. You're the number one."

Demi nods. He isn't going to disagree with this.

"But I reckon you are going to need help, backup, you know. Miguel is clever; he will go with you, share the risk, help you carry the money. He knows the area too."

"What about Baz? Baz watch my back. I don't work without Baz."

Eduardo's eyes flick toward Baz and he studies her for a moment, then smiles at her again. "She's so quiet I forget she's standing right here beside us. Sure Baz can be in the team, but I want Miguel there too." He looks at Fay.

"Sure. Good for Miguel. Time he learned a few more tricks."

"OK," says Demi, but with obvious reluctance, "but how about a little detail? How we going to get there and come away? Don't expect us taking the tram up north side and partying all the way back down to the Barrio with all your daddy's cash in a sack. We not so dumb, y'know."

"I have a car and I have a driver. He's very good. You could come along for the ride, Mother. It'll be like sitting in a taxi."

"No. I done my share. This is not what I do." Her voice is final.

"You don't trust me?"

"Course I trust you."

Eduardo holds up his hands, recognizing that there will be no persuading her. "It's not important. Course you don't need to be there at all; you be here, ready to count the bills."

She smiles. "I can count bills."

"OK," continues Eduardo. "We do the business tomorrow night. My father got a meeting set up tomorrow night back at the house and"—he rubs his hands together—"that means more honey in the pot. It gives me time to put my end in place: car, driver, all that." He looks at his expensive watch and makes a calculation. "So, two in the morning, the driver will pick you up outside the Barrio, in Agua by the fountain. You drive uptown. Thirty minutes. You find the window open. You do the business. Drive back. Ditch the car. You back here no later than four. Two hours. And that's it. Fay hides the money. I meet up with you that evening, here. This is a no-risk venture."

Baz wonders what a venture is. But whatever it is she doesn't believe it has no risk. Everything has risk, but there is one good thing in all this: she and Demi have tomorrow. Fay won't make them work if they have to be up all night robbing the Captain's house. They have their clear day to find Raoul and get him off the Mountain.

The boys come back and there is more talk and more drinking, though Baz notices the young man has no more than that one glass of watered wine. Baz herself keeps quiet and lets the others talk. She knows one thing that the others don't: the old life is over. It was all right when she didn't know about the Mountain, when she only cared about pleasing Fay, pleasing Demi. Maybe this boy is all he says he is and this job is as easy as he promises. Maybe Fay will pay Señor Moro whatever it is he says she owes him. But there is one certainty: she and Demi cannot stay in the Barrio. Sooner or later Señor Moro will want more, and the Captain won't stop until he has found who has robbed him. And there is always the ring hidden away in Fay's special place, the ring that seemed full of promise but has made everything worse. It looked like it had the sky tucked up inside it, but that ring just a trap, a lie; it would bring them nothing but bad time. If Fay sold her baby all that time back, sold it for money, wasn't she still the same person? Wouldn't she do the same thing now? Sell them all if she had to?

After tomorrow night, if she and Demi get a share or even if they don't, the two of them have to leave, make a life somewhere else. She knows this. She just hopes she can persuade Demi.

Chapter Twelve

EDUARDO LEAVES. He won't let Fay walk him through the Barrio so she sends Miguel and Giacco just so he doesn't lose his way. She goes down to see him off.

"She in love with that boy of hers," Demi says. "The way he come in, like he own us all already." And then he falls silent when Fay comes back in. They talk a little while more. Baz wants to know what the real story is about the time she gave the baby away. She wonders really if Fay didn't care, if she did it just for the money. She knows she is hard now, but then, when she was so young, was she maybe different then? But when Baz tries to get her to tell the story again Fay waves her hand. "We done enough talk about that time. Leave it, hey, Baz. You just think about what we do when we get all this money." So they talk about the robbery some more, at least Fay and Demi talk and Baz listens, then after a while Fay goes to her room.

The two boys come back and Giacco turns on the TV again. Baz tugs Demi's arm. "I'm goin. Can we talk 'bout something?"

"Sure," he says. "I'll walk with you." And they slip out of the den.

*   *   *

The night air is thick with musky smells from the Barrio: cooking fires, open drains, and always the fat, greasy stink of the dead river. Far in the distance, somewhere over the mountains to the north, the sky ripples with lightning. The storm has moved on, taking away its promise of rain.

"You promise we go find Raoul."

Demi is leaning against the carcass of an old Volkswagen

Beetle, dumped on the shore a long while back. In the half-light of a full moon it looks like a big turtle.

"Raoul goin to survive a coupla days. He don't need us throwing everythin away. Better if we do this thing first. Then go for Raoul."

Baz doesn't want to hear this. She wants Demi and her to think the same, to want the same things. Sometimes they do, and then she's happy; most times Demi goes his own way and she follows. This time she wants him to see what she sees. "You forget too easy, Demi. You forget a thing when it's not right in front of you. You forget Raoul." The words taste bitter in her mouth, make her want to spit.

He shrugs. Demi always shrugs to seem he doesn't care about anything.

She turns and starts walking away from him up the river to her corner where she can cut out to the hulk of the pilot boat. Demi often comes down this far with her, never any farther.

"I don't forget him," he says, his voice half calling, half keeping hushed. "I just got to do this thing. You know that. Fay tell you to do something like this, you do it too."

She's not really listening to what he's saying. "Always gonna be somethin in front of you stoppin you doin what's a right thing."

She hears his muttered curse and the *tang* of his fist banging the wreck. Then his feet slapping the hard mud as he runs after her. He grabs her arm. "If something happen . . . we get late, we find trouble and they ready to roll uptown—she goin to get someone else to do this thing. You want that? This a chance for us—you heard her say that, Bazzie, come on. Think what it mean if we get this, we maybe make big-time."

Baz remembers the hand that let her go. "What's big-time,

Demi? What's so special 'bout it, if it mean someone you like you just let go." She shakes off his arm and starts to walk quickly.

He doesn't follow this time. "You one stubborn girl!" Then when she doesn't answer and doesn't stop, he calls out, "OK. OK, I promise. I don't break any promise, you know that. Don't make me mad, Baz. We get this business out the way, then we got money in our pockets and everythin get a whole lot easier."

"You go make your robbing with Fay, Demi. I gonna find Raoul. I go on my own."

"You so stubborn!" he shouts. She can almost imagine him stamping his foot like he did sometimes when he was cross with Fay about something she wouldn't let him do, back in the time before they moved to the Barrio. "I bet a mule got more sense than you!"

Just before the bend in the bank she stops, listening to see if he's going to change his mind. There's nothing but the rumble of the city and the shreds of music and the calling of the Barrio. She looks round but can't see him anymore. He'll have gone back. His mind full of all the money he thinks he's going to scoop up.

She turns and picks her way through the softening mud to her safe place.

On the sloping deck she stoops and picks up the last of her plastic water bottles, shaking it and frowning. The end of her supply. She dribbles the warm water, rubbing it onto her feet, between her toes, digging out the gray slimy mud with her fingers, leaving the last drops to clean her hands. Tomorrow, after she has found Raoul and rescued him from the hill of rubbish, she must carry more bottles out to the boat.

She scrabbles up to the foredeck, her feet drying almost instantly in the warmth of the air and the heat from the deck. Upstream she can see lights on the bridge she must cross tomorrow, trucks driving north maybe, rich folk going home to some estate they got tucked away in the upcountry. Maybe that's where the river used to come from before they took all the water away with the big dam. She's seen a picture of the dam. Mama Bali showed her one time. It was on old and yellowy newspaper and it didn't look like much of anything. Mama kept the article because she said it made her laugh. It said that the great Barrier del Norte would bring water and electricity to every home in the city, and it also said that in less than a year the river would flow as free as it always had done, deep and wide enough to bring the boats back to the city. The newspaper was older than Baz and the river was as dry now as it had always been. Baz doesn't see much that's funny in that. As far as she is concerned, the only time the river flows is in her dream. Mama says someday someone is going to blow up the dam and she prays every night for that to happen so the flood will come sweeping down through the city and wash all the dirt away. Then she won't have to clean her windows and front step three times a day.

Baz has no doubts she will find Raoul. She is so certain of this because it is a right thing and right things are as thin and hard and sharp as that blue stone Demi stole. But finding is one thing; getting him away from that place, the Mountain, that will be hard.

Holding the rusted railing she raises herself up on her toes and then lifts her right leg behind her, arching her back, lifting her chin, closing her eyes, seeing the dancers on Mama Bali's wall. If she could dance, she could be in a picture like one of those; if she could dance, maybe she could fly too like it seemed they could. Fly across the river and find Raoul, fly back and scoop up Demi before he did something foolish just because

Fay tells him to, so foolish that the hard man catches him and locks him up in the Castle.

That night, lying on her scuffed-up nest of old clothes and thin plastic cushions, the sky above her a square of velvet black pricked with stars, she wonders what it will be like to leave Fay, to leave the Barrio, to leave it for good, because when she finds Raoul there will be no going back. Fay isn't safe anymore. Fay will let them all go, Baz and Demi too.

She turns over, her eyes wide-open, staring through the darkness, seeing nothing, feeling her hip bone pressing through thin blankets to the bobbled metal of the floor. Tomorrow will be a day without Demi. She turns again and tries to sleep, but sleep doesn't come. He let go my hand, she tells herself. He let go my hand. I asked him to come with me but he let me go.

When sleep finally does come, there is no feathered flight in her dreams, no flooding water sweeping down the dead river washing everything cleaner than Mama Bali's front step. Just a jumble of restless thoughts, and when she wakes she feels exhausted. Her eyes are sore and all her body's aching like she's been struggling through hot pitch, through sinking mud, and somewhere outside in the thinning darkness she's aware of a voice calling out. For a moment she thinks she's still sleeping and this is a bird calling, but her eyes are open and the calling, she suddenly realizes, isn't plaintive; someone is screaming her name, and whoever it is is terrified.

For a moment she lies still. Then she's frantically scrabbling up the ladder to the deck and slithering down the slope to the railing. She stares out toward the gray shapeless mass of the shoreline. There's the call again, closer, near the buoy she uses as a marker across the mud.

"Baz!"

It's Demi! He came after all! Then she feels a sudden tight band of panic. He came and now something terrible is happening to him and she can't see him, she can't see him anywhere. But he must be there, somewhere, out on the mud.

And then she picks him out. He's off the path by some yards and struggling, arms waving like he's fighting to keep upright, slowly being sucked down.

"Keep still," she shouts. "Don't move. I'm coming."

She races back down below and then a few moments later reemerges, clutching a bundle knotted together with one of her cotton blankets. Hiking the bundle over her shoulder she swarms down the side and slithers through the narrow patch of soft mud by the boat, reaches her path and then, moving as swiftly as she can, she zigs and zags her way toward Demi.

By the time she's at the buoy, the mud is almost up to his waist. "Baz, get me some help. Fay she gonna know what to do."

"No." There's not time. "Stay still," she says, slipping the bundle off her shoulder and undoing it. She has two of her thin plastic cushions and a couple of the cotton blankets. She twists them and knots them together, making a cord about three meters long, and then, holding the cushions in one hand, the makeshift rescue rope in her other, she walks cautiously away from the buoy. After only two steps, she feels the dry skin of the mud crack and her foot goes straight down to over her ankle. Quickly she takes two more strides, not letting the mud get a grip. Then she spins one of the cushions so it lands just within Demi's reach and the second one down in front of herself.

"Throw yourself on that, like me here." And she sprawls down spread-eagled, the cushion under her chest and stomach, taking some of her weight. It won't keep her above the surface forever, but maybe long enough to pull Demi out.

"Can't," he says.

"Lean like you gonna fall."

He leans. His legs don't come up but his weight pushing him forward allows him to just reach the cushion. "This old thing gonna do me nothin, Baz. What you thinkin?" The mud is over his waist, darkening his belly, touching his chest.

"Stretch your arms out like you swimmin," she says. Her own cushion is already an inch down in the mud and she's keeping so still she's hardly breathing. They'll have to be quick, and she doesn't even know if her plan will work. But she makes her voice steady. If Demi starts thrashing about, he'll go quicker than a rat down a sewer.

"I getting mud in my face, Baz."

"Keep you head up and catch this, Demi, and hold it tight." She's coiled her makeshift rope and now she swings it forward in an overarm loop, hoping it will unravel before hitting the surface. It does, and Demi just can touch the end with the tip of his fingers but he can't get a grip on it.

"Reach it, Demi! Come on," she hisses. "You so smart, you catch it. You tell me you half magic, now the time you show it . . ." She badgers and mocks, and Demi strains and sinks a little lower. "Use your arm, Demi. Pull into the mud with one hand and stretch with the other." She sees his eyes wide and frightened but he does what she says, flinging his left arm forward, his hand scooped forward like he wants to haul the riverbed up to the surface and at the same time he lets his face go flat down into the mud, giving himself maybe half an inch more while his right hand stretches for the blanket.

Baz has her eyes closed. This is it. For a moment there's nothing and then she feels the blanket tugging. He has it. "Steady," she says. "Steady. Get your other hand on it."

There's a splutter and grunting and then another jolt. "I got it," he says, and she starts to pull, one hand slowly and then the other, and Demi begins to inch up from the mud, a black and glistening face, only the whites of his eyes showing and his teeth in a tight grimace. And then there's a soft, slow, squelching suck and his feet come free and somehow, with the cushion acting like a sled and Baz hauling on the rope, hand over hand, the distance closes until they are face-to-face.

"Why you got to hide out on this place, Baz?" His face is a mud mask, and his voice sour and breathy from the effort of dragging himself free. "You nothing but difficult." And he spits and grimaces, and then tries to clear gobs of mud from around his mouth but only manages to swallow more of the filth.

She picks up the plastic cushions and winds in her cloth rope and then, without waiting to see if he's following, she sets off on her invisible path to the hard shore. Over her shoulder she says, "You make it sound like you wasn't coming with me. Then you turn up and get yourself in a fix. Lucky you got me; river swallow you whole. You so small you don't leave no trace."

He's too tired to rise to the bait but wearily follows after. Once on the shore, she pulls out three plastic bottles of washing water from her store under a deserted riverside shack and patiently pours the water into his cupped hands so he can wash the worst of the mud from his face and arms. "Fay see you coming out?"

"Snoring like a hog. Took too much wine last night." And then the terror of his near drowning slipping away from him, his old manner starts to strut back: "Could've snuck by her even if she awake. You forget what Demi can do."

"I don't forget your big mouth go right along with your big feet." She splashes out the last of the water and then looks at him critically. "Nobody gonna give us a lift, you stinking of that mud."

"Give me five," he says. "I got some clean clothes still and I'll haul a bucket from Lucien."

So she waits while he runs off. The sun is well up from the horizon now. The sky is a hard blue—another burning day in the city. Behind her the Barrio stirs into life. She tidies away her three bottles, telling herself to remember to refill them as soon as she gets back. Then she sits down cross-legged in the scrap of shadow thrown by the hut, resting her hands on her knees, noticing the way her fingers are trembling, feeling her heart still banging in her skinny chest. Was it a sign? This river trying to pull them down—was that a sign? And if so, what did it mean? Maybe this old river doesn't like the way she runs across it, sleeps in her boat, maybe the river thinks it time she move on out of there. But she didn't let him go and she could have done; if the muddy old river had really wanted to pull him down she would have had to let the rope slip through her hands . . . either that or be pulled down along with him. Maybe the river was telling her this: you never let go. No matter what happens.

Chapter Thirteen

ONLY THE WEEKLY BUS that goes all the way to the upcountry crosses the city's most northern bridge, and that doesn't run for another three days. So Baz and Demi pick up a tram on the far side of the Barrio and take it to the last stop in district ten, two stops farther than Basquat, and then they walk.

They reach the bridge and stop to look over. The river has a bit more life in it up here but it's still little more than a shallow stream sluicing over the mud. Looking south toward the city all Baz can see through the midday dust and haze is a scumbly scratchwork of buildings. It's the other way, up to the north and east, that there are the hills and clean green land Baz dreams of. That's where she wishes that they were going, but they're not. The Mountain is a lot closer, maybe only half an hour from where they are, if they are lucky and pick the right truck. They share a drink and settle down to wait.

Plenty of trucks go this way. They go bumping and wheezing along the highway, trailing smoke, heading up to the farmlands. But they're looking for trash carts, or maybe those big compressor trucks; the city has a fleet of those for crushing the rich folk's dirt pure flat.

"Fay see you when you went back?"

"She saw me."

"Weren't so good at creepin by her then?"

Demi rolls his eyes and flaps his hand, like he's sweeping a fly away. "What you expect? She open her eyes. She see me . . ."

Baz interrupts. She's not thinking of teasing him, bursting the bubble Demi spends half his time walking around in. "She want to know what you an' me doin?"

"She want to know."

"You tell her!"

Baz doesn't show very much, not to Fay, not to the others, but with Demi it's different, except when they're working. He can read her like she can read him. It's just that with Demi most of the time his attention is on himself. This time though he sees her eyes widen and hears the worry in her voice. "I tell her we go looking for new streets, check this house she so keen on us robbin."

He makes it sound like nothing, telling a lie like that; but it's not nothing. They don't lie to Fay, because Fay has a way of finding out. Kids come, and some lie and some cheat. It always happens. And then they go, like Pickpack. "Nobody safe unless Fay safe." That's what she always tells them. "And if you tell Fay anything and she find it isn't so, then that's when Fay don't feel safe." She talks about herself in the third person like that as if this fierce and dangerous person isn't her really, but someone who only comes out of the dark corners of the den when a child tells her a lie. "And when Fay don't feel safe then there's nothing for you here and the shady man can come and take you away." And her voice when she says this doesn't sound like her normal voice, which can be husky and warm and sweet as bean stew, but cold like a needle finding its way into your heart.

Demi has turned away. He always gets fidgety when Baz has her eyes on him, but she carries on studying his face while he stares down the road, watching the approaching cloud of dust that signals another truck.

"What she say when you tell her you goin to check this house?"

"Nothin. That what she want to hear."

"But she'll ask when we get back. We going to have to go

and check it—how we do that if we're looking out this way for Raoul?"

"Don't fret, Baz. We can go look; nothin so difficult. I know how to find this house she got in mind, and she don't care so much. She just tell me to get her an aspirin and not make so much noise. Me, I don't make noise. Since when I make noise? But I bring her aspirin and then she tell me one more thing. She say we both gotta be back to meet this somebody boy she got comin round later." He breaks off and bounces up and down on his toes. It's his I-don't-care bounce. It means something bothers him but he doesn't want to think about it. "Miguel was up too," he says abruptly. "Saw him checking through all the other boys' stuff. You right 'bout him, Baz. He's got rat in his veins. I told him if he touch my stuff, I bury him in the river."

"You an expert on that now?"

"Expert at escaping from tricky situation, that's me."

"How you puff out your chest, Demi! You worry me when you do that. Get so full of air one day you gonna get lifted up like some balloon and blow right away."

"Flyin. I could do that." He grins and then leaps up and steps out into the road waving his hand up and down—not flying, of course, but flapping a stop sign with both hands.

With a grinding squeal of brakes, a monster city garbage-disposal truck pulls up beside the two children and a window rolls down. The face at the window has just the same glinting dark glasses that policemen wear. His hair is cropped into gray stubble, but he has an oversize shaggy mustache that droops round the corners of his mouth and his voice is slow, a big country drawl. "Where you heading?"

Demi jerks his head the way they want to go, over the bridge and up. "Mountain," he says.

"Is where I'm going," says the man. "Come up." He swings open the door and Demi scrabbles up first and Baz follows. As soon as the door is shut he shoves the truck into gear and pulls out. "District six," he says, "every day. Could do the run blind." He glances at them. "Not so many people travel out this way. Not so many at all. You got family out there or something?" He's a big man, his belly straining at the seams of his sweaty denim shirt. The truck's steering wheel is like a toy in his hands. His breath smells of onion.

"Sort of," says Demi.

Baz thinks that's a good answer because family's what she thinks Raoul is. Demi is changing, thinking a bit more like she does maybe, and a little less like Fay. If he was still thinking like Fay, she'd be traveling out on this truck on her own.

The driver doesn't think it's so good though. "I never heard of no *sort-of* family," he says. "My family say that about me, I gonna kick their ass." He laughs and Baz wonders what kind of a family he has that kicking ass should make him laugh. "You been out this way before?" He glances at them, maybe trying to judge what kind of place they come from. They're both neat, now that Demi's washed up and in clean clothes again, a bit scuffed up from the walk maybe but they don't look bad. Not how they should look if they were riffraff kids whom the police felt they could sweep out of sight with no one paying any mind to how they did it.

"Rat got your tongue?" says the driver. "I askin you been out to the Mountain before?" They both shake their heads.

"No, señor," says Demi. "Just enjoying the ride. We don't often get to sit up in a truck fine as this."

"I mind my business," says the driver, "but someone come and sit up in my cab then I expect a little conversation." He flashes a smile at them, perhaps to show he means no harm, but to Baz the smile is full of yellow teeth and his eyes don't wrinkle up the way Mama Bali's do when she smiles. She doesn't want to talk to him; she wants to look out of the window, across the dusty river plain up to the hills hazily stretching out along the horizon. He's too big; too big for the cab. She's got room on the seat all right, but she feels squashed by his presence. His loud country drawl seems to soak up the air, making it hard to breathe.

Demi's not bothered though. He reckons he's the equal of any man in the city, even the mayor. Forgets he's only half grown though.

"Many people working on the Mountain?" asks Demi.

"Plenty. Got some living in houses right inside the wire. Like living in your office." He laughs again and shakes his head as if he can't believe such foolishness. "Sometimes looks like an anthill with all that sifting and sorting. They got paper this an' plastic that; they got rag an' glass an' rubber. Recycling, you see. Recycle the whole city! Good money from bad dirt." He shakes his head. "Me, I tried growing maize and sweet potato, keep some cattle. And did I make money? No. Six to feed and nothing but bad debts in my pockets. But they can squeeze money out the dirt. Ain't no sense to the way the world runs, not to my way of thinking."

"They get pay then, these families?" Baz catches a different note in Demi's voice. Money interests Demi all right.

Baz, remembering the little that Lucien had told them, isn't surprised when the driver laughs. "Pay? Maybe you think they got pension too?" He rolls himself a cigarette with one hand and tips it into his mouth. "Money come from that Mountain, but it goes to the man that owns the Mountain—he's the one that's got money in his pocket. Private business. Soon as I make a little money, goin to buy my own truck, have my own business. You want to be a free agent, you got to have money. Anyone tell you that yet?"

"They tell us," says Demi.

"And they're right," he says, jabbing his stogy rollup in Demi's direction. "You look like smart kids. You got ambition too, I bet."

"Yes, sir," says Demi. "We got ambition. We going to do big things, Baz an' me. We goin to—"

Baz presses her elbow into him and, ignoring his angry look, says, "We going to maybe start an eatin place. A body got to eat." She doesn't want him to tell this man anything, not one thing.

The driver, though, is nodding. "That's a fact," he says. "A place to eat, that's an idea, indeed it is." He pauses and draws on his rollup cigarette. "But what's that got to do with coming out this way? Nobody much comes out this way. So you tell me, you got someone out on the Mountain, maybe someone who get in a little trouble? Cos I hear all kind of thing, you know, kids like you—no, maybe I should say not like you, but 'bout your age—get a little close to the police, maybe been in the Castle for a night or two, end up working the Mountain." He says it casually, but it makes Baz go tight in her belly. "You got someone like that?" he asks again.

"Sure," says Demi, blabbing it out before Baz can stop him. "This boy always getting in trouble, got a mouth bigger than your garage, señor, but we just hopin he not get behind any wire." He breaks off abruptly because Baz has pinched him. "We just come to see, you know." He gives her a stony look. Then he turns back to the man. "This is a good ride for us, you know; we are grateful, señor. Maybe we can hook up on the way back."

Baz looks away. He's so confident all the time. Thinks he knows everything. Maybe he's king in the street, but there are times he's so dazzled by himself he can't think straight. This man is not what he pretends to be. She's as certain of that as she can be. All his questions. She closes her eyes and prays Demi's careful and watches what he says.

"Maybe we can," says the driver. "No problem to me. You on the track, I pick you up—simple." He picks a shred of tobacco from his lip and wipes it away on his shirt. "So this friend of yours got a name? Maybe I heard things I can tell you. Maybe your friend from the Barrio, hey? I got a lot of friends in the Barrio. It's a good quarter, no matter what anybody say."

"Yeah," says Demi, "he from the Barrio, but he never do harm to no one, this boy."

"What's his name?"

"Raoul," says Demi.

Baz opens her eyes. Big Raoul with his smile so wide you could slip it in a frying pan and cook it like a tortilla. Who could help liking Raoul? How could Fay let him go? Fay's got a little poison in her heart, that's how. And now Demi has given away Raoul's name to this driver with long yellow teeth. Too much, he's giving away too much. She looks out of the window and tries to think good things. Maybe the families living out at the Mountain have taken Raoul in. Maybe they won't need to do any rescuing. Maybe. Maybe. Sometimes life seems like a whole string of "maybes," but they never seem to turn into anything real. Lucien had a family and they just put him out on the side of the road to die, so what chance is there that Raoul is going to find some kindness in a place with people like that?

The driver blows out a thin stream of smoke. "No, I never heard talk of no Raoul, but that don't mean nothing. I just shed my load and turn round for the city." He glances at them and, catching Baz leaning forward and looking at him, says, "You a funny thing. You a boy or girl, you?"

Demi laughs at that. Can't help himself. "Half the Barrio askin that question," he says, and laughs some more till Baz jabs him.

"Girl," she says. "I can look after myself."

Demi shakes his right hand in the air, loose-fingered, like she's a danger. "Got a kick like a mule!"

"You never even seen a mule!" she says, annoyed that he's joking with this man.

"Bet you can," says the man, nodding, and then repeats himself, "bet *you* can." She has the feeling it's himself he's thinking about, not her. He doesn't laugh and doesn't smile either, not like Demi. "What they call you?"

"This Baz; me, I'm Demi."

"All right, Baz, I tell you what I do. I like you kids. You good people. You looking for your friend. I like that. I tell you I drive you to the depot—I got friends there. I talk to them, ask some questions and maybe, maybe for a little consideration, they find this Raoul friend of yours, maybe they even let him walk right out of the gates. How about that?" And he stares so long and hard at them, with his bushy eyebrow raised up over the rim of his dark glasses, that Baz gets nervous he'll drive them right off the road.

"That's a big favor for us," says Demi.

The driver grunts. "It's nothing. People got to help each other."

His words sound greasy to Baz. She's surprised Demi doesn't feel the same as her. She doesn't believe he'll do any of the things he's offering, but there's nothing she can say. All she can

do is sit and hear his talk, and hope Demi doesn't say something that gets them in real trouble.

"This the kind of consideration you thinking of?" Demi lays
a ten on the dashboard and the driver smiles.

"I knew soon as I laid eyes on you that you two got class."
He picks up the bill and slips it into his shirt pocket. Then grinds
the butt of his rollup into the ashtray. He falls quiet then, just
humming a little to himself. Baz watches dirt-poor fields flowing past them. Scraggy trees and dry irrigation ditches quarter
the dead land. "Unless they put some water in the river," the
driver says at length, "this whole country going to die of thirst."

It turns out that his small farm in the uplands dried out soon
after the dam was built but he was one of the lucky ones, he
says, lucky to find a job in the city, lucky to hold on to it.

They turn off the highway and snake down a track, past a
scattering of shacks, a wire compound piled with wrecked and
rusting cars with an old spindly crane pecking at the wrecks,
lifting them up and slamming them down, glass spraying out
like flecks of water caught in the sun. It makes Baz think of one
of those long-beaked birds she sees stalking the soft mud. Their
driver beeps his horn long and loud and a hand waves from
way up the crane and then they are past.

A few moments later the driver winds down his window
and the stale air in the cab thickens with a sweet and acrid
smell that makes Baz gag. "Smell that?" he says. "Gets in your
hair, in your skin. That's the Mountain. Live out here too long
and no one gonna marry you cos you just gonna smell of rot."
He laughs again, and Baz turns her head so she doesn't have to
see his teeth. "There she is."

Right up ahead is a reeking hill of waste. All over it are glowing bugs of fire. Like eyes, Baz thinks. And from each one thin

smoke trickles up into the windless sky like strands of hair. And on the hill's skull-like dome she can see figures moving slowly.

Demi sucks in his breath and crosses himself. Baz has never ever seen him do that before. "That look like hell," he says.

"The city's mess got to go somewhere," the driver says, and begins to slow the truck down. To the right are yet more of those burnt fields; ahead is a depot and parking lot, and a truck pulling away from it, and then behind that a whole cluster of shanty roofs, running right up to the foot of the Mountain. Only thing between them and the trash is the wire fence, and in places it looks like the Mountain has grown so big it threatens to topple right over the fence and come down on those houses, swallow them up. Something else Baz sees, something she hadn't expected: two men lounging up against the outer wall of the depot. Men in suits. Men with guns under their arms. Men in sharp suits that deal in hurt. What will they do if they recognize Demi and her?

"Stop!" she says suddenly, buckling forward and gripping her tummy. "I got sick in my belly."

"You hold on! I don't want sick in my cab." He slams on the brakes and swings the truck over to the shoulder. Baz shoves open the door and tumbles down onto the dirt road, retching and coughing and spitting.

Demi jumps down after her. "You OK, Baz? What happen?"

"The air, maybe," shouts the driver. "When she's all right, you just walk on down to the depot. Only a couple o' hundred yards. Take your time. She'll be fine." Without waiting for a reply he pulls the door to, revs up the engine and roars away, leaving them in a choking cloud of white dust.

Chapter Fourteen

THE DUST IS IN THEIR EYES, nose and hair. Demi flaps his hands and curses and coughs, but Baz is upright, squinting through the haze of grit as soon as the truck pulls away. She knows they have to move quickly; they have a few moments before the air clears and the driver is telling the men at the depot all about them and those two suited men will be able to see every move they make. How can they disappear? It's too far to get to the parking lot and lose themselves among all the trucks and work-sheds. Anyhow, they would have to cross the road and go right by the depot. To the right are the fields of dried-out cotton. No shelter other than the odd stunted acacia tree . . .

She grabs Demi. The ditch right between them and the field is deep enough for them to keep out of sight just by stooping. In fact there's a whole network of these old dried-out irrigation ditches running round each field. If they're lucky, they could get right up to the wire.

"This way," she says, already moving off the road, jerking his arm hard to make him follow her.

"What? I thought you sick. What . . . ?" Half resisting, half letting himself be dragged, his eyes streaming from the dirt kicked up by the truck, Demi tumbles awkwardly into the ditch beside Baz. His hands are grazed and his jeans torn at the knee. "Baz! What you do? Look! You want to step in dirt nobody stoppin you, but you leave me be. That man save us a long walk and he tell us 'bout this place. All we had to do was sit tight, pay a little dollar and we drive home with Raoul. You make us look stupid now!" He smacks his leg and flinches. "How am I gonna do business with bust hand? You tell me . . . Wait, where you goin?"

Baz is moving as fast as she can along the overgrown ditch. Prickly thorns tear at her arms and snag in her clothes. She keeps low, using hands and feet to scuttle like a monkey. She can hear Demi following, still muttering but keeping up. Only a few meters to go before they can cut right away from the road, run between the fields and then zigzag away from the depot. Maybe the driver won't talk; maybe they won't hunt for them. More maybes. The sun beats down; the narrow irrigation ditch holds the heat like a stove. Baz feels her face swell and burn; flies swarm out of the grasses, stinging her arms and legs and neck.

End of the first field. She scuttles to the right.

Still no pursuit.

Who would be this crazy to run after them? Why would those suited men care if two kids catch a lift on a truck? But Baz knows they would, course they would. No one gonna visit the Mountain unless they got business or they mean trouble. Children inside the wire are OK cos they slaves, working the dirt pile, livin in the filth; but children outside the wire, children who been askin questions, are trouble. And for sure they gonna be a nice dollar bonus for any shady man who snatch them up, get two more workers, two more slaves.

End of second field—left.

Keep going. Her breath comes in ragged gasps. End of the field. Another turn and the way is blocked. The ditch here has been reinforced with concrete and an iron gate blocks the way. She slumps back along the side wall and Demi collapses beside her. Cautiously she inches her head up over the lip of the ditch and takes stock.

The depot roof is just visible three hundred meters back

across the way they've come. Two short fields away is the high wire fence and beyond that the stinking Mountain itself. She can see people on it, bent-backed, moving slowly, stiffly, their heads and hands and legs muffled in rag; grown men, women or children, she couldn't tell.

"Baz! Slow down. Now you tell me, you explain. I come here. I find out 'bout this place an' I got money. Look!"

She turns back. Demi is holding a wad of notes in his fist. "This my money. Not Fay's. Mine. That driver say he goin to help and you run off like a rat. Why you so crazy?"

"You tell him too much."

His mouth is open to complain more, and then he snaps it shut, his eyes black and angry. Demi is never angry with her, nor she with him. This is a first time. She feels herself tighten, her eyes smart, but she is right. He must listen to her even though he is older. On the street he tells her because it is his element; here they are equal.

"How we even know if Raoul in this place?"

"We don't find out by knocking on that big gate and askin that man. You seen them at the depot? You seen the shady man, standing there waiting on the truck?"

Demi frowns. "What man?"

"With a gun. Señor Moro's man. You think it so smart go askin them 'bout Raoul?"

The anger goes out of his eyes. He shrugs and turns away, looking back to the depot. He doesn't like to be the one with no idea about what to do. "Fay gonna kill us if we not back tonight—you know that, Baz."

Baz hadn't thought about Fay at all, other than wondering how she could have let Raoul be taken away like she had. "Fay not going to kill no one."

"She kill me. She want me to go robbing tonight. This fancy house you and me supposed to be checking out right now. That's what I tell her this morning. I didn't say nothing 'bout crossing the river and finding no Raoul. And this boy of hers she so sweet about all of a sudden, the one rat-Miguel bring round . . ." He breaks off. "Baz, you reckon Fay ever goin to turn me an' you away?"

"I don't know, Demi." They don't have time for this. She turns back, as if the Mountain is pulling her round. "You going to help, or you goin to hitch a ride back, because I'm looking for Raoul."

He pulls a face. "What you think? Girl like you couldn't find an egg in a chicken nest unless you got Demi lookin with you."

Tense as she is, she can't help herself smiling. "Come on then. We climb round this thing," she says, indicating the iron barrier, "then we get to the wire. Maybe all we got to do is ask people on the inside. They not going to give us away."

"No," he says, "got a better plan." Demi always has to have a better plan, but she agrees with what he proposes. It makes no sense for the two of them to do the same thing. If she goes to the wire, maybe even finds a way in and onto the Mountain, he'll cut back, get in close to the depot to see what kind of security these shady men are involved in. If the coast is clear, he'll cross the track, cut through the parking lot. "Nose around a little."

"Like a dog."

"No dog as smart as me," he says. "I come find you here. Give me half hour; you go no place else." He points a warning finger at her before turning and running back part of the way they've come. She doesn't wait for him to go out of sight before scrabbling up the bank, tummy-wriggling across the dirt, and then sliding back down into the ditch on the other side of the barrier. Then, head low, she makes her way toward the wire. At the edge of the field, where her ditch connects with another, she stops. This is as close as she can get. No more than ten paces from the wire.

The Mountain rises behind the security fence like some giant swollen-backed rat: a cancerous and pocked mound of slag, glinting with scraps of tin, stinking with smoldering garbage, piles of old tires, broken furniture and plastic, plastic, plastic everywhere, fluttering like snake heads in the hot rising air and hanging in tangled slimy ribbons from the wire.

She climbs out of the ditch and slowly straightens herself, feeling horribly exposed. Birds lift up from the wire and circle overhead, their crying harsh and angry. The people working this side of the Mountain one by one stop what they are doing and turn to look at her. She feels rather than sees their eyes hidden behind their muffled faces. What are they going to think, seeing a figure crawling out of a ditch to come and stare in at them like they're some animals? Her neck is raw and burning in the sun. She keeps her gaze fixed on those inside, though every muscle in her body is aching to turn, to check that no shady man is walking across the field toward her. It's too late for turning, too late for running.

She lifts a hand. No one moves. She steps across a worn, narrow track just wide enough for a motorcycle that runs right alongside the wire. She registers the tire tracks but her attention is on the people. "I'm looking for a boy," she says to them.

Someone snickers and coughs. The cough turns into a hacking retch, and a figure a little to the left buckles to his knees. No one pays him any attention. She grips the wire with her right hand.

"A boy, maybe two day ago, brought here by the man. The man in suit."

"Moro," says one figure, and spits. That's a good sign, surely. They will help. They must.

They start to shuffle forward, the older ones, she sees, moving cautiously, the children more quickly, stumbling sometimes, their feet suddenly sinking, all of them dragging sacks. One falls and gives a cry, struggling up, clutching his arm, and then continues down the slope toward Baz. As they move, disturbing the ground, the smell thickens, the air rancid with gas. Baz covers her mouth with her forearm. Rats ripple out from the rubbish.

It's the children who crowd the wire, four of them, their eyes watery and staring at her like she's a dish they could feed on. The older ones stay back, halfway down the slope. One of them has a stick that he raises and shakes at Baz; she doesn't know if it's a warning, a welcome or some attempt to make her vanish in a puff of smoke. He reminds her of an old old man, dry as paper, down in the Chinese quarter of the Barrio, who people said did magic.

"You got watch." A boy with a hoarse voice is staring at her arm.

"Soft skin," says another, a girl. The rag muffling her face has slipped a little and Baz tries not to stare at the angry blisters crowding her forehead.

"You want my watch." She strips it from her wrist. It's cheap, plastic, but it works.

The first speaker holds out his hand. He's lost the little finger and the wound is raw, seeping. She lets the watch drop and quickly withdraws her hand. A half smile flickers across his face. "Scare you get grab, eh, pretty girl-boy?" Then he looks at the watch and shoves away one of the others who's come too close. "Got a cell phone?"

She shakes her head.

The girl's eyes have never left Baz's face. "Who this boy you lookin for?"

"Raoul. Big. Maybe thirteen. Laughs." This didn't look a place where anyone spent time laughing.

"Laugh?" she says. "Two day ago they bring a boy who try to laugh, but he sick now."

"Where is he?"

The girl shrugs. The older ones have lost interest; even the boys who had crowded down to see Baz are now slowly making their way back up the steep and unsteady slope, occasionally stopping to investigate some bit of rubber or rag, sometimes adding what they find to the collection in their sack.

"Please, you can't go," pleads Baz. "Help me."

"Why?" she says, turning back. "You can't hurt me."

For a moment Baz doesn't think she has heard right. "I don't want to hurt anyone."

The girl gives a laugh. "You on the outside. You want to come here, have my life?" She doesn't wait for a reply but begins to climb away from Baz.

"Please," calls Baz.

One of the boys farther up the slope mimics her. "Pliz . . . plizz."

They don't care. Why should they? Her fingers tighten on the rusty wire fence. "Please," she begs. The girl ignores her. Why can't she tell how much this means, how much Baz would give? Suddenly she shakes the wire. "Take me to him," she calls. "Please. If you know where he is, take me to him. I'll climb the wire. I'll get in somehow."

The girl stops. A rat noses up to her foot but she ignores it, her attention wholly on Baz, and Baz, who had really only noticed the blistering on the girl's forehead before, now sees that her eyes are like dark pools. She thinks they are pools of hurt.

Then, from somewhere behind her, Baz hears the whine of a motorcycle.

"Go! You must hide. They catch you, you gonna be like us. Go quick!" says the girl. "They come round, these men, check there are no breaks. Check no one runs. Go hide. Now."

"But Raoul—what about him? Can't I get in?"

"No!" Her voice suddenly fierce. "Hide and then I bring the boy."

"How long?"

"I bring him," she says curtly. "You wait."

The sound of the bike is louder, an angry buzzing.

The girl abruptly turns and scrambles, quickly this time, up the slope while Baz sprints back to the ditch, jumps down out of sight and then cautiously lifts herself, peering through the dry scratchy grasses.

A moment later the bike comes into view, traveling slowly along the bumpy track. One rider only: black short-sleeve shirt, not one of the shiny-suit boys. His face is masked by goggles against the dirt and there's a gun slung across his back. His head is tilted toward the wire, not out to the fields. Not looking for her and Demi then. The bike trundles on, picking up speed, round a corner and is out of sight.

A movement on the brow of the mountain catches her attention. One, two, three figures making their way back down to the wire. She climbs out and runs to meet them. Two holding the third, his arms round their shoulders, his head flopped down so she can't see his face, and them struggling, having to half carry him. And the one in the middle is dressed differently, not a bundle of rags and sacking, but like her, like Demi, except the T-shirt is ripped from shoulder to stomach and stained brown.

They stop a foot from the wire. "Is this the boy?" It's the same girl of course, but she's bound up her face again so that only her eyes show. The other helper is the boy with the husky voice to whom Baz gave her watch. He doesn't acknowledge Baz, just unhooks the boy's arm and leaves him propped against the girl and immediately begins to climb away from them. The boy groans faintly and lifts his head; his face is feverish, glistening with sweat, his eyes dull, unseeing, but it is Raoul. His lip is puffed out and scabby, black with dried blood, and there's more blood by his right ear. She remembers what Señor Moro had said: "Boy like that a good worker, strong . . . good for the Mountain." Poor Raoul, good for nothing now maybe. This is what Lucien told her: you get unlucky, something happens, you take a fall, a bad cut and you get sick easy.

"Yes!" she says to the girl. "Thank you. Thank you."

"He try to climb the gate," the girl says. "First night. When they pull him down he tell the men he got business in the city. They all laugh. Then they beat him." The girl undrapes Raoul and lowers him to the ground. "I come back," she says, "when you go."

"But we take him, Demi and me."

"Demi?" she says. "Demi someone you got who can walk through wire fence to get this boy? Maybe he can work miracle—take us all away." Her voice is mocking. "I come back when you go."

Then she too moves away.

"How long before that motorcycle come round again?" calls Baz, her eyes on Raoul, crumpled almost to nothing.

"Come round anytime."

Baz waits a moment, listening for the telltale whine, but there's nothing behind the crying of the circling birds and the regular thump of a machine over toward the depot. She stoops, reaching through the wire to touch Raoul. "Raoul? Raoul! It's me. Baz. Raoul, we come to get you! What happen?"

The boy lifts his head slightly and his eyes seem to focus, blinking against the light. Baz holds up a hand to shade his face from the sun. "Baz." His voice is nothing more than a half breath. "I'm so sick, Baz. Couldn't even juggle a purse from a blind man." He tries to laugh but coughs, spitting up a gob of bright red blood, the only bright color on the Mountain.

Only two days and he's like this! "What happen you, Raoul? How you get like this?" He doesn't answer. "We come to get you," she repeats helplessly, feeling tears pricking her eyes. And Baz never cries. Never. Where was Demi? If he was here, together they could do something.

"Fay lose time for me, Baz. Give me to the man . . . They beat me some when I . . ." He coughs again, another ball of red spit.

"Shh," she says.

His eyes dull, his head drops onto his chest, his body slumps against the wire.

She touches his damp hair, his burning face.

*   *   *

And this is how Demi finds her: her head close to Raoul's, her hand on his neck, the wire separating them.

Demi's agitated, bouncing on his toes, his head constantly moving, taking in everything. "You right about that driver-man. He must have told on us; they skinning the village looking for us. We got to move, Baz, get out of this place." His eyes settle on Raoul. "He bad, yeah?"

"We can't leave him," she says.

"This boy not going anywhere, Baz. He got a pulse even?"

"I don't know." Her voice is small.

"Let me see."

He bends down beside her, moves her hand away and presses his fingers in against the side of Raoul's neck. Then he looks at her and shakes his head. "Hardly nothing."

"We can't leave him, Demi! How can we?"

He squints up the Mountain, not wanting to answer her. The sun has moved round and is almost directly in their eyes. Three figures appear over the brow and stand, black shapes, like crows, vultures. Demi has seen vultures on TV and knows how they live. A rat scuttles over Raoul's leg. He doesn't move. Demi bangs the wire, but the rat is unconcerned. It's sleek, healthy. It disappears down a crack beneath a worn-smooth car tire.

"Some things can't be changed, Baz. Come on. He don't know nothing. Come on, leave him. He got no pain now."

Somewhere over toward the depot a horn sounds, blaring, loud, startling a spray of scavenging gulls into the air. Half a moment later Baz hears the whine of the bike again. A higher pitch, she realizes, moving faster. Not routine this time.

She lets him take her hand, guide her to her feet. She lets him hurry her back away from the wire. Neither of them looks back. Demi because he doesn't want to see anymore; Baz because she can't.

Chapter Fifteen

DEMI CROUCHES; Baz leans against the sloping bank of the ditch, staring up at the sky. The sun glares down. No forgiveness.

They should move.

They hear the bike kick to a stop, the engine killed, the man's voice shouting, "Boy! Move back, eh." And then abrupt silence.

Ten, fifteen paces away, that's all they are. If the guard is suspicious, decides to check around, he'll find them easy enough, but they don't want to move. Demi has his eyes glued to the guard's motorcycle. If he can get his hands on it, it would be their ticket back to the city, a whole lot faster than walking, safer than hitching a ride. He can ride a bike, no problem. He scans the ditch looking for something, anything he can use—a few lumps of fist-size concrete down by the barrier, some scraps of wood from the acacia tree, nothing that would do as a club. Baz just doesn't want to move. She's not thinking about the bike, or the guard. She just wants to feel the sun burning her up. She doesn't have to look back at the wire to see Raoul's slumped shape.

"What's this fat slug doing here? He sick? Dead?" The guard's voice is oddly high. It doesn't go with the gear.

They can't hear the reply, but there must have been one from the girl, keeping her word to Baz and coming back for Raoul.

"Take him to the gate," says the guard. "You know what you supposed to do with someone sick. Just move him, eh? Hey, tell me—he the one they call Raoul?"

Baz eases herself up to the rim of the ditch, lying beside

Demi. The young guard is standing well back from the wire, his goggles pushed back onto his forehead; the gun is cradled in his hands, finger on the trigger. What's he so scared of, this macho man? wonders Baz. What's he think? Those children go bustin the wire to bite at him or something? Or maybe he just think he can shoot away the sickness they got in there.

"You certain? No one come round? Two kids, maybe."

The guard takes a couple of steps back, putting more space between himself and the figures who, Baz sees, have come down to Raoul and are now hauling him upright into a sitting position. The guard turns his back on the wire, and stares out to where Baz and Demi lie hidden. He doesn't move for a moment. "You just come this way, señor, come this way and I take your bike from you," murmurs Demi.

"Bike not the same as a purse, Demi."

"His bike got a whole lot o' tool bag at the back. Maybe for this fence. Cutters maybe."

She looks at him in surprise. "What you thinkin?"

"What about if you go standing up, Baz, and then running back down this ditch. What he gonna do?"

"Gonna ride me down."

Demi scoops two of the bits of concrete and hefts them in his palm. "That's what I reckonin too. You wanna try it? Get ourselves a bike and maybe get through the wire and all."

It's a risk, but she and Demi run risks all the time. It's what they do. "You think he use his gun?"

"No. He want to catch us—what's he want dead thief like you for?" He grins at her. "You ready?"

She nods. "Now?"

"Go!"

She takes a breath, then jumps to her feet. She stands for a full second facing the man, like she's been caught in a set of headlights, dazzled. Then she runs, not in the ditch but along the top; she can go faster on the top.

"Hey! You! Stop!"

Demi holds his breath as the guard swings his gun up, takes aim for what seems a lifetime but isn't anything more than a heartbeat. Then, changing his mind, he curses loudly and jumps onto the bike, kicking it into life, and skids away across the rough field toward Baz, the front wheel high off the ground, the back wheel bouncing on the bumpy track.

Baz is sprinting fast, jigging right, left, taking no chances, but keeping right on the rim of the ditch, ready to jump down.

The bike is almost directly in front of Demi when Demi springs up, his left arm pointing at the man, his right arm arced right back, the lump of concrete tight in his grip. The man, startled, yanks the handlebars to the right and the back wheel slides round, spraying a whole cloud of dirt at Demi. But for a split second Demi doesn't move; he's like stone, eyes narrowed, and then he hurls his missile, not at the man but straight at the front wheel, praying that it won't just glance off the tire. It's got to hit the wheel dead on, knock it sideways.

There's a crack. A grinding roar, and the bike flips right and then left as the man overcorrects. Then he slams on the front brake, jerking the back wheel so far off the ground that the bike cartwheels and slews across the dirt on its side.

Baz, hearing the sound of the crash, spins round and sees Demi snatching the gun from the ground. The driver is face-down, one arm splayed out. She wonders if he's dead but by the time she reaches them, only a few moments later, the man has raised his bloody face and is glaring at Demi, who's standing over him, impassively pointing the muzzle of the gun straight at him. The bike's engine is still roaring, its back wheel spinning and spraying dirt and stones up into the air. She turns off the engine and pockets the key.

The silence is a relief. Now the man's ragged breathing seems loud as he inches his way out from under his bike, cursing all the time.

"Tha's enough," says Demi when the man has dragged himself clear. "Don't move more 'n that."

"You shoot me," pants the man, "and you got big trouble."

"I shoot and you one dead piece of dirt," says Demi. "You think I care 'bout any of you friends? You think they care 'bout you either? You think that, you more stupid 'n you look."

Without being told to, Baz checks the tool bag and pulls out a long strip of thin wire and some oily rags. Then between them they bind the man's arms and his legs, taking his belt off to tie his ankles. They ignore his cursing. Baz tries to ignore the way her hands are trembling.

In half a minute the man's bundled up on his side on the ground. He's so angry she can see the vein throbbing at his temple. Demi is cool, tells him if he wants to shout then they will just have to stuff his face with a dirty rag, so he needs to do a bit of thinking and a little less foul-mouth cursing.

"I shout. You bet I shout," hisses the man. "I shout, then I tear you head off you shoulders, you Barrio scum. I know you."

"You don't know me," says Demi, "but I don't want to hear you talk no more." He pokes the gun at the man's mouth and Baz flinches. This is a Demi she hasn't ever seen, hard, bad as them maybe. The man falls silent. "OK, now open you mouth again." The man obeys. "Gag him," he says to Baz.

She wads up one of the rags and pushes it into his mouth. Then she ties the second rag round his mouth as a gag. The man's eyes bulge with fury but he's still, his eyes glued to the barrel of the gun. "This a whole lot better than the bullet you wanted to give us, I reckon," Demi says to him.

With that, they haul him to the ditch and roll him down into it. Then while Demi tips up the tool bag, looking for wire cutters, Baz runs back toward the fence, where the girl and the boy with the missing finger are standing beside Raoul's unmoving body, watching them. Baz is straining to be there instantly, running faster than she's ever run before. They can do it. They can get him on the bike, get him to the city, clean him up. Bit of medicine. Mama Bali will know.

She bangs into the wire and then stares at Raoul's still face. Half a second later Demi is beside her, snapping at the wire. One strand and another. "Hey, Raoul," says Demi, "we got you, boy. We got you."

But they haven't got him.

"You too late," says the girl. "He's dead. You want to take his body, go ahead. We got enough here without one more."

"What you sayin?" Demi angrily snaps another strand. "We got you, Raoul." Then, abruptly, he throws down the cutters and turns his back on the ragged hole he's made. Baz reaches through the tear in the fence and touches Raoul's hand. Maybe he understood that they came back for him, that they didn't let him go, not really.

She looks up at the girl. "You want to come with us, climb through the wire, you and him?"

"Where we gonna go?" says the girl. "You got a job we can do? You got a place we can live? You got food?"

"Come on, Baz." Demi's voice sounds washed out. "They gonna come looking for their man any time now. We got to move."

Baz ignores him. "No one should do what you have to do," she says to the girl. "You come. You come on the bike. You and the boy. I can run."

"We got family," she says. "We can't leave." She and the boy turn away and begin to drag Raoul back up the slope.

Then Baz turns away too.

"You OK, Baz?" Demi looks worried. "You can't do nothin more."

She nods and Demi takes her hand and they run stumbling a little back to the bike. He hauls it upright and straddles it. It's too big for him, but he manages, motioning her to get on behind him. He flicks the ignition, kicks the starter and turns the throttle. The bike roars. "Hold tight, Baz." She holds him round the waist. He jerks it into gear and they lurch off, nearly falling, and then Demi gets the knack, changes gear. They don't race but cut across the field, finding tracks across the ditch, all the time leaving the Mountain behind them.

"They gonna follow us, Demi? You told that driver we looking for Raoul. You give him our names. This place all belong to Señor Moro. They gonna tie us back to Fay."

Demi doesn't answer. Maybe he didn't hear. Baz reckons he did, just doesn't want to think about all the trouble they're piling up. She's not blaming him; it was her fault they came out looking for Raoul. She holds Demi tightly and leans her face against his back. There is nothing good in this day; and the worst thing is it's not over: tonight they have the job, robbing the Captain. And it's easy, so easy—that's what Fay and the angel-boy kept saying. Easy, just a straight road to the Castle, that's what Baz thinks.

Once they are well out of sight of the depot Demi cuts down to the main road. Here he turns the throttle up and, with the sun beginning to sink down below the horizon, they accelerate down the highway toward the north bridge and the city.

Chapter Sixteen

THE SUN'S HANGING LOW over the river when Baz and Demi cross the last ditch before reaching the den. They are sticky with sweat and their bellies tight with hunger, and nerves too maybe. They are in good time but Fay's twitchy. She's standing by the window, the last of the sunlight flaming her hair, her face pale, expression strained. The air in the den is thick with the smell of her tobacco.

"Where you and Baz been? You know we got this business tonight," she says sharply, lighting another black cigarillo.

"Told you," says Demi. "Uptown."

"You lyin to me, Demi? Look at me." Fay always says you can tell when a body's lying to you when you see their face.

"What fool gonna to tell you lies, Fay?"

"Baz?" she asks.

Baz wants to tell Fay right there how they found Raoul and how he'd been sick and hurt and frightened, and now he's lying dead on a hill of stinking rubbish. And she wants to ask her did she know when she let Moro's men take him that that was what would happen to him.

She doesn't though.

"Cat got your tongue, Baz?"

"Uptown. Looking for this house for tonight."

"You got anything to show me then?" she asks.

"We didn't do business today."

Fay blinks. To Baz she looks like a white-faced bird. "Why you all scuffed up? You got dirt and your jeans all torn. Looks to me like you been out of the city."

"Got in a scrap—some boys in the neighborhood. Had to run." Demi shrugs. Things like this happen all the time.

Fay considers this, then says, "You steal a bike, motorcycle?" Baz holds her face still.

"Motorcycle? What you dreamin on, Fay? We take purses. Maybe some jewel if we get lucky. What we gonna do with a motorcycle? You got no garage, Fay, not unless you got some business interests you not told us about." Another jab of the spike, but at least Demi's playing easy, like he's joking, but this is not joke time. The men at the depot, Moro's men, they put two and two together quickly if they contacted Fay already.

Fay doesn't smile at Demi's back talk, but she doesn't get snappy either—she's still a little fuzzy round the edges. "Plenty thing I don't tell some fool child like you about." That's the truth, thinks Baz, but she lets herself relax a little. Fay doesn't think they would have gone out of town without telling her; she doesn't think they are the ones Moro's men are already trying to track down. If she thinks it's them, her voice would have more ice in it than in that whole block Demi tried to bring back the other day.

"Sol, go take a look round the Barrio, see if there's an old motorcycle leaning up against a wall some place, maybe on the bank, upriver a bit," she says, looking at Baz, because upriver she knows is where Baz has her hideaway. She consults a scrap of paper and then gives Sol the plate number, and Sol, without looking at Demi, leaves the den.

"You better hope he find nothing," Fay says. The smoke from her cigarillo curls round her pale face and makes her look like a witch.

Baz shrugs and turns away toward the window. Sol won't find it by looking in the Barrio, but even so she can't help worrying. She had tried to persuade Demi to dump it in the river, but Demi refused. "Waited all my life for bike like this, Baz.

What you think I want to get rid of it so quick when I can be the flash boy down main street?"

"You want the world lookin at you?"

"World can look at me if it want."

In the end though, they agreed to hide it under the bridge. They covered it with rubbish and bits of plastic and it should be safe there.

Demi had taken the ignition key, and then they had made the long walk back into the city, getting back to the den just as the day was fading, and with just enough time to spare before the night's expedition.

Neither of them had expected to face questions from Fay about their stolen bike. As if echoing Baz's thoughts, Demi says, "Why you care if I go stealing bikes anyway? You turn parish priest all of a sudden, Fay?"

Fay takes a pull on her black cigarillo. "Because," she says carefully, like she's finding her way round the edges of the words, "the man who lose this bike ask me—say two wild Barrio kids take it. Two boys, but sound like you two. Sound to me like he want more than his bike back, sound like he want to go teaching those thieving rats a lesson. Sound like he mean to catch 'em before they find their way back to the Barrio."

Of course he meant to catch them; they had left him trussed up like a chicken. No shady man was going to like that. He'd kill them if he ever found them.

Demi pulls a face. "Man lose a bike to a couple o' kids don't deserve to have a bike in the first place."

At last Fay's expression softens. She rubs her face and then stubs out the half-smoked cigarillo. "Demi," she says, "you beginnin to sound like some old teacher, and one thing I don't need is teacher." Then shrugging slightly she adds, "It's what I tell him too."

Demi slumps into a chair, puts his feet up on the table. "This man someone important, Fay?"

Fay brushes the question aside. "I don't care where you an' Baz been so long as you don't cause me problem. You cause me problem, you get treated like everyone else, Demi." She lifts up the bottle from beside her chair, looks at it, frowns and then puts it down again.

The bell jangles and a moment later Sol comes into the room. He looks at Fay. "You seen anythin?" she asks.

"Shady men all over," he says, "but I seen no bike. Not anywhere. No one seen one."

"Good boy," she says to Sol, but it is Demi's cheek she pats. Maybe she is thinking that Demi is too smart to cause trouble with Moro and his men. But Fay is wrong, and sometime, Baz knows, she'll find out how they lied to her.

They told a lie, but they saw the truth about where children go when they get passed on to the shady man; and Baz feels shame for all the time she hasn't cared, has kept herself hidden away in her private place out on the mud river.

Fay takes a call on her cell phone and they both watch her. "Yes," she says. "Of course I'm goin to tell them." She looks at her wristwatch. "Yes. We got all the time we need." Her voice softens. "I'll be here," she says, and then clicks off the phone.

"Eduardo," she says. Baz didn't need telling. "Says the driver will be in Agua at two. You just go to the fountain. He'll be there."

"He got a name, this driver?"

"Domino."

Baz thinks of the game: old men slapping their black-and-white pieces down on the bar table. *Snap. Clack.* Like gunshots.

Demi's restless, moving round the den, peering from the window, flicking the TV on, turning it off. "What kind of car?"

Fay shrugs. Cars aren't her thing. "Big. Looks beat up but Eduardo say it got a good engine. You'll be fine."

She cooks up a light meal and then hustles around them, fussing them into dark-colored clothes, wanting them to sleep so they won't be too tired. They have never seen her like this. But though they are both tired neither of them feels like sleep and Fay agrees that they can just rest till it's time.

Baz tugs Demi's arm and they slip out of the den and go up onto the flat roof. Baz has brought a couple of cushions and they sit down on these, leaning back to look out over the flickering lights of the Barrio.

Baz looks at Demi's profile. He's hunched up and she can tell he's frowning, lost in his thoughts. She thinks how he flickers like the lightning they get in these hot day storms. Flickers in the way he can move down a street, through a crowd so fast you hardly see him. His mood flickers too. One minute so full of himself he could swell up like a balloon and float away, and now this—all shuffled down and small.

"Fay different," he says. "Barrio different. What happen?"

Raoul happened, is what she thinks, but he doesn't want to hear about that. He wants her to explain why Fay is the way she is so she tries to tell him what she thinks: "Reckon Fay got some monkey on her back and she give away most everything to get rid of that monkey." She pauses, trying to find the words for what she feels is happening. "She think that hard angel-boy gonna turn everything right, but if tonight don't work, everything come falling down, I reckon."

"Angel—you callin him that?"

She makes a pulling-apart gesture with her hands: "Angel one part, wolf the other."

Demi laughs. "You never seen no wolf! Where you hear about wolf? We got dog in this city, but we got no wolf."

"Got no angel too," she says, "but it don't stop him being that thing."

Demi's quiet again, then says, "Fay's blood child want something a whole lot more than the money we gonna take, but whatever it is he keeping it close."

"Keeping it from Fay?"

"I reckon."

She thinks Demi is maybe right, but she doesn't care about the money, never has.

They sit in silence for a little while. It's good on the roof, second best to her hideaway. Better in some ways because you are up above the Barrio; there are lights burning away on the streets, and now the clouds have pulled away to show the stars. Better than any TV. And there's warmth in the air but it's not so close that you can hardly breathe. And Demi is beside her and he's quiet.

She tries not to worry about the job. Whatever happens they'll be together, and nobody works better than them. She knows that, but it is what comes after that she can't help thinking about. Despite all Demi's raging and stomping and puffing, he's Fay's boy, and Baz is terrified he won't be willing to leave her. And then what happens? She can't stay, won't stay. Staying would mean having to forget Raoul, forget Raoul dying against the wire all because Fay let him go. She's never going to forget that. Never. If Demi won't leave with her, she will go alone.

She takes a deep breath. "Demi," she says, "this thing tonight . . ." She breaks off.

"Don't fret. You don't need to come tonight. I just only testin him."

"No, I don't mean that."

"Baz." He turns to face her. "I don't need you at my back. Not tonight. OK? This is different business. We haven't done this thing before, going in somebody house, poking about like some rat. This a Miguel job, but I can do it. So don't fret. If Eduardo"—he says the name as if it tastes sour—"is telling half a truth, we gonna be OK. We get money to keep Moro off of Fay's back. That man like the devil or something."

"Fay deal with him."

"Everyone got to deal with the devil sometime."

"Who told you that?"

"No one. I been thinking."

"You?" she teases. "You going to be complainin your head hurt tomorrow."

He laughs but doesn't say anything.

"Demi, when this job done, we leave this place, hey?"

"The Barrio?"

"Yes."

"Fay sayin same thing."

"Fay say it but she don't mean it, Demi. Fay stuck here, and now she think she found her boy she stuck here forever. But we free to go. If we stay we gonna get lost. I feel it, Demi. I dream it."

Demi laughs but not unkindly and touches her arm. "I sometime think you got a whole head stuff full of dream. You dreamin when I found you with that old dog. Now you dreamin again, Baz. Leave tomorrow to tomorrow. Let's just see what happen." He leans against her a little and they fall into a silence as warm as the night air.

*　　*　　*

At twenty to two Miguel steps up onto the roof, telling them it's time to go. There is nothing to collect or organize, just the slip of paper with the code for the safe, but Fay still fusses. For a moment Baz thinks she's going to give them a hug, hold them tight before letting them go, but the moment, if it existed at all, passes, and Fay just takes Demi's hand in hers. "Remember the rule," she says. "Come back safe but if it's not safe . . ."

"We know, Fay, don't come back at all. Nothing change, hey."

"Good boys. Baz, watch his back and . . ." It is as if she doesn't want them to leave, not quite yet; there is something else—Baz can see it in the anxious look in her eyes, and then realizes it is not for them that she's fretting, not really.

"It's OK, Fay," she says simply. "Whatever happen, Eduardo gonna be sleepin in his bed. He won't come to harm."

Demi looks at her, surprised. "What you thinking?" Then catching on, nods. "Sure, like a bug in a rug."

Fay's expression softens; the three of them have been together for a long time and sometimes it helps not to have some things said openly. "That's good. That's good. No need to make problem. You do this thing, neat and tidy."

"You won't see no stitch. You won't see no tear." Demi picks up the old words; it seems a long time since they have heard the refrain they used to chant before a hard day's thieving. And so they leave. Demi with a swagger, Miguel like a shadow close behind him and Baz last, not looking back at Fay, but knowing she's framed in the doorway, her hair wild as fire, her face pale with tiredness but with a tiny worm of hope. Maybe, like Baz, she feels that something new is coming out of this night, something that will let her break away from her life. Maybe she hopes she can be a mother again. Maybe.

Chapter Seventeen

THE THREE OF THEM, Baz, Demi and Miguel, Demi leading, slip through the sleeping Barrio, winding their way through the shoulder-wide alleys until they emerge into the wide-open space of Agua. On the far side the lights are still on in a few of the bars. Moro's Slow Bar has its name in pale blue watery light across its window. It looks so small from where Baz is standing she feels like she could almost hold it in her fist and crush it.

Just one car is parked by the fountain, large and old with a long flat trunk and fins.

"What kind of bad-man car they give us?" says Demi. "The policeman see this, he gonna haul it over first thing. Bet it got a motor that sound like dirt." A shadowy figure is leaning up against the side, the orange glow of his cigarette an occasional pulse as they walk toward him.

"Domino?"

The man doesn't answer, just opens the rear door for them. Miguel slides in first and Baz follows. Demi walks round the other side and climbs in the front. Domino shrugs, closes the door on Baz and then gets in. As Demi predicted, the engine grumbles throatily.

"You must be some kind of genius make a thing as old as this work," says Demi.

Domino flicks the butt of his cigarette out of the window, reaches into his shirt pocket and pulls out another one, and lights it. His face looks like polished wood, expressionless. His arms are thick, ropy with muscle, his fingers short. He looks like a fighter to Baz, not a driver, but at least he's not one of the swaggering sharp-suited shady men who live in Moro's pocket.

"You want a Mercedes, you pay for one," he says, the cigarette hanging from the corner of his mouth like in the old movies.

"We get to ride a Mercedes, you out of job, I reckon."

Domino doesn't answer and when Demi tries to draw him on Eduardo Dolucca—"You know this Eduardo long time, yeh?"—Domino remains silent, and there is such a heaviness in his silence that neither Demi, Baz nor Miguel say anything at all on the whole drive up through the city.

They rumble slowly along the city's glittering main street, every shopwindow selling a promise of the good life. Demi flips on the radio without asking the man. He picks a station playing jerky street music, but turns it down soft and then sits there nodding to the beat.

The city is not so big when you drive through it at night. The streets are like black ribbons, running in long lines east to west, south to north. Square glassy buildings give way to older houses with black-bellied balconies and steep steps down to the pavement, and these in turn dissolve as the city becomes, even in this early-morning darkness, brighter, newer, so new in places it's still being built. Here in the northern suburbs the streets are stamped with high white walls behind which the rich live in their cool, pale-colored houses. Heavy gates lead to courtyards and watery green gardens. But the passengers in the slow-moving car see nothing of the inside, only the walls, their eyes scanning now for the house of Dolucca. Via de Peone. No numbers anywhere, but Domino knows where he's going. Baz tries to track the lefts and rights; never go anywhere unless you have an exit, a way back to safety. No trams come this far north—buses maybe. Whoever heard of running from a robbery and catching a bus? If the policeman's coming for you, you better find something faster than an outer-city bus.

They pull in at the edge of the road. "This one, right here," murmurs Domino, tilting his head in the direction of a small building set into the outer wall. "Gate lodge. Main house beyond that. All you got to do is get in through that window."

There's one small window up on the first floor; the rest of the lodge must look out on to the garden.

Domino pulls away from the curb. "We go round the block one time," he says, "check everything clear."

There is nothing, just a lone dog moving briskly along the sidewalk. Halfway down the street, the road has been dug up where they are fixing drains or laying cable. There's a mess of timbers and tools propped inside the warning barrier. A house on the left has its gate open. And in the parallel street Baz spots one light on. But there are no moving cars, no patrols.

Domino U-turns and comes back down their road and pulls up outside the Dolucca house. Demi is eyeing the window. "Too high to jump. Miguel?"

"Too high," he agrees.

"Baz, you OK if we give you a lift?"

"Sure. You want me to open the gate?"

Demi is staring at the house and the wall and the gate, like there might be some secret way in Eduardo hasn't told them about. He shakes his head. "He didn't say nothin about a gate. Don't go near that gate. You stay by the window and you catch my hand when I run at the wall. I catch your hand and swing up. Miguel, wait below, give us warning whistle if we get a patrol car coming by. You OK with that?"

Miguel nods. "I stand in by the gate, shadow hide me OK."

"Good. You gonna keep the engine running, Domino. The boy said we won't be more than five."

Domino gives him his wooden look. "I come back for you."

Then, maybe sensing that Demi is about to rage at him, he says, by way of explanation, "Safer to keep moving; any policeman going to check a car pulled up like this."

He's right. The streets are bare; not a car pulled up anywhere— all safely tucked away in their garages, behind their gates. Baz nods at Demi. "OK," he says curtly, then ducks out of the car and the other two follow suit. "You wait till we are in. Then you give us five." Demi is all business, like when it's just him and Baz working on their own. Baz wonders what this silent man thinks, taking orders from a boy, a boy probably ten years younger than him. Maybe he doesn't care, maybe it's just a job to him— taxi. Except if they get stopped by the police, he'll end up in the Castle along with them.

Baz doesn't hear the driver's answer, but the car sits rumbling softly as Demi slips her a flashlight and then the two boys run and put their backs to the wall and cup their hands together. Baz doesn't get nervous working the street, just focused, all eyes, spotting, spotting, watching. But this is different. You can hide in the daylight, hide in the noise of traffic, bustle of people, appear and disappear like magic. Demi's the best, but she can do it too. But this is darkness and shadow, not light; silence, just a dog howling now, in another street, picked up by a ragged chorus of barks scattered from houses up and down their street. They freeze. If the Dolucca house has a guard dog it is a heavy sleeper. The barking dies away.

Baz takes a breath, gauges exactly where the sill of the window is, bounces up on her toes, nods to the boys and then runs lightly toward them, jumps, feels the hands solid under her right foot and instantly propelling her straight up. Her hands grip the sill and in one easy movement she is stooping in through the opening.

As she flicks on the flashlight she hears the car rumble slowly away. The air is cool. Air-conditioning. The pencil beam picks out a short corridor, a weird spotted carpet, stairs at the end and two doors off the corridor. No footsteps, no lights shining under the closed doors. She leans out of the window, hears the light patter of Demi running, touching the wall with the toe of his sneaker, the slap of his hand on her wrist, and then he's tumbling in through the window, somehow landing on his feet, knees bent, head swiveling, up, down, just as she had done.

He touches her arm and she follows him along the corridor and down the stairs into some kind of a day room. There's a bar counter along one wall, easy chairs, round table. All of one wall is window looking out on to the garden and swimming pool. The pool's water glows cool and blue with underwater lighting; it takes Baz's breath clean away. She's never seen anything like it, not for real, scuzzy images on the little TV, but not in a house that people . . . that that boy actually lives in.

She hears Demi moving about behind her. "Gimme light, Baz," he whispers. He's studying a box fixed to the wall to the right of the little stairway they have just come down. The alarm. She runs the pencil beam across the switches. "OK. I know how to do it. Now we get the safe. Behind the bar, he say."

Everything is exactly how Eduardo had told them it would be. The safe sits like a lumpy black fridge under the bar counter. The dial clicks as they spin it to the numbers on the slip of paper and then swings open. Demi makes a little puffing sound of surprise when he sees the space stacked with razor-neat towers of dollar bills. "What we doin being thief, Baz?" he whispers. "Policeman got all the money in the world and he don't got no one chasing him."

She spreads open the mouth of the cotton sack she's brought and methodically begins to scoop in the bundles of money.

"Why that boy want to give up all this?" says Demi. "Give it up and come to the Barrio. You believe it because he want to be with his mother, with Fay?"

"Dunno. Maybe jealous. Maybe they don't treat him good." She thinks she would find it hard to give up the pool; she keeps looking over her shoulder at it, at its silken stillness.

"You believe his story?"

"He got something in mind. We do this now, but you got to start thinking 'bout what I said." She pushes the last stack into the bag and draws the neck tight.

"What you say?"

"Demi, up on the roof. I tol' you: movin on. Fay give us some of this money and we start up on our own. You come with me an' we can manage." She hikes up the sack and hugs it to her chest while Demi closes the door of the safe, spins the dial to lock it.

"Let's go." They skip out from behind the bar. Demi goes to the alarm. "Thirty second from when I set the alarm back, Baz. Go to the window and signal Miguel and then tell me if Domino ready and waiting." He looks at his watch.

"Demi, what you think?"

"Baz! Do what I say. Go!"

With one last look at the dreaming pool she hurries up the stairs. When she leans out of the window, Miguel slides out from the shadow of the gate. She waves. He lifts his hand. The darkened car is there, throbbing quietly. She goes to the head of the stairs. "OK, Demi."

"Throw Miguel the bag and then jump. I'm gonna count to five then turn the alarm back on. Go!"

She runs back counting. *Four. Three. Two. One.* The alarm is on. Thirty seconds now. She holds out the bag and Miguel raises his hands to catch it. Four seconds. She lets it go, slings one leg over the sill. Twelve. Easy. Sees Miguel throwing the sack into the back of the car and scramble in. Hears Demi's feet on the stairs, swivels round to hook out her other leg and at the same time drops down so she's just holding the sill with her hands. With her nose to the white wall she sees the sudden illumination of the car's headlights being switched on and hears the gentle rumble turn to a racing growl. And as she falls she registers the squeal of hot rubber burning on the road. She lands easily, steps back and spins round and sees the sharklike car already at the corner, turning, a glimpse of a face at the back window, and gone. Miguel. Why did they have to bring him? Why did Eduardo want him there? So he would do just this, of course. Eduardo didn't want Demi any more than Demi wanted Eduardo.

The window above bulges with the black shape of Demi, crouching like a monkey. And then the alarm howls like a nightmare. Lights blaze on and the house burns white in the darkness of the long street.

Demi jumps face forward, straight down, landing badly, right leg buckling. He gives a grunt of pain and curses. She grabs his arm and hauls him up. Beyond the gate they can hear shouting. In the distance a siren begins to wail. Dogs bark.

"They made a monkey out of me!"

"You a monkey, you'd jump better than that. Can you run?"

"No one faster."

"Split?"

Rule number one. If you got to run, run alone.

"Split."

She touches his arm. His face is twisted in a grimace. "Mama Bali. OK?"

"OK." She watches him moving in a fast hobble down the edge of the road.

She turns her back and runs in the opposite direction. The policeman's siren is closer. Any second now there's gonna be a man finding the open window. She runs as fast as she can. The street is too long, too straight. She needs a low wall, an open gate. Anywhere to hide, just till the heat cools. Nothing. And then almost without thought she registers the roadworks, with tools stacked in one corner. She vaults the barrier and drops into the shallow hole, crouches and looks back to see Demi picked out, a small black silhouette caught in the beam of a police car. She sees his head swivel and then his hands lift slowly up in front of him, almost like he's meaning to push the light away. At the same instant, a barrel-chested man in long boxer shorts bursts out from the Dolucca gate. He doesn't shout or call, just swings his arm straight and there's the crack of a gunshot.

She sees Demi drop.

She feels such a thump in her heart she gasps and slides down into the bottom of the hole and crawls blindly under a scrap of tarpaulin and squeezes her eyes tight against this, the worst dream-time a body can have.

There are raised voices, the slamming of a car door. One boy, maybe dead; one man's house robbed. One man! This is the captain of police! This man can snap his fingers and you disappear. And they pick up one boy? They're never going to think this one boy did this on his own. So what are they going to think? What?

Baz lies tight as a nut in its shell, eyes shut, ears stretched wide, thoughts jigging up and down like her heart. She wishes she could squeeze her heart in her fist—stop it drumming so loud.

A car drives slowly down the road.

They're searching now, got their flashlights playing along the shadowy places, checking any open gate, any little place a mouse can squeeze in and hide. Sure they're going to search this hole in the road, it'll be under their nose.

The patrol car is close. Stops. A beam splashes brightly into Baz's sparse hiding space; she can feel the light against the squeezed-tight lids of her eyes.

"Nothing."

An answering voice.

Then: "No. Wasting our time. You think a gang going to pull a robbery and not have a car? You think that, you got your brain in your belly . . . No. You dumb-neck, didn't you hear the Captain son say he recognize the boy, say he's one of Señor Moro's scum, run errand for him?"

A whistle of surprise from the driver. More words.

"And nothing taken. Didn't get nothing, the Captain say. Not a thing. If they think we going to bust our asses hunting shadow, they got another think coming. Let's go."

Dark.

The car pulls away. For a few moments she hears the squeal of its tires as it U-turns down the end of the street and then accelerates back and past her to the Dolucca house. More voices. More doors clunking open and then, at long last, silence. Baz doesn't move. Baz doesn't blink. She hardly breathes. Her bones ache. Her face, pressed into the stony side of the hole, hurts, but her heart slows.

More time.

She unlocks her fist. She pulls the tarpaulin away from her face and opens her eyes. Still dark. Still quiet. She lifts her head and winces. Her neck is stiff. She bites her lip and slowly unlocks herself. Free!

How long. An hour? Two? Sun comes up quickly. She has to go now while it's still dark. She stands and then instantly ducks again. Lights blaze in the Dolucca house. At the gate she sees two policemen standing guard.

She has no choice. She has to go. She eases herself up wormlike, squirming over the lip of the hole, wriggling across to the darker shadow of the wall. She is all right. The men standing in the pool of light thrown by the house won't see anything, but she still keeps low, a stooping run, scuttling, like a lone rat back to its nest.

The street is long and dark.

And what kind of refuge is Fay's nest going to offer? Didn't they dump her and Demi, throw them away like so much trash?

Chapter Eighteen

FOR TWO HOURS SHE WALKS, keeping off the main highway, shrinking into a doorway any time she hears a car. Her eyes sting. Her feet hurt. And then there's a thin rim of light at the edge of the sky. Moments later she feels the warmth of the sun on her neck and the day has come. She feels like weeping, but what's the point? Fay taught them not to cry a long time ago. "Tears don't do you no good." Angrily she rubs the heel of her hand into her eye and tells herself to stop fussing; nobody snatched her. She's free.

More cars. More people filtering out of their houses. But it's a long walk into town. Finally she reaches a stop with workers lining up to climb on a bus to take them to the center. Wearily she clambers on and tucks herself into a seat in the corner. Her head tips against the window and her eyes close.

*   *   *

It takes another hour to get to Agua, and then she slips back into the Barrio. It closes round her, like a shawl, and she feels safe.

It is still early so no one is about; the Barrio works to a different clock to the rest of the city. Even Mama Bali's door is shut and the rusty iron shutter swung across her window. She cuts down to Lucien's square.

"Haul a bucket for you, Baz?"

She gives him his two cents and then sloshes the water on her face and neck while he hunkers down, his bony legs sticking out on either side of his chin so he looks like a big stick insect.

He watches her wash. "Somethin happen, Baz?"

"Somethin."

There's so much she can't even rehearse it all in her own mind, let alone spill it out to Lucien.

He nods; he can read bad news on a body's face. "Demi?"

She uses her hands to wipe the wet from her face, then dries her hands on the back of her jeans. "Demi get pick up by the policeman." She tries to keep it casual, like it's no big deal, but there's a tremor in her voice. She turns away. "I got to see Fay," she says. "Thanks for hauling the bucket, Lucien."

"Anytime, Baz." Then, when she's already ten paces down the slip of an alley that leads to the ditch you have to cross to get to their building on the old river front, he calls out, "You let go his hand, did you, Baz?"

She didn't let go his hand. She didn't! She rubs her forearm angrily across her itching nose and smarting eyes. He ran the wrong way, that was all; it could have been her the Captain saw. It could have been her caught in the light. He said to go separate. It was the rule. She didn't let go.

She reaches the building and snatches the warning rope by the entrance. She hears the jangle way up in the belly of the building and then she clambers up the stairs, up to their door. Without hesitating she pushes it open and goes right in.

"Where you been?" The den is gray with the smoke from her black cigars. The boys are curled up on their mats, sleeping still, but Fay, wild as a witch woman, is standing by the door to her room. She's a mess. Her hair is like a storm raging round her head, her face is pinched tight, her eyes red rimmed. Her shirt's untucked, one sleeve rolled up to her elbow, and she's gripping her bare arm so tight it's like she's only just holding herself in place. "Where are they? You tell me, missy. You tell me." She hasn't ever called Baz "missy" in her life. "No one come, no one phone me. This the day Moro gonna come! Where that money gone?" The last question is a whispery shriek.

"I got no money," Baz says, her voice steady.

"What you mean? You know what he threaten. You want to work for that man?" Fay marches straight at her and slaps her hard in the face. "Where Demi? Why Demi not here? You never don't come back without him."

"You think I don't know that."

Fay's hand jerks up again. "Baz, you start talking fast this minute or I swear I gonna break something and you right in my way for breakin."

Baz looks at her. The veins on her hands and on the side of her neck are ropy. For the first time Baz sees something in Fay she's not seen before, something behind the rage, the steely strength that has let her forge a life in this hard place; she sees confusion, panic maybe. She can rage all she likes. She doesn't frighten Baz, not anymore.

"Domino and Miguel run out and leave Demi and me for the hard man to catch. I seen Miguel looking back. They got the money. You plan it like that with your Eduardo boy? You decide the time come for me and Demi to get move on?"

"No! You crazy!" She scrapes her hands up through her hair so it stands up like bat wings. "And Miguel gone in that car?"

Baz nods.

"No one here tell him do that!" She snatches Baz's hand, holds it in hers, stares at her, like she can read a secret that Baz is keeping from her. But there is no secret, only truth in Baz's face. The storm vanishes. "Always truth," she half whispers. "You never even one time tell a lie to me, Baz." Instead of another slap, she touches Baz's face. "Come." She makes Baz sit and pours her a glass of water. Then she puts on a kettle to make coffee. She puts bread and cold meat, half a tomato on a plate in front of Baz and makes her eat, and as she eats, picking at the food, she listens to what she says.

"Poor Demi. You sure they took him?"

"They took him."

"You think that man got him with the gun?"

"I just seen him fall." She looks at the piece of bread in her hand and then puts it back on the plate. Instead of blanking out the memory, as she has done through all the long hours she lay in the hole and then the equally long trek home, she tries to recall all the detail of what she did see. Did he lift his head? No, but she recalls seeing them move his body, not one man at his feet and the other at his head, not slinging him in the back like they would have were he a corpse ready to be tipped out on a dump, but one on each arm, folding him into the backseat. Was that it? Maybe. "I think maybe he just fell. He hurt himself jumping from the window. They took him."

"Demi gone to the Castle," Fay says half to herself. She looks at Baz. "Poor Demi. Him so quick and neat. Like he born in a charm. Always like that, ever since the time he came to me . . ." She stops.

Baz stares at her.

Fay reaches across the table and grips Baz's hand again. "He won't tell them nothing about his Fay, will he, Baz?"

"No! Demi never do that. How we gonna get him out the Castle, Fay?" Fay doesn't answer. Baz leans forward, ideas forming as she speaks. "We go right now. What d'you say? I ask question. Say I lost my brother. They got no proof he was robbing; no one see him jump. No one see us take anything, and he got no money."

Fay tightens her grip on her hand. "Don't be fool, girl. No one visit the Castle—not if they come from the Barrio."

"You know people, Fay, and you got money put by for bad time like this. You got to help him."

"Help him!" She sits back in her chair as if stung. "I help him all my life. What he doing walk right in the arm of the hard man! Crazy boy!" She waves away Baz's objections. "Don't tell me nothing. I know how it is. He know how it is. Better if Demi dead than go in that place." Her voice drops and she glances at the still-sleeping boys. "They make him talk, and we all gone." She now seems hardly aware of Baz, her pale eyes focusing on things only she can see: her fears, her plans washing away, old age creeping toward her crookbacked and toothless.

Baz stares at her, unable to understand the way Fay seems to turn into different people right in front of her; and this one . . . this one disgusts her. She pushes back her chair. "Demi dead? What you sayin? You do nothing. You think you safe, Fay? You got your child back. Maybe he got your money tuck away safe somewhere. Maybe you think of that. Maybe your angel-boy done you a big-time wrong."

Fay looks at Baz as if she is the crazy one. "Don't be fool, Baz. Maybe Eduardo done his own thinking is all. Or maybe his driver take a notion an' we got to find him an' shake him down. Go make some food for the boys. I got business to do."

"What business?"

"Find where that money gone."

"And Demi?"

"Forget Demi. I deal with Demi."

Fay abruptly leaves the table and, pulling her cell phone from her trouser pocket, goes into her room. Private business then, business she doesn't want Baz to hear; business with Eduardo.

Baz sits for a moment, thinking hard. Everything is speed now. The longer the police have Demi, the less chance he will ever go free. Fay's shut the door on Demi. He's a threat. And Fay has only two ways of dealing with threat: remove it or run away—find a new place, a different city. She won't run, thinks Baz. Not without getting her hands on that money. So who is she phoning right now? Baz's mind is icy, just like the block that Demi ran through the Barrio with. There's only one man who has fingers that can reach into every little crevice of the city, reach into the Castle itself, into the cells. Señor Moro. It will just be a whisper from one man to another to another, and Demi will not even see the danger coming. And then he'll be dead, like Raoul, and Fay'll be safe.

She quickly stokes up the stove and puts fresh water on to make the boys' hot drink, her mind racing. If she is going to do anything, she will need money, a lot of money; only money is going to open a prison door. The ring! If Fay hasn't fenced it, it'll still be in that secret hiding place in the cellar that Demi told her about.

"Hey, Fay!" she knocks on Fay's door. "Going down to Mama's for milk."

Fay pulls open the door of her little room. She's sitting on the edge of her bed, the cell phone to her ear. "Don't be long. I got a message I want you to carry."

"Just getting milk, maybe bread."

"You not thinking any fool thought 'bout Demi anymore?"

Baz shakes her head.

"Good. I take care of Demi. You more like me than him, Baz. Keep your head cool." Fay studies her for a moment, maybe seeing only a reflection of herself. Baz returns the look, but her eyes are so dark and soft they give nothing away, not a hint of the ice in her mind. Fay waves her hand as a voice comes on the phone and pushes the door to with her foot.

Flashlight. She no longer has the one she used last night. Fay has another by the sink, but she'll see it gone. Matches then. She won't miss matches, nor a stump of candle. She glances at the boys. Not a stir. Swiftly she scoops up what she needs and hurries out of the den.

*   *   *

The stairs down to the cellars of the warehouse are narrow and steep, the smell dank and sickly. She hears the scratchy scuttle of rat, and the whisper of something else moving. Snake maybe. Snakes like the dark warmth of a cellar. She lights the candle and carefully but quickly makes her way down. Demi had real nerve to hide down here in the dark, waiting to spy on Fay.

She holds the candle up high and scans the wall to the right. It's scabby with some of the original plaster and mold and dirt, patched with rough concrete blocks. Where did he say? The corner. Fay had pulled out a brick or stone and reached right into the wall, her whole arm getting swallowed up, that's what he said. Then she had pulled out a box.

She runs her hands across the wall, looking for a place where her hands don't come away with so much dirt. She taps. The wall is thick, solid. She taps again and again. Pauses. Listens carefully, her ear to the wall. Maybe. Yes. She holds up the candle, finds the crack around a half block and eases it out. There is a space between the outer and inner walls, maybe a foot wide. She holds her breath and reaches down and down, as far as she can. Nothing. Fay's got longer arms. She tries again, squeezing her face against the wall, pushing so hard the skin on her shoulder pinches and tears. She grunts with frustration but keeps trying, the sweat pouring down her face. Then, as she is pulling her hand back up, thinking that the only way for her to get what she needs is something she can reach down with, or maybe a piece of iron so she can lever out more of the wall, she touches a shelf about a foot down on the inner wall. She lets her fingers run along it. Something furry brushes her fingers but she keeps moving her hand along the shelf . . . and then her fingers tap against smooth metal.

A box!

She grips it but it's heavy and awkward, and it's difficult with only one hand, but she grits her teeth and, holding it as tightly as she can, inch by inch, she brings it up to the opening.

The warning bell jangles. She hesitates and then quickly lifts the box out of the hole and lays it on the floor. Holding up the candle she unlatches the lid and looks inside.

Fay's treasure.

Chapter Nineteen

BAZ COCKS HER HEAD and listens. Whoever has come into the building must have gone up to Fay. Early though. Early for business.

She stares into the open box. There's money, old bills stacked and held together with rubber bands. Not as much as they took from Dolucca, not at all, but some hundreds, maybe a thousand. Not enough for Fay to retire on, or to take them all north as she had promised. There are coins, watches and credit cards too, and a stash of little sealed plastic bags. And there is the ring. It glitters at her in the candlelight. She holds it up and thinks of the Captain's wife in her little bitty dress and her bangles on her arms. The ring she wanted so much. Why? Didn't she have enough already? She remembers the way when she and Demi had held it up to the light that first time, it had seemed as if somehow it had the sky right inside.

Quickly she makes a decision. She peels off two fifties, folds them into a tight square and puts that and the ring in her trouser pocket, closes the lid of the box, slips it back into the hole and then fits the block back in place.

Thief.

It feels different to steal from someone you know. A bad feeling. It doesn't stop her though. She slips lightly up the stairs and then, checking to see if the coast is clear, she turns left and sprints along the baked mud shore, up to the bend in the river.

*   *   *

Twenty-five minutes later she is standing outside Mama Bali's kitchen.

"What the matter, child? You been stomping in that river again? You all mud. No! You not comin in here," she says, shooing Baz out from the doorway and onto the step. "You wait now." And a moment later comes out with a bucket slopping with water. "Step your feet in that. You wantin milk?"

Baz nods and sluices water over feet and the bottom part of her jeans. She should have changed—her T-shirt is stained and sweaty.

Mama stands there, her fists on her fat hips, watching her wash. Baz sometimes feels Mama is too big for the Barrio, too wide for its tangle of threading alleyways. "I never seen you so scuffed up, girl. Wha' happen? Where's that Demi? You two like peas in a pod . . . I say somethin?"

"No." She slips her wet feet into the sneakers. Then she straightens. "Policeman took Demi." She tries to keep her voice steady but it is hard. "Took him to the Castle, I reckon."

Mama doesn't say anything for a moment, then she sighs. "And that boy thought he could walk on water . . . Come inside, Baz." She leads her into the kitchen and sits her down. Then goes behind the bar and pours out a bowl of steaming coffee and hot milk and sets it down before her.

Mama lowers herself onto the stool facing Baz. "How much you wanna tell, eh?"

Baz sips her drink and describes the robbery and the betrayal by Domino. She tells her about the boy, Fay's lost and found son, the robbery and the betrayal, and how she is now terrified that someone is going to have Demi killed. When she is done she says, "How can we get Demi out of that place, Mama?"

Mama shakes her head. "We? What you think I can do? I know 'bout coffee and I know 'bout beans and how to keep my head up in this place, but I never done any business with the policemen in this city, not for long long time. What Fay say?"

"Fay? Fay prefer Demi die than he live a day in that place and tell people about her. But Demi never goin to say nothin. Demi never goin 'gainst Fay . . ." Baz stops herself and Mama exhales softly but doesn't say anything. Baz laces her fingers round the small bowl she's been drinking from. "If I don't get Demi out of there, Demi not goin to live. Fay do nothing for him now . . ." But what she really fears is much worse than this, much worse than doing nothing.

"Demi got burned, Bazzie." Mama reaches across the table, touching Baz's hand with her own, just as Fay had done. "That what happen when you do what you do. I don't say a thing, but that what happen. Happen to you too one time. Meantime, you got life. All a body can do is take what she got."

Just because a person looks like a mountain and has a smile and a kind word for scuffed rats like Baz and Demi doesn't mean that they can pull a miracle. Doesn't mean they can beat down the door of the Castle. Baz looks at her without blinking, and Mama turns her head away. Baz doesn't expect miracles, never did, not from anyone except maybe Demi, but she wants advice. She makes a quick decision, reaches into her pocket, pulls out the ring and places it on the plastic tabletop. "This one thing I got."

Mama blows out her fat cheeks. "Put it away, child. That ring don't bring you nothin but trouble. Sooner you get rid of it, safer you gonna be. Moro got his men turnin everything this way, that way lookin for that ring. Barrio gone crazy. And this job you tell me 'bout—the Captain's house—I think Fay lose her mind! Everything going to come down on us hard—tell you that for nothing, Baz."

"You think that Captain wife help me if I give the ring back?"

"Maybe. Maybe her husband do something if she ask him, but most folk only put themselves out when you offer them what they really want."

"Maybe she really want this old ring back. Can't I just tell her I got this ring?"

"Don't tell her what you got—just say you got something she wants. Phone her. But be careful, you know. See what she say; see what she willing to do. Maybe she want to meet you, but if she do, you make sure you choose the place and you get there long time before her and you make sure there are no uniform waiting to snap you up."

Baz nods and tightens her hand round the ring, making a fist. She's not looking at Mama but at her hand. "I think Fay gonna get Demi killed," she says suddenly. "I think she gonna talk to someone she know . . ."

Mama Bali puts her hand up to Baz's mouth. "You do what you can. That's all a body can do. Go. Phone this woman. Maybe you get lucky, Baz."

*   *   *

Baz has to go all the way to the other side of Agua to find a pay phone that works and that has a directory. She finds a hundred Doluccas and then squinting at the letters identifies the right address. She calls.

"Hallo."

"Can I talk with Señora Dolucca?"

"Who is this? Do I know you?" The voice is male but young. Eduardo. What is he doing answering the phone? How come he's sitting in that fancy house and Demi's slapped in the

Castle, maybe dead. A hot, airless cell. Bars. Maybe thieves. Maybe murderers. Maybe no one to look out for him. Eduardo has set it all up. It was never just the driver and Miguel but Fay's boy himself. He has some plan—stir everything up, get everyone fighting each other, and somehow he get all the money to himself; she and Demi nothing to him . . . Baz glares at the phone, and then stills herself.

She ignores his questions. "Señora Dolucca, please." She's heard them talk, telling cabdrivers and porters this thing and that thing; she's seen their fancy ways and how they sail through the city getting touched by nothing, getting stopped by no one. She doesn't answer his questions. She makes her voice firm and strong, a don't-mess-with-me voice. Nobody, not even Demi, has heard her sound like this.

"Your business?"

"Señora Dolucca."

There are voices in the background. "One moment."

Then a woman comes to the phone. "Hello."

Baz pictures her, still in the yellow hat she was wearing when Demi worked his magic. She can almost hear the jangle of the silver bracelets on her skinny wrist. Is she a smart woman or foolish? Baz doesn't think she's that smart, bringing up a boy like Eduardo. This woman's got money though, got a fancy house, likes to have precious things.

"Hello. Who is this?"

"I got something you want," says Baz.

"Scuse me?"

She takes a deep breath. "You got one chance to see what it is. You go to Caliossa Street and you go to the bar on the corner. I find you. You bring anyone, you tell your husband, the Captain, you tell your boy . . ." She pauses. ". . . Your boy, the

boy you bring into your family when he's a baby; you got a
little girl . . ."

"Stop! How do you know this?"

Voices in the background.

"Tell them go away. This is private."

She hears the sound of the phone being held away from the
woman's face, a hand perhaps partly covering the mouthpiece.
Her voice muffled, but Baz can hear what she says. "No," she
says. "Fine," she says.

Baz holds the phone tight. She listens carefully. If there is a
click, it means someone else is picking up the phone. No. Just
the woman's breathing.

"Hello. Hello, are you there?"

This is good; the woman is startled, maybe a little nervous,
but she hasn't called for anyone, hasn't put down the phone.
"You want to meet me, you come to Bar Centrale, Caliossa
Street. One hour from now. It is easy. Safe. You know it. You
come alone and I give you this precious thing—I don't want no
money." Baz pauses, hears the sound of the woman breathing
down the end of the phone. Traffic rumbles behind her. Something prompts her to say, "And I tell you something 'bout your
family. Something you don't know. But you come alone. You
understand me, Señora Dolucca. I can see if you come alone or
not."

The voice at the other end of the line hesitates. Then, "How
will I know you?"

"You don't, but I know you, Señora Dolucca." She puts the
phone down. One hour. OK. She needs to wash, buy a new top
and jeans in the market. But she must hurry and be there in quick
time. Mama Bali is right—she has to see that the place is clean
before she shows herself to this woman. Too easy for Señora

Dolucca to tell her husband. Too easy for her husband to put some man in there, some hard man in easy clothes. But it's not a problem if she's there first, watching everyone coming in. She can spot any hard man no matter what he's wearing, and if one comes through the door she'll slip away, make another plan.

She swings up onto a tram. Caliossa Street is midway between smart town and her district. Not a bad area, but not too good either; she doesn't want Señora Dolucca to feel too safe. The bar, Centrale, is one Fay used for a while: Baz and Demi spent long hours waiting outside for her. It is popular, all come and go. But smart. She hopes they don't fuss her. She runs her fingers through her short hair and looks at her reflection in the tram's window. The face looking back is so faint she can hardly see herself, like she's half disappeared.

Fifteen minutes later she is outside the bar. She hangs back a moment and then swiftly follows in on the heels of a couple, obviously husband and wife. Could be her parents, maybe, except they're smart folk; they don't have the flat brown skin of those from upcountry, like Baz does.

A waiter raises his eyebrows. "Excuse me," he says to the couple, "is this child with you?" Baz doesn't wait to be questioned. Without hurrying she wanders off to an empty table by the window. Perfect.

The waiter follows her as she knew he would. "You can't sit here." He sweeps a cloth over the table as if he wants to sweep her away with the crumbs.

She smiles at him, a big smile, the biggest she can manage. Demi says when she smiles her eyes get so big they make him dizzy. She doesn't know whether this is a good thing, but this is the smile she gives the waiter and she pulls out one of Fay's dollar notes from her pocket and smooths it on the table. Fifty.

The waiter's eyes widen slightly.

"Coke, please," she says.

The waiter ducks his head slightly and then weaves off through the tables. She slips the note back in her pocket. A Coke only costs ninety cents. He is a fool if he thinks he's going to get a forty-nine-dollar tip from her, but money is still magic, makes things happen. She wishes she had a thousand times as much—then the magic might lift Demi out of the Castle.

The Coke arrives and as she sips it, she carefully looks round the room, checking each table. Safe. Then she watches the street, looking for Señora Dolucca, looking out for the hidden policeman in his easy clothes.

People stream by, some swinging into the café. Her Coke is almost finished when she sees her. She's walking down the street all tippy-toe on high heels, peppermint-green jacket and peppermint-green skirt and peppermint-green bag swinging on her shoulder. The lady must live in those ice-cool shops on the main street, spending all her money to look this way. She's wearing big dark glasses and looking behind her every so often.

Inside the bar, Señora Dolucca scans the tables, ignoring the waiter who's asking her questions. Her eyes pass over Baz and settle on a single woman over in the corner. Baz sees her hesitating and then start toward her. Swiftly Baz gets up. "Señora Dolucca," she says. "Here, I have a place for you."

The police captain's wife stops suddenly, almost as if she's been stung. "You?" she hesitates. "I thought it was a woman who spoke to me this morning."

"Come," says Baz, and instinctively she holds out her hand to guide the older woman through the tables, and the woman, perhaps to her own surprise, allows her hand to be taken. "Maybe you want coffee, maybe cool drink? I buy you something."

The dark glasses close her in like a pair of shutters, but her fingers are tight on her bag and the bag's clutched to her side like a wing. Her head turns, scanning the bar again. "You bring me here and then you buy me a drink?" Her voice wavers a little. Nervy.

An effort for her to come to this place on her own, not knowing who she is meeting, worrying that there is some threat hanging over her life, over her children.

"You want someone else to talk to you?" says Baz. "You want a man maybe . . ."

"No." She sits, then lifts her hand and the waiter is at her side. A woman like this never has to wait for service. "Tea," she says, "jasmine. You have that?" The waiter ducks his head.

There is a pause. The smart woman and the girl, on either side of the small round table, their knees almost touching, waiting for the waiter to come back. Baz keeps her face still. She is not sure how to begin. Her face gives away nothing; her hands rest lightly on the table. She sips her Coke. Her eyes never leave the woman's face.

This woman the key, she thinks, the key gonna unlock me Demi. But how does she begin? Has this woman really come all this way just for a ring, a jewel? Baz doesn't think so. She has already registered Señora Dolucca's street value: pretty ear studs, good quality; bracelets, four, silver, and a pretty wristwatch; no chain or necklace; handbag, expensive. She sees the way the woman's middle finger, the one with a fat yellow stone on the knuckle, picks at her thumbnail. How she fingers the catch of her bag and then swiftly pulls out a packet of menthol cigarettes, taps one out and lights it. Baz decides to wait, let the woman ask the questions.

"This precious thing . . . ," Señora Dolucca says, puffing out a stream of smoke. "Are you going to tell me what it is?"

Baz ignores the question. "You tell your husband, the big captain, what you doing?"

Señora Dolucca shakes her head and then the waiter sweeps down on them, placing the cup of jasmine tea and a tiny saucer of thin black chocolates. He slips the tab under the saucer, and then with a little half bow to the elegant woman, he disappears back into the bar.

"What do you know about my family?" says Señora Dolucca suddenly.

This is it. Baz feels like she's playing that card game she plays sometimes with Demi and Señora Dolucca has just let her see her hand. She picks up one of the thin chocolates. The waiter didn't bring chocolate when she was sitting on her own. "I know many thing about your family." She leans forward and lowers her voice. "I know your husband do business that not police business." The chocolate softens in her fingers so she quickly eats it. It tastes like heaven must taste. Without thinking, she reaches for another.

The woman is very still. She has not sipped her tea.

"You worry 'bout your children?"

"Are you threatening my children?" Her voice is thin, brittle with anger and fear. "Last night. You know what happened last night, at my house. Do you know that?"

"I know."

"What did it mean?"

Baz doesn't blink. It meant taking a whole lot of money. It meant some bad business happened with the two rats driving off in the car and Demi getting taken. That's what it meant. It meant Demi getting shot. Demi getting dragged to the Castle and Baz having to hide and do nothing to help because there had been nothing that she could do. It meant seeing Fay stepping out of her big-sister skin and now becoming this other person, a person who doesn't seem to care about Demi, doesn't care about anything but herself. Doesn't care if Demi dies. Maybe worse, maybe hopes Demi dies, his mouth closed up good.

And maybe it meant more than all this. Maybe this was part of Eduardo's plan, getting rid of Demi. Why not? Getting rid of Baz too, why not? Doesn't he want Fay to himself, the mother who let him go? And doesn't she want him?

The woman's skinny hand suddenly grips Baz's wrist like a claw, nails digging into her flesh. "You tell me now. What did it mean? Who do you work for? You a messenger from one of my husband's . . . business partners? Does it mean something about my family?"

"It mean a lot to you, Señora Dolucca, if you lose your boy, or your girl maybe. That hurt you, hurt you worse than you hurtin my wrist right now."

She lets go, pulling her hand away as if it was Baz's skin that was burning her rather than the other way round. "What do you want?"

Baz blinks. She holds herself tight as a drum. She is saying the right things to this woman. She feels like she is pushing at the door and the door is inching open. "A boy got hisself shot last night, right by your house. Got hisself shot; got hisself taken to the Castle. That boy not much older 'n me." She keeps her voice cold and steady as a knife. "You understanding me?"

"You think I can help you!"

"You . . . your husband. Yes. You can help me."

"My husband!" she gives a bitter laugh.

"OK, you. You can get this boy out of the Castle." She takes a breath. "Think if it happen to your children. Think what you feel then."

"My children don't break the law."

"Bad thing happen all the time," Baz says wearily, and thinks of Raoul, of Demi.

Perhaps Señora Dolucca hears something else behind Baz's plain statement. "And if I can't help?" she says.

Not if I won't, but if I can't. The door is a little more open. Just one more small push and the woman will do what she asks. "You know how thief come into your home last night?"

Señora Dolucca puffs at her cigarette. She doesn't answer.

"You got big high gate. You got big high wall. You got alarm. You got big police-captain husband. You think you safe? Nobody ever safe. Thief come into your room easy. Thief come in any room thief want. Because someone always tell thief how."

The woman flinches. "Who?"

Baz shakes her head. "Come with me. Come. You let that boy go and nobody come near your home again. Nobody come near your children."

"Do you think I am stupid? How can I trust what you say? You! A child!" She grinds out her cigarette.

Baz reaches into her pocket. This is everything. She pulls out the ring and puts it on the table. "This my good faith," Baz says. She keeps a finger on the ring. "What you give me in return? You help me get my brother?"

The woman is very still. Slowly she takes off her dark glasses. Baz sees her eyes are rimmed with red, the skin round her left eye is discolored, a little yellow, an old bruise. "Where did you get this?" She stops. "The boy? Is this the same boy, the one stole from me?" Suddenly she laughs and shakes her head. "And he is your brother?" She studies Baz, as if really looking at her for the first time. "I remember him, the boy. He is not so like you. You are from the country. Why is he so important to you? Someone tell you to do this? Someone older than you? Your mother maybe? His mother?" Baz doesn't answer. "No. You don't have family, do you? Except for him." She picks up the ring. "And you would return this to me? I could just take it from you. I could call out. I could say you tried to steal it from me. I could do any of these things and what could you do?"

Baz doesn't look at the ring. She looks at Señora Dolucca, holds her eye.

After a moment the police captain's wife gently pushes the ring back to Baz. "Keep it safe. I will come with you to the Castle. I want to see this boy again. Maybe we can do something." She replaces her glasses and lifts her hand. The waiter appears and she pays the bill. Baz slips the ring back in her pocket. "The ring," Señora Dolucca says, standing up, "is that the precious thing?"

Baz shakes her head. "No." She had thought this woman would be foolish, a spoiled rich woman, a woman to do business with, to feel nothing for. It is different now, now she has agreed to help, now Baz has seen the yellow bruise staining her eye.

"I didn't think so. It is something you know, something you can tell me."

"It is not a good thing," says Baz.

"No, I didn't think it would be. Do you always tell the truth?"

Baz thinks for a second. "Always."

"All right. Tell me this—when I know this thing that you can tell me, will it make my family safe, me knowing?"

"Maybe."

Señora Dolucca gives a wry smile. "You're a closed-up little thing, aren't you? Like a clam."

Baz doesn't know what a clam is.

The woman holds out her hand. "We'll get a taxi, all right?"

Baz feels her heart give a lurch. So easy. She just go with this woman and they get Demi, just like going in a shop; for this woman maybe all life is like going in a shop, get what you want. But they are going to the Castle.

Without thinking, Baz takes her hand and they walk out of the bar together.

Chapter Twenty

SEÑORA DOLUCCA ONLY HAS TO LIFT a hand and a taxi glides up to the pavement. She gets in and Baz slides in after her. This woman, she thinks, never had to run for any tram, never swung up on the back step, sweeping round a corner, leaving trouble behind. This woman just catch a taxi.

"Bolivar Street," she says. "Police headquarters."

Baz sees the driver's eyes in the mirror. "You want the Castle?"

"Yes," says Señora Dolucca, a hint of impatience in her voice. She takes out her purse, checks herself in a little mirror and then snaps it shut. She doesn't look out of the window. She doesn't look at Baz. The taxi is big and new, the seats shiny black. There is enough room, Baz reckons, for a small family to sit in the wide space between her and Señora Dolucca. She is nervous. She tries not to be. She sits very still, looking out of the window, seeing the smart shops sweeping by. Would this woman who has everything give her to the policeman? Would she say, if you search this girl, you will find a ring, a ring she stole? Would she say this, or would she help get Demi?

She pulls the ring out of her back pocket, looks at it for a moment and then quickly makes up her mind. Without saying anything, she touches Señora Dolucca's arm and holds the ring up for her to take. The woman looks at it and at Baz, then shrugs slightly. She slips it on her finger, glances at it and then looks out of the window.

Perhaps, thinks Baz, for her the ring is not so much. Then she wonders what Demi will say when she tells him she gave the ring back. Even if it was to help rescue him, will he understand?

She is not sure, but what does it matter? It is better to do something, not just let things happen.

The taxi slows and swings right at a set of lights, onto a long tree-lined avenue: Bolivar Street. This is the street of government ministries; and different people walk here—no rich women holding shiny shopping bags but men in suits, men in uniforms. The buildings are tall and old with elegant windows and curved iron balconies. One building, however, is different. She knows even without looking exactly where it is because she remembers from that time when Demi took her here to show her. It is exactly midway down the street, on the right, a pale ghostly gray. It was once the old presidential palace; now it is the Castle.

The taxi pulls up and Baz takes a deep breath. Some things you cannot know till they happen.

Señora Dolucca pays the fare, gets out and smooths her skirt. She looks back at Baz, her face expressionless behind the dark glasses. "Come."

Baz slides across and gets out. Although she's wearing new jeans, she feels scruffy beside this woman; everyone is going to see what she is—she might as well have SHE-THIEF written on her T-shirt. She is from the Barrio; nothing washes that from you, not here. The man in uniform knows; he can smell you.

"Come," says Señora Dolucca again, and perhaps sensing that the one thing Baz doesn't want to do is to climb these steps and pass the two armed policemen standing either side of the big-mouth door, she takes Baz's hand again and Baz steels herself, and then together they go into the Castle.

Inside is a wide, echoing hall with a marble floor and a high ceiling. An ugly plastic-topped counter runs down the right-hand side, staffed by three shirtsleeved policemen. A thick black line has been daubed on the floor, and behind this men and women queue. There is no easy talking here, no greetings. They wait, head down or staring straight ahead, locked up with their own personal business. And when they reach the counter they lean forward and mutter to the bored official behind the desk who, Baz sees, sometimes writes something down in the ledger he has in front of him.

Uniformed men saunter through the middle of the hall, chatting, smoking, ignoring the public, heading for duty on the streets or through one of the inner doors, perhaps to the cells and interview rooms.

Señora Dolucca takes in the scene with a glance and, ignoring the waiting queues, walks straight up to the desk. The man she cuts in front of starts forward ready to jostle, complaining loudly. People turn; the official looks up annoyed, sees Señora Dolucca, sees the man and presses a buzzer on the desk. Instantly two policemen zero in and without a word they take an arm each of the still-protesting man and frog-march him out to the street. Baz wonders how many hours he must have been standing there waiting his turn; he was a fool this man—anyone can see that Señora Dolucca is a rich woman, important; what point is there in complaining here in the Castle? He should have known. Señora Dolucca doesn't turn her head.

"Señora, yes, can I help you?" He is polite but not that interested. Baz sees that he is looking past Señora Dolucca to the door where the ejected man is still arguing and one of the policemen has drawn his club. Farther along the counter Baz sees that an elderly woman is fumbling in her basket. She takes out one, two notes, crumpled dollar bills. She smooths them, as if unwilling to let them go, and then slides them across to the official dealing with her, who folds them into the ledger without a word and then curtly waves her away.

"My husband is Captain Dolucca," says Señora Dolucca.

The police official is suddenly attentive. "Yes, señora, I am sorry, I didn't recognize you. I do not think we have met. I . . ."

Señora Dolucca snaps open her bag and shows him her papers.

"Of course, thank you, señora. Please." He presses the buzzer and Baz wonders for a split second if he is going to have them both ejected like the complaining man, but when an officer comes hurrying over, he snaps an order at him: "Chair, iced tea." And then to the police captain's wife he says, "Surely you did not need to come here, señora. A call, or a word to your husband . . ."

"I wish to see someone here."

"Ah, of course, an officer, but again a call, unless of course . . ." The man is fumbling, trying to understand why she, of all the privileged people in the city, should come here. He looks past her, noticing Baz for the first time.

"There was a boy arrested last night . . ."

The chair and iced tea arrive and Señora Dolucca sits down. She ignores the tea.

"So many . . ." The man raises his hands apologetically, as if it is his fault that crimes are committed in the city.

"And he was shot."

"Maybe he is dead, señora . . ."

Señora Dolucca is not a patient woman. "What is this? You have records of arrests. This was an incident at my house. My husband was involved in dealing with it. The boy's name is . . ."

"Demi," says Baz.

"Ah yes." The man writes this down and looks up again.

"This is his name," says Baz. "I do not think he has another one."

The man nods and carefully underlines the name Baz has given her, as if this will somehow conjure the boy up for them. Then he flicks back through the last couple of pages in his ledger.

"You have no computer? You are police headquarters and you still use pens and pencils. No wonder we have problem here."

"We have," says the man, "but not in reception, not for this." He indicates the people waiting. "It is not necessary."

"And for arrests? When you have a child brought in. You think it is not necessary? And when that child is shot, you think it is not necessary?"

"Señora, please. My job is this; I do not make these decisions."

"This I can see," says Señora Dolucca shortly. "Well? Have you found anything?"

He shakes his head. "One moment, please." He picks up the phone and taps two numbers. Then he turns sideways in his chair and talks quietly so that Baz can catch only the odd word he is saying.

Señora Dolucca sits stiffly in the chair, her hands on her purse. Baz knows what it is: this is not her world. When she wants something, it is done. Whatever difficulty she has in her life, it is not this, not queuing, and waiting, and dealing with officials.

The man puts down the phone. "I am sorry. I cannot help you, señora. There is nothing." He holds up his hand as if to stop another icy outburst. "It happens sometimes. One incident followed immediately by another and so on, so that the first one is forgotten, or missed. Human nature. The patrol is tired. Of course it is not right, but it happens."

"And a boy who is shot is forgotten too?"

Baz remembers the boy at Norte, the one who ran. This is Demi, maybe.

The man is very uncomfortable. "You can try the morgue, señora. Or maybe, it is possible, if the wound is not so bad, they take him to the hospital."

"Which one?"

"Wait, please." He dials again and tries one number, then another. "San Lucia Hospital. They have a boy brought in last night. Maybe it is this one you are looking for. They do not have a name yet."

"It is the military hospital?"

"Yes, all the services. It has a secure wing. This is where that boy will be." He stands up.

"Thank you." Señora Dolucca gets up and then hesitates. "You do not think he could be here somewhere? I believe many people are held here."

The man's face is expressionless. "We have no medical care here. A prisoner who needed treatment would have to be taken elsewhere."

Baz turns away. If Demi is in the Castle, he is dying in some corner of a cell. And what can she do? What more can she do? She cannot run through this hall, push past policemen, bang on doors. She can only do this, use the Captain's wife to ask and to look.

"Yes," says Señora Dolucca. "We will try the hospital."

"Perhaps I can arrange a car to take you there . . ."

"No, I do not think so." She unclips her purse. "I understand there is a charity I can make a small contribution to. You have been helpful."

"Of course, señora."

She folds two bills into the ledger. "This was a discreet visit, you understand. You need not record it in your book."

"No need at all." He slides the bills into his pocket and then, as Señora Dolucca and Baz walk back toward the entrance, he gestures for the next person to come up to the counter.

Down on the pavement Señora Dolucca fumbles in her purse for her cigarettes, taps one out of the pack, lights it and then draws on it deeply. "That place . . ." she says more to herself than to Baz, and she shudders. She takes another draw and then drops the cigarette and grinds it out with the heel of her expensive green shoe. "You are a very silent child, aren't you?"

Baz doesn't think of herself as a child. "Do you know this hospital?"

"Yes."

"And we go there now."

"Yes. I think we should find this boy and perhaps if we are lucky it will be your brother, and if it's not perhaps we can help the child, find him a lawyer."

Baz turns away. If it is not Demi, Baz doesn't know what she will do. Except she will go to the morgue, see if Demi's there, see him one last time. She tries to shake this thought out of her mind.

*　　*　　*

Another taxi ride; another part of the city. A pale green slab of a building set back from the road, surrounded by a dusty garden and a high wall. There's a wide entrance with a security barrier that dips up and down as cars and ambulances come and go. Right by the entrance is a small newsstand; across the street is a café-bar with tables outside. A bored soldier stands by the barrier, glancing at those entering, stopping no one. Their taxi takes them right in and up to the front of the building.

Reception here is very different to the Castle's. The duty officer logs their visit, taking their names, and is duly respectful to Señora Dolucca. At the medical desk a nurse identifies the patient they wish to see as Renaldo Balta. "Very sick," she says.

Renaldo is never a name that Demi has used. Her heart sinks but she stands patiently beside Señora Dolucca; all this must be done. You cannot give up. You cannot let go till the very last hope has gone.

They are given visitor tags and directed up a flight of stairs and along a dull green corridor at the end of which is a small office and a gray metal gate blocking off the secure wing. A cheerful, round-faced officer steps out of his little cubbyhole office to greet them. He straightens his uniform, trying to tuck his shirt in, his large belly swelling against the buttons.

A lazy man, thinks Baz. A man who likes an easy life. In his office a small television is murmuring the latest episode of *La Reglia*, the city's favorite soap—even Fay's hooked on it. Beside it another screen shows a corridor with numbered doors. As she watches the image flicks to the inside of one room, where a man is sitting up in bed staring out of the window, and then to another, empty, and then back to the corridor again. "Ah," he says to Baz, "you're like me. *La Reglia*, eh? I have to know what is happening all the time." He checks their passes and then takes them through the barred gate into the secure section of the hospital but seems unwilling to let them go.

"Popular boy, this one," he says. "You are the second visitor he has today. For a boy like that, you wouldn't think there would be anyone at all. From the Barrio, plain as a pig's tail." And he would have gone on chatting, except Señora Dolucca pats his arm and tells him in a surprisingly gentle voice that they have little time. "Of course, of course. Room seventeen. Go in—it is not locked." Baz sees the way his eyes follow Señora Dolucca as she clacks down the corridor ahead of them, her hips swinging a little in her expensive dress. For this man, Señora Dolucca must seem like one of those perfect creatures from the soap. As Baz slips by him almost unnoticed, she tucks the thought in the back of her mind that this might be useful.

The door clunks shut behind them.

Chapter Twenty-one

Señora Dolucca takes off her glasses and gestures for Baz to go in ahead of her.

Despite the brightness of the day, the room is so gloomy Baz can barely make out the figure lying in the bed. A dark head on a white pillow that shifts as she steps into the room. Baz holds her breath. A ceiling fan stirs the thick air. The figure groans faintly. She hesitates, takes a breath and then soundlessly moves up to the bed.

For a moment she still cannot tell whether it is him or not as this boy has his face turned toward the darkened window. Gently she reaches out and touches him, just the tips of her fingers on the back of his neck. The boy stirs, rolls his head and then she sees the outline of his face, the whites of his eyes, staring up at the ceiling and the slow whirring of the fan.

"Demi!" It is half a cry, half a whisper. "Demi." She doesn't touch him again, just stands close to the bed, looking down.

He turns his head a little more and she can see dark rings under his eyes, and his face looks pinched, his breathing a little ragged. "Baz," he says, "you come lookin for me."

"What you thinkin?" she says softly, trying to hide her concern. "I gotta come find you—such a fool boy to get snatch up like that."

And then, to her surprise, he grins and whispers, "They maybe catch me this one time, but they do not put me in the Castle. And I got a deal if I want it, Baz—ticket out of here."

"You play-actin all this hurt!"

"Some. Bullet got me here. Went right through." He touches

his left arm and then, wincing, pulls himself up into a sitting position. "Reckon I can still run quicker 'n you."

She wants to know who this other visitor was: Señor Moro? The police? Maybe the Captain himself. The hard man making deals with a boy from the Barrio. Maybe. Demi got a lot to tell.

"You make a deal?"

"Deal been put on the table. I pick it up if I want. Gimme some water, Baz."

She hands him the glass. "Who give you this deal?"

He shifts his head slightly, takes a sip and then sees the figure of Señora Dolucca framed by the light of the doorway. "Who this with you, Baz? Who do you bring?"

"The Captain's wife, Demi. She bring me here. And I give her back the ring, Demi."

"She knows?"

"She know all thing, all thing but one."

He looks at her without saying anything for a moment. Then, his tone almost careless, "You give her that ring. You kidding me. After all the trouble I took."

"You just trouble for anybody round you. I the one that have to run halfway round the city to bring this home; then I got to do the same to get you back from trouble."

"Open the shutter, Baz. It always seem nighttime in here."

She goes over, pulls the wooden shutter open and bright sunlight floods in through the barred window. Blinking, Demi pulls himself up so he's leaning against his pillows.

"You some fool girl," he teases, and then in a quieter voice, "and you find where Fay keep her treasure hidden, hey? She gonna rage when she find the ring gone."

Baz shrugs. Fay doesn't figure in her thinking now, except

she needs to get Demi away from her, right away from this place, because there's no home for them now in the Barrio.

"So this is him?" Señora Dolucca has come up beside Baz. She has slipped her black glasses back on. "He is very small. What is a small child like you doing trying to rob the city's police captain? Who makes you do this thing?" She is not cross, Baz can tell, but puzzled.

Demi is silent for a moment, as if gathering strength. "I'm not so small," he says. "I am fast, and I know much thing in this city."

"When you stole this," she holds up the ring, "you didn't know who my husband was, did you?"

"If your husband standing beside you I know him but you just got the little girl with the skinny sharp eyes—that's who you got."

"Yes." Her mouth curves slightly into a smile and Baz can tell that she likes this boy, this thief who stole from her. "And you got this girl. Is she as important to you as you are to her?"

"She!" He coughs and then winces. "Baz! Hey, I find her, I give her name—course she can't miss me, what she do on the street without me?" Baz folds her arms and waits. Sick, flat on his back in hospital with a prison guard down the corridor and the boy is trying to strut. "So I gotta look out for her all the time," he says, satisfied. "This is it."

Baz pulls a face. Not even a bullet can put a stop to his big talk. "You got more hot air puffing out your head than Ching Chang laundry!"

"Well," says Señora Dolucca to Baz, "I'm happy you found him and you found him here, not in that other place. And I have my ring, so that is one half of what was agreed between us." She slips it back on her finger. "So now you tell me this thing about my family, yes?"

"Yes." Baz hesitates; this truth she is about to tell could be the big wave that sweeps them all away, but she has promised, and this woman has done more to help them than she ever imagined she would. "You must do one more thing, please. When I tell you this, it makes much danger for me and Demi. Much danger, you understand. You must make promise that you say nothing, nothing to anyone, not your husband, your daughter, anyone. Just for a little while."

"How long?"

How long? She doesn't know. "Two days," she says, hoping this will be long enough.

Señora Dolucca goes over to the window and taps out a cigarette. "Two days," she says. "All right, now tell me." She clicks a silver lighter and inhales sharply.

And so Baz tells her while Señora Dolucca nervously smokes her menthol cigarette. She tells how they know their boy is adopted and that they know who his mother is. The woman is very still, listening carefully. She takes off her glasses, revealing her yellowing sore eye. "All this I know," she says tiredly. "Is there more?" Baz explains as simply as she can what Fay is to them and to the other children who work for her. "My husband, the Captain," she says with a short laugh, "always helping girls on the street. He says he gives them a chance, make a new life. He knew your Fay before she came to our door with the baby. I know this. He is what he is, but she, she become a mother of thieves?"

"Yes." Baz glances at Demi. "Your boy should be lucky to have family," she says, "but he doesn't want what he has. He want more. He want to be like his blood mother. He want to be thief." She doesn't know this for sure, but he is playing sweet to Fay, he is telling lies, playing with their lives; whatever it is that he plans, it is not going to be for the benefit of this woman.

"No!" Señora Dolucca looks as if she's been stung. "He is a good boy, kind to us, to his sister, to me . . ."

"And to your husband?" says Demi. "Is it so good between him and Eduardo?"

"You know his name?" she says almost to herself, then she shakes her head. "I don't know, boys and their fathers, sometimes at this age it is not so good."

Baz waits for a moment and then continues. "He plan for us to thief your house. He plan it with Fay. He plan to take all your husband money, his dirt money, money criminal give him. You know? Then I think he plan for us to be caught." She looks down, not wanting to see this woman's hurt face.

"Why would he do this?"

She shrugs.

"Is there more?"

Before Baz can answer, Demi gives out a soft moan and clutches at her wrist and she is suddenly frightened again. "What is it? Where is the hurt, Demi? You don't tell us nothin."

He pulls her toward him and then faintly whispers, "Make her go, Baz." Then he closes his eyes.

"The wound is bad," she says to Señora Dolucca. "He must sleep. Then take medicine."

"I should go. I must collect my daughter, but I promised to help."

"You have helped."

"No, helps to get him, your brother, safe. This is not safe here." She fiddles with her purse. "I can give you this. It might help." She gives Baz a card with a phone number and a hundred-dollar note, and after a moment two more.

Fat as a pig leg, Baz thinks, and she takes the card and the money without hesitation. Maybe she can bribe the guard, maybe buy a car to take them somewhere safe.

Having been so calm at the meeting and then in control at the Castle, it is strange to see this woman nervous now, but she is. She no longer knows what to say to them. The knowledge is perhaps more than she expected. Or perhaps it is just what she suspected but didn't want to hear. Perhaps she wants to help them, but more importantly she wants to help herself. She promises to come back. She says she will try to talk to her husband, but she doesn't convince Baz. Baz has seen young women with eyes bruised like Señora Dolucca. She has seen the Captain on the television, and she thinks he is just the man to punch his woman.

When she has gone, Baz looks at the bills in her hand and almost laughs. She and Demi spend their lives risking everything to steal money like this and then here it is in her hand when she has done nothing. No, that is not true; she has returned something they had stolen and for that they are given more money than she has ever had.

She turns back to Demi, and Demi, pretending to be half dead a moment ago, is sitting up in bed in his white hospital smock, grinning and looking so pleased with himself that if he were a cockerel he would be crowing. "How much she give you, Baz? You some sneak-rat. I never seen nobody string a mark good as you."

"I make a deal with her is all. Hey," she says as Demi pulls back the sheet and swings his legs off the bed and onto the floor. "Stop that!"

"You think I gonna stick around this place, you not so smart as I just think you are."

His left arm is wrapped up tight with bandages. It must have bled badly; she can see the orange stain showing through.

He holds it up proudly. "Doctor say any shot can kill a man but this only small bullet. See? Nothin. Nothin to stop me from getting on my feet, Baz. You figured out some way we can get from here?"

"What! You think I got a car outside?"

"We got motorcycle hid. You get that here, then no one catch us."

It's dream talk. This isn't the Castle, but the windows are barred, the corridor locked and guarded, and unless Demi's learned how to turn himself into a puff of smoke so he can drift out through an air vent maybe, he's not going anywhere. The uniform man will come for him soon enough, put him in jail if they want, put him in the Castle. With the money she can try bribing the guard, but this is something she has never done—and wouldn't the man see the money and just take it from her? That would be the way in the Barrio. "What was the deal the man pull with you?" she says. "Maybe that something better than you dreaming you can get up and walk out this door?"

"You know who come calling before you?"

Baz waits.

"Fay boy, that who."

He nods, seeing her expression of surprise. Then he tells her how Eduardo came walking in as if he was the president himself, waving a pass at the guard, who saluted him and even offered to bring tea if he wanted. It was Eduardo who offered the deal: all Demi has to do is admit that the robbery was planned by Moro, that's all. Simple. And then Eduardo will arrange his release.

"He can do this?"

Demi shrugs. "What I got to lose? They come and question me, and I tell them what he want. What's it to me if Moro get stung for this? We got no love for that man. He take Raoul and the other boy, you know that."

Baz is trying to understand why this is so important to Eduardo. Of course he doesn't want Demi to tell the truth, the truth that now Señora Dolucca knows, but he does want to stir up big trouble in the Barrio. If the Captain thinks that Moro is double-dealing with him, maybe he will try to close this man down. She looks at Demi. "Eduardo is looking to make war between the police and Moro, yes?"

"I reckon."

"Then he take the Barrio for himself. You think Fay know all this?"

Demi pulls his I-don't-care face but Baz presses him. She wants to know. If they are going to survive, they need to understand. The war will bring trouble to everyone, not just the hard men but to people like Mama Bali; everyone in the Barrio will get hurt. There's always been a call to pull the whole place down, raze it to the ground and build something new, plenty of talk in the papers but never anything more than that. Is that what Eduardo wants? No, he just wants to take Moro's place and be the king. But he's too young—who's going to work for him? No one, unless he proves to be more ruthless, more organized and smarter than Moro himself.

And maybe he is, thinks Baz. He knows as much as the Captain. He knows who pays who and for what. And now, thanks to the robbery, he has a war chest to pay for his own hard men. She wonders about Fay too. Fay never wanted to do anything but a little business, make her way out of the slum, but this boy has changed things. She wants *him* now, she wants her boy, wants to be a real mother. Baz thinks she is too late. Baz thinks that one thing Eduardo can do without is a mother like Fay. He will use her as he has used them, and then he'll get rid of her. Didn't she give him away? The angel-boy wouldn't forgive that. He'll punish them all: the Dolucca family, Fay and the whole city, maybe. She and Demi are just flies for him to swat out the way. This is what she figures out and what she tells Demi. "No way Eduardo let you out of here alive," she says. "You know too much. Maybe better you say nothin, Demi. Stall him an' we get you out of here . . ."

"Baz, I already agree to do what he ask an' put the finger on Moro. An' I figure it out: it's a good thing, Baz. The king goin to come down, Baz. Maybe he had all these people in his pocket, like the Captain, but I bet they all waiting on the chance to bring him down. This the time now. Nothin stopping it now. It already begun, Baz. Policeman come for Moro anytime now; then we got war in the Barrio. Big time. Moro's men goin to fight. Everyone run like chicken." He is suddenly excited. "This maybe our chance, Baz. Time to move; you want that?" She nods. "Fay not going to know what to do," continues Demi. "We can take what's ours, Baz. You took the ring. We take some of what she owe us, start again. Maybe start business." He's off, another fantastic future unrolling, but he's still got a hole in his arm and bars on the window. He finds it easy to forget things like that. Baz forgets nothing. The Mountain is always there, stinking on the far side of the river. And Raoul is always there too, behind the wire.

But then what choice is there? "When does Eduardo come back to see you?"

There is a sound at the door, and Demi rolls back into bed and lies flat just as the guard comes in. He's flustered, his round face shiny with sweat. "Time," he says. He glances at the shape of Demi and then points at Baz. "You go. The Captain wife ask to let you stay a little, but now you go quick time, OK. Back way for you, girl. This thief got more visitor." He wipes his sleeve across his face. "The Captain coming up. I'd like to know what this thief done to get so many visitor."

"He just got bad luck," Baz says. She leaves without a backward glance at Demi, following the guard down the corridor in the opposite direction to the way they came in. The end of the corridor is blocked by a door-shaped iron gate, which he unlocks. The key, Baz notes, was just loose in his jacket pocket. Where would this man keep his keys? In his little office? Or maybe take them home. And that gives her an idea.

"Señor," she says, "I know you gotta hurry but . . ." She holds up one of the bills Señora Dolucca gave her, a big bill, one hundred.

He eyes it greedily. "Got a tongue now, have you?" he says, glancing nervously over his shoulder as if the Captain might be standing there watching, and then he quickly pockets the bill.

"You let me in later. I bring a little food for you, somethin sweet."

"OK."

"Maybe the Captain wife cook you little something; she probably best cook this side of the city." She lets her voice go a little soft and whiny. "You like sweet things, hey? And then you let me see my brother. What do you say?"

"OK. OK."

"You on duty all the time here?"

"Sure. All the time. Long day. No one else want this job, but keeping sick people locked up is not so hard."

"You go home nights, I bet."

"I go home nights. Now go, before you lose me this job. Then you come back this time tomorrow. If the boy still here, I let you in. This same time, you got it?"

She stops herself from smiling. Of course. It's three and that's when the soap he likes finishes. That was why he let her alone so long this afternoon—he was glued to the TV. Three in the afternoon. That was OK. A quiet time in the city, businessmen taking their lunch, sleeping.

"Thank you," she says, edging around his belly and through the door. He closes the gate behind her and hurries back to his office, buttoning his jacket as he goes.

The gate is at the top of a steep flight of steps that she quickly goes down. At the foot of the steps is a small service area that opens out into a yard for delivery trucks, but at the moment the place is empty and the back gate leading into it is locked. She slips out and follows the building round to the right till she gets back to the main entrance, where an ambulance is just drawing up beside a parked police car. Two officers lounge against the car, smoking, clearly waiting for the Captain who, she presumes, is at this moment with Demi.

She walks, slowly now, toward the gate. Two doctors pass her. The guard doesn't even look at them, just flips the barrier up and leaves it up for Baz too.

Once outside, she crosses the street, finds a café and sits down at a table outside. The proprietor, a thick-shouldered man with a bristly square-cut mustache, eyes her suspiciously but she asks politely for an iced juice and puts the coins on the table so that he sees she can pay. He nods and the drink is brought. Discreetly Baz tucks the roll of money Señora Dolucca gave her into her waistband, and then, slowly sipping her drink, she looks across the street to the gate of the military hospital, and she thinks.

Once Demi has done what Eduardo has instructed him to do and told the Captain the story Eduardo wants him to tell—that Señor Moro arranged the theft—what then? Will they use Demi as a witness in a trial against Moro? Maybe. But would the Captain ever want a trial? Maybe not. No, he's just going to want to know who is trying to rob him, and when he finds it is this man he does business with, whose pocket he's been sitting in, then he's going to want to kill that man. And as for Demi, once the Captain is satisfied that he has squeezed out every bit of information that Demi has, he'll give orders and Demi, like any other street boy unlucky enough to fall into the hands of the police, will simply disappear, and then, a day, maybe two days later, his body will be found somewhere, a dump on the edge of town, under a bridge somewhere, or maybe he won't be found at all.

This is the way things are, and it is better, Baz knows, to face this and not just to hope that the problems will go away.

Baz cannot go back to the den. She has stolen from Fay, and Fay will find out sooner rather than later. Now that Raoul is gone there is no one she can even half trust among the boys; in fact she'll be best keeping well out of their way. She wonders if Fay knows where Demi is; it is possible. What is certain is that the boy, Eduardo, is not telling his birth mother everything.

The yellow sun edges across the sky, and the shadow moves along the hospital wall; the guard at the entrance comes to the end of his duty and is relieved by another soldier, who unslings his rifle and pulls a stool into the shade, sitting there, leaning his back against the wall of the sentry box.

Baz sips her drink slowly and concentrates on the good things. They are not so many, but they are important. Demi is not in the Castle and he is not so badly hurt: he can walk though maybe he cannot run. The hospital is not difficult to enter and leave. The officer who is in charge of Demi's wing is soft and lazy and he has already agreed to let her in again. She has money; she doesn't know how much, but it is enough to make some things happen. And there is the rich woman who gave them the money, though Baz doesn't think she'll be able to help them more; she has too many troubles of her own.

Time is something that Baz doesn't think she has much of. It's possible that the Captain will decide to take Demi out of the hospital at any time. It is possible that he will take him away this day; why not?

She knows what she must do. She goes into the café and finds the washroom. She is lucky—there is a small piece of soap, softened with use, left in the corner of the basin. She squeezes it into a disc and slips it into her pocket. With this she will make a key. She knows it can be done, and Mama Bali will know someone who will do it for her. Then she will walk Demi down the corridor and out of the service gate while the fat guard watches his TV. Not so difficult.

But first she must get the key from the guard. For this she must be quick. She flexes her fingers. As quick as Demi.

She goes back to her table and waits and watches. Twenty minutes pass. The proprietor comes and stands by her table so she orders a dish of beans and eats, discovering that she is hungry after all, not having had anything other than a little piece of chocolate since early that morning.

After half an hour the police car pulls up at the barrier. She stands up and runs to the corner so that she can see who is in the car. No Demi, just the Captain sitting alone in the back, staring grimly ahead, and the two officers in the front. There can only be one reason that the Captain is looking like that: Demi must have told him he was betrayed by Moro, and the Captain is now thinking what he must do.

Soon there will be war in the Barrio.

She returns to her table, finishes her dish of beans and waits.

Chapter Twenty-two

SHE LINGERS AT THE BAR for as long as she can, buying a small coffee and slowly sipping the bitter black liquid, then ordering ice cream, but then, once she has spun her time out to an hour, the proprietor comes back and puts her bill on the table. Though she has money, he doesn't like her there. "You wait for your uncle someplace else," he says rudely. "I need this table for my evening custom."

She knows better than to make a fuss. A burly man like this could tip her out of her seat, even hit her, and no one would say anything, everyone would presume that she had done something wrong. Children without parents are always suspect. Silently she takes out some money, making sure it is exact. Then she gets up and leaves. She walks the street down to the corner on one side and then back up on the other, the side of the hospital entrance, stopping by the newspaper vendor.

He's a small, gray-haired stick of a man with the same flat brown coloring that she has, and he is as full of chat as the proprietor was silent. He tells her about his village and asks her about hers. She makes up a story that is maybe a little like the truth—that she lives with her mother who works as a cleaner in an office and her uncle who has a job in the hospital, though she has to be a little vague when he wants to know exactly what this uncle of hers does. "I know many working here," he says, almost proudly. "Been at this pitch ten years, see them come and go every day. See a few prisoner come and go too. They got a lock-up wing in there, you know that . . ." He doesn't seem to mind that she doesn't tell him much; it's the company he likes, and she makes herself useful, running to get him coffee in a paper cup and undoing the bundle of afternoon papers and setting them out on the stand. She tells him she is waiting for her uncle to come off duty, and he lets her sit on a stool in the shade of his stand.

Three hours pass and the vendor packs up, wishes Baz well. "One more year," he tells her, "and then I go home. Here"—he digs out a slip of paper from his shirt pocket, a ten-cent ticket for the Providente, the national lottery—"my investment. One a week—maybe I go back a rich man. You come and visit me again, I buy you a ticket." Then, tucking the day's newspaper under his arm, he heads off back to his room out on the edge of the city.

Baz moves back across the street and stands just in the entrance of an alley. At seven o'clock the sun sets and the street lights come on. Two hours later there is a sudden flurry of movement and a small group of military personnel leave the building, then some nurses and finally, on his own, her mark, the fat guard. She stretches and steps out on to the near-empty street. She leaves a gap of twenty paces and keeps to her side. She is careful because she is always careful, but he never looks back. Why should he? He, like her friend the newspaper man, has done his day's work and has only one thought: getting home.

When he turns left down toward Centrale she skips through the traffic and closes in on him. There are more people here, strolling to or from the bars or queuing at the tram stops. She chooses her moment, just when he has to thread past a group of noisy office workers, and brushes up against him, feels the hard shape of the gate key and would have slipped her hand into his pocket right then but she senses that one of the office workers, a woman, has noticed her. Here a lone child in a street crowd means thief. Baz drops her head, avoiding the woman's eyes, and pushes on away from the guard, making for a shop a couple of paces to the left. Then half a second later steps back onto the pavement. The woman and her friends are still there, but none is looking her way; the guard is a little way along the street.

She's careful. Demi says a good thief is invisible. A good thief doesn't hang round street corners; he's busy, like everyone else, he's doing something, going somewhere. A good thief knows what a mark is going to do even before the mark does. A good thief sees the opportunity and then is so fast you got to catch him on film and play the film in slow motion to see the way his hand moves. That's what Demi says, though he got seen by the little girl. Demi says you got to be lucky too.

Her round-faced guard isn't in so much of a hurry. He plods along, his head turning every so often, sometime looking at girls, most time looking at the cafés and restaurants as he passes by them. She knows what's on his mind, and she knows just where he's going to stop: Brastoliris, the pastry shop. Sure enough, he pauses for a moment to scan the gold-crusted pastries and then, making up his mind, steps in through the door.

Baz stands back a little, in the half shadow to the right of the shopfront. This is it. He will come out fumbling at the paper bag, too greedy to wait till he gets home before taking a bite, and he'll eat as he walks onto the tram stop, which is only twenty meters down the road.

She will have to be very fast. She has to steal the key, make an impression of it in the soap and then return the key before he gets home. She will have to be lucky too.

A moment later he comes out, pausing again so close to her that she can smell the mix of sweat and the sharp ammonia tang from the hospital, so close that she can hear the way he breathes, short, greedy. He is not a man who could run after a sick dog let alone one of Fay's quick-footed thieves. He fumbles at the paper bag, as she knew he would, and then just as the pastry is entering his wide mouth, his head tilted back a little so he catches all of it, Baz holds her breath, steps up so close she is part of his shadow, slips her hand into his pocket, catches the barrel of the key between her two forefingers and is back in the shadow before his second bite. The guard gives a little grunt of pleasure and steps forward across the pavement to the tram stop, as Baz, never taking her eyes off her mark, presses the key hard into the soap, hoping that the impression will be good enough.

She wishes she could look under the light to see if the job is good enough, but it would be a foolish risk and anyhow she has no time. A tram has turned the corner and swung into their stop. She gives one last press, and then as the tram is pulling away she runs lightly after it and swings up onto the back.

After a twenty-five minute ride across town, in the direction of the river, Baz begins to wonder if he will go as far as Agua, but two stops before that, at Amaro Street, he steps down and she quickly follows. This is a rougher area and the guard is more alert, walking quickly, keeping in the light, bustling through a small group of youths hanging out on a street corner. One of them, noticing his uniform, calls out an insult, which the guard ignores. He is not a man who looks for trouble. The youths laugh and one of them flicks the butt of his cigarette after him. Baz skirts them, all her senses alert now, not for police but for anyone who might cause her trouble, very aware of the roll of bills tucked into her waistband.

When he stops at a fruit and vegetable shop and starts to

feel melons, she breaks into a run, passing him just at the moment he has both hands engaged, one holding out the melon he's selected and the other with the coin to pay for it. Without a break in her stride, she slips the key into his pocket and, keeping the same pace, reaches the corner, turns into the side street and then stops, waits for a couple of seconds and looks back.

Nothing. Not a flicker.

Good. Good as Demi anytime, she thinks, then feels a flush of guilt. Demi's got the locked door, the barred gate; Demi's the one looking at the high white walls of the Castle if she doesn't come through, and she's got so much more to do.

She catches a ride on another tram and swings off at Agua. It's late and the wide space is deserted and quiet, even the fountain has stopped running. She walks quickly by Moro's bar, glimpsing a few customers, their heads bowed together, drinking and talking, no sign of the dark-suited shady men. Maybe this is the still time before the storm, she thinks. The air is heavy and sticky, and after the sharp edge of working the mark she's suddenly tired. It happens; nerves tighten like wire before you make the move and then when you have the sweet thing in your hand—the purse, or the fat wallet that you show Demi or Demi shows you—you feel good but tired like you've been hard running. This night the air sticks in her throat and there's nothing to show but the mark of a key on a bar of soap; not much, not enough to lighten her step.

Rather than cut across the square where even in the poor light she would be visible, she takes the long way round the western edges until she reaches the alley that winds into the heart of the Barrio and then heads straight to Mama Bali's. It's dark as death in the Barrio, but she doesn't need to see. She runs the tip of her finger along the sides of the alleys, ducking left or right without thinking; just her finger and her feet telling her what to do.

Mama's door is shut, bolted up tight, and there's no light showing in her kitchen either. Baz doesn't like to make noise; you make a noise in this place and somebody is going to come looking, maybe someone who'll do you harm. But she doesn't have any choice. She raps on the door and presses herself into the deep darkness of the doorway.

Somewhere a tinny radio plays old folk music. Closer she hears someone cough up a lungful of spit, and a voice grumbling, hoarse, cursing, gritty as dirt.

Then, after a minute and banging one time more on the door, she hears the scuffling waddle of Mama coming down the narrow stair from the single room she has above the kitchen. "Who?" she calls.

"Baz," Baz says, quiet as she can, half looking over her shoulder, expecting the shady man to come, grab her by the neck, grab and twist, but if there's someone there, back up the alley a little way, she doesn't see him. And then the door opens and there is Mama Bali in a yellow cotton gown big as a tent, her eyes wide with worry.

She stares past Baz into the darkness and then grabs her, pulling her inside. "What you do, foolish child? Half the Barrio up and lookin for you. Fay got everythin stir up like a nest of ant gone crazy."

"I done that business, Mama," says Baz quietly as Mama bolts her front door and pulls a shutter over it.

"Tsk. You got no business. You just child; child don't got business. You sit there. You look like you got hurt. You hurt, Baz?"

"No hurt, Mama."

Mama lights up a lamp and gives Baz a long look, then, satisfied that no visible harm has been done to the girl, she puts the lamp down on the counter. "Stay put," she says, turning on the gas and putting milk on to warm. "I get you something."

*   *   *

Around the walls, Mama Bali's scrapbook of dancers ripped from the pages of old magazines seem to come to life. How come they so free? thinks Baz, and as she always does, she wonders what it would be like to move like that. Jump so high could spin right over the Castle wall maybe. To the right of the entrance into the kitchen, Mama has been pinning up some more recent cutouts from the paper. One headline is so thick and black it seems to scowl its accusation from the wall: "**You, Thief, Stole Our City Water!**" and then pictures of the dam, and grainy faces of people Baz doesn't know.

"You seen bad thing?" says Mama, spooning rum into a mug of hot milk.

"Bad an' good."

"Here, this give you some bite, girl. You lookin like a lost dog." She settles her bulk down onto a stool, having first poured herself the same drink as she gave Baz but with three times the rum.

Baz sips and tells her what's happened. Mama nods and gives her opinion on everything, cursing the uniform man in the Castle, feeling sorry for the Captain's wife, and clutching Baz's hand when she describes Demi with his bandaged arm all alone in the military hospital.

"You better get him out o' there quick time, Baz. No child gonna stay long in that place. I know that in my bone. They take him out o' there and your Demi on a tightrope to heaven."

"I know," she says. "I don't need your telling, Mama. I need you help me." Baz pulls out the soap with the key shape molded into it. "You take this to the lockman, Mama. He never do nothing for child like me, but he do it for you, you ask for me. This is the key that let Demi free, Mama."

Mama looks at the mold but doesn't take it. Instead she slops another spoon of rum into her cup. "What you want, Baz? I got this place. This place all I got. You don't know what you askin. You know I help you any way I can, child, but I got to keep out of Barrio business. If I mess up, this kitchen burn down and me along with it. Baz, truth is you and Demi Barrio business now. I go to that locksmith, he going to tell half the Barrio what I ask him to do." She wipes the hem of her nightgown across her sweating face. "Go uptown, Baz. I get you a number, I get you name and tomorrow we cut the key."

"Tomorrow too late, Mama. What you just say? Get Demi out o' there quick time. This quick time now. I got money. You pay the man and he keep his mouth shout. Money more important than meddling—everyone know that in the Barrio."

Mama Bali narrows her eyes. "How much you got?"

"Enough." After Demi, Mama is the person Baz likes most in the world. One time it would have been Fay, but Fay's a different person now. Yes, she likes Mama, almost trusts her even, but a body's a fool to put their whole trust into anyone in the Barrio. "How much you need?"

"Twenty for the key, I reckon, same again to buy him silence. You got that kind of dollar?"

Baz nods. "Sure."

She turns her back and then unfolds a fifty. "I'm not looking for change, Mama."

Mama folds the bill into her cleavage. Then shakes her head.

"You remember this, Baz. You remember this time, and if I ever get to be old woman, you come see me, you and Demi. You keep wolf from my door, that's what you got to do; you hear me?"

Baz nods. She understands what Mama is saying; she knows the danger and she knows if you ask a favor, you got to give one back.

"All right then." Mama climbs up to her room, dresses herself in a black dress and wraps a black scarf round her head. She takes the soap and folds it into a cloth, then she slides back the bolts to the door, eases it open and listens for a moment. Silence. Not the faintest scuffle of foot on dirt. If there's anyone close by, they're not even breathing. Mama steps out into the night. Baz makes to follow her, but she won't have it. "You bolt that door an' you let no one in but me. You hear me?"

"I hear."

"Good." Mama's teeth and eyes gleam white in the darkness. Then she turns and is swallowed by the alley.

Baz locks the door and goes back into the kitchen. She sits and waits, trying not to worry; trying to trust her friend. She doesn't think Mama will betray her. She doesn't think she will go get Fay, but how can she know what Fay's been promising or threatening? She stares at the door and waits and tries not to think. Her eyes are heavy and the rum is warm in her veins.

Chapter Twenty-three

RAIN THRUMS DOWN on the steel deck and hisses onto the mud, thunder rumbles and somewhere upriver the great dam begins to spiderweb with cracks that ripple and bulge into gaping mouths that roar . . .

Baz jolts awake. Her mouth is dry. The door to the alley is rattling. She can hear someone hissing her name.

She jumps up, runs to the door and pulls it open and Mama looms in, huge and black as the night itself, pushing past Baz, going straight to the bottle of rum that she had used earlier.

Baz closes the door and snaps the bolt across. "What happen?" she asks. "You get it cut, like you say? The man give you problem? What happen?"

Mama puts the mug down, unwraps the black scarf from her head and dabs her face. She's breathing heavily as if she's been running. Nobody's ever seen Mama do anything but move slow and steady all the time she's lived in the Barrio, but times change. She shakes her head at Baz, takes another long pull at the mug and then puts it down on the counter. "I pay for the key." She produces it from a fold in her scarf. "Here"—gesturing for Baz to take it—"he make a mile of fussin but he cut the key; this the best I do for you, Baz. That man a snake, so you get from here before they burn me down."

"Someone see you?"

She waves her hand tiredly. "You dreamin? This the Barrio, child. Half the world know my business. Go get Demi and then hide someplace till everything quieten down again. Go on, go!" She has her two hands placed on her knees, her head up looking straight at Baz. No anger, no betrayal. This is how it is.

Baz nods and looks at the gray barrel key. "Hope this works, eh."

"Hope 'bout the only thing we got." She doesn't move from her stool.

"You lock the door behind me?"

Mama waves her hand like she's brushing away a dirt fly. "Go."

Baz slips out, quickly closing the door to cut out the frame of light and then, just as Mama had earlier, she stands stock still, listening. She doesn't see Mama putting her hands up to her face, not wanting to see her leaving.

Baz hears feet running, leather soles. Only Moro's men wear leather sole shoe, wear the smart suits. She cocks her head. It's hard to know which way they're coming from, maybe from both ways. She makes up her mind, takes ten quick steps back to the right, the way she came in, then finds the place where she and Demi used to climb up onto the rooftop.

She scrambles up and over a mess of pipes, pulling herself onto the flat surface just as weaving sticks of light stab down the alley. And then she picks out the men: two, no, three of them, jogging easily, silent, heads turning like they're sniffing out whatever's hiding in the doorways or skulking down behind grates. Baz squeezes her cheek down on the warm concrete of the roof and listens to their shoes slapping the dirt.

Half a moment later there's silence. They're at Mama's, have to be. They don't call out or bang on the door, but Baz knows what they're doing.

She doesn't have to see to know they just use their fingertips to push the unbolted door open. Doesn't have to see to know that Mama will still be sitting there on the stool waiting for them to come.

She gets to her feet and moves catlike along crazy rooftops, avoiding corrugated tin and stepping lightly over skylights covered with stretched plastic and wire; she jumps a narrow gap, squeezes past a stack of hot pipes, crosses one more roof and then comes to a stop by the dome. Her and Demi's safe place. If anyone comes for her here, they must have Demi leading them; and Demi's leading no one nowhere. She's safe.

She sinks down onto her haunches and then leans back against the curve of the dome. Mama won't tell them anything. Mama will make up some story; she'll bluster at them and give them mouth. Mama's the heart of the Barrio, her kitchen the only one that does business all the time. No one will hurt Mama.

She hears shouting in the distance, padding feet; she sees two splashes of flashlight and then right beneath her there's someone murmuring into a cell phone. And then nothing but silence again, broken from time to time by the odd call, and the muffled traffic way back up in the city.

Baz closes her eyes and tries to sleep but sleep doesn't come; the hours pass slowly. Above, the stars prickle the black sky, silvery clean; around and below her the Barrio straggles out in every direction, just a tangle, she thinks, nothing but a mess of streets running nowhere. Twice she is startled upright by a scream; one time it's nothing but a cat fight, the other she's not so sure. It sounds hurt; it makes her shiver. She stays just where she is. Fay already has half the Barrio looking for her. No one steals from Fay. She'll hunt Baz down and she'll rage, and then, who knows, maybe she'll give her to Moro. Baz tells herself she'll die rather than be given to Moro. And this is how she spends the night, her back against the dome, her knees hugged tight, staring out over the black thread-needle streets of the slum.

Half an hour before sunup, the Barrio begins to stir. People move and cough and call out; a few of those with work in the city make their way toward Agua; those that stay light fires and begin their chores. She's half tempted to try her luck and leave now but it will be safer later: more people moving about, easier to hide then, to spot the shady man hanging around on a corner, to keep an eye out for Fay's boys. Instead she sits cross-legged, facing the river, waiting for the sun and working out what she will do.

The sun comes up all yellow and tired-looking, and even with a haze over the dead river she can just make out the square flat block of Fay's building. No one will be stirring there yet. The room will be thick and airless. The boys will be curled up around the silent TV, and Fay, her hair like orange flame all tangled about her pale face, will be lying still as a corpse on her narrow bed, her eyes open but seeing nothing, making plans. One time she'd have shared her plans with Demi and Baz, three of them at the table and Demi always eager to get going.

Slowly Baz gets to her feet, careful to stand back from the edge of the roof, and stretches, raises herself up on her toes, turns slowly, arms out, like one of those dancers on Mama's wall; then she sees the smoke and she stiffens.

It's thick and oily black, rising right from the direction of Mama's kitchen, but no one's hauling buckets from Lucien's well, no one's running or yelling. Why not? Accidents often happen in the Barrio. Places burn. And though no fire chief is going to try bringing a truck down into the Barrio's warren of alleys, neighbors always help, if only to see that their own place doesn't burn too; and people are going to run half a mile to help Mama unless Señor Moro has one of his men standing some place in that alley, leaning against a wall, arms folded. Nobody is going to help Mama if the shady man blocking the way.

Nobody except Lucien. He'd help, no matter what. He owes everything to Mama. Baz can see his little square from the north side of her roof. She can see the well and now she can see Lucien too, standing, hand shading his eyes, staring at the smoke. But even he's not running. Maybe he hasn't figured it's Mama in trouble.

And then almost without thinking Baz slithers down from the roof. She'll tell him. He'll let her hide up in his little place while he checks out what has happened. He'll help, Lucien will. He always offers to help when she goes for the water. Always. She cuts through the covered alley, through the Ching Chang house, and glances left and right. All clear. She starts down the wider lane that leads to the well. Then she hears the shout. "Baz, hey! What you doin? Fay half crazy with worry for you." She stops and looks back.

Miguel! So he came back after all. He's running toward her, trying to hide his eagerness to catch her by furrowing his brows, looking concerned; to Baz he just looks like one hungry rat: ragged, torn shirt flapping, mouth open. She wonders who he's working for.

Instinctively she sprints in the opposite direction.

"Baz! Wait! Fay say we got to find you!"

She skids left, elbows a bin of garbage out of the way, slips down a skinny gap between two buildings, but it's not narrow enough. Miguel is there, pushing himself after her. "Baz. What you doin? You wanna make Fay think you hidin something from her? Baz, wait . . ."

She pops out of the gap, elbows and knees scraped raw, and runs down the lane that takes her to the well. She can almost hear the greasy *plip* of Miguel emerging from the darkness behind her. "Baz, you makin one mistake."

She sees Lucien looking her way, puzzled. His eyes widening as he takes in Miguel hard on her heels, his expression changing as Miguel reaches out and grabs at Baz, spinning her round so she slams up against the side of the lane. Miguel doesn't notice Lucien—why would he? Nobody minds anybody else's business down here. Kids scrapping; they do it all the time.

Miguel is small but he's all sinew and muscle screwed up tight, and he is hungry, hungry to be number one for Fay, number one for Eduardo. If Miguel had a gun or a knife he would kill, except nobody told him to kill, just find her, bring her back. "You comin with me," he pants, one hand gripping at her neck, the other twisting her arm up behind her, and he won't let go though she's kicking hard and butting him with her head, catching him one smack on the chin with her forehead. There's blood running on his lip, but he doesn't even notice. "Comin with me, Baz. You comin with me."

He doesn't register Lucien running toward them. Lucien may be skinny and sick but he's been hauling buckets of water from his old well for a few years now, and when he swings his fist down against the side of Miguel's head, Miguel snaps back like he's been slugged by the world's boxing heavyweight champion. He staggers back and something drops from his pocket—a cell phone—but he's not aware of it. He's blinking and holding his head, and the blood is trickling down his mouth and it's as if he's seeing Lucien for the first time. "You!" he hisses, and Baz doesn't know whether it's directed at her or Lucien. "You nothin now." He spits up a gob of red with a scrap of tooth and turns away and starts to run unsteadily back toward the den.

Baz is leaning up against the wall, breathing hard, looking at Lucien like she's never seen him before either. Lucien, frightened of his own shadow, living on scraps of nothing and half cents for his dirty water. Lucien, with all his sores and scabs, stepping out of nowhere to save her. She blinks. "Nobody done that for me no time; not Demi, not anyone. You just save me, Lucien." In the background she's half aware of a banging, like people hitting doors, or clanging lids of pans.

Lucien turns away, looking down at the hand that dealt the blow and then shrugging slightly. "I see him hurtin' you." Then he stoops and picks up the cell phone that had dropped out of Miguel's pocket. "He'll come looking for this, I reckon."

"He gonna come lookin for you, Lucien; gonna come with a whole lot o' trouble unless Fay stop him."

Lucien shrugs. "Hey, you want this, Baz? I got no one to call. You call someone maybe." The banging noise is louder. He frowns.

She takes the phone, almost without thinking. "You seen the fire. I know you seen it. That's Mama's kitchen. You got to go an' see if she's all right, Lucien."

He nods, his expression troubled. "She come see me last night. Tell me if I see any trouble over her place not to come see what happenin. Made me swear." He wipes his skinny wrist across his forehead. "I seen the smoke and I just goin to go, no matter what she say, Baz, and then you and him happen right in my yard. Maybe I'll go now." He's almost two foot taller than her and so thin he makes everyone else in the Barrio look about as fat as uptown folk; he's wearing an old faded shirt that Mama passed him; it's clean but it's almost got more holes than cotton to it now. One tear runs from his shoulder down to his elbow and one of his sores shows right through. "You think I should go, Baz?"

There's the piercing sound of a whistle and the sudden crack of a rifle shot. The banging dies away and instead they can hearing calling and crying.

She knows what this is: it's the beginning of the trouble Eduardo has started. Eduardo's war, and she doesn't want to be caught up in it. "Course you got to go. We both got to, Lucien. That's police trouble. They comin in the Barrio, that's what happenin. I got to run or I gonna get trap in here and then no one gonna get Demi." She gives him a little push. "Go, Lucien."

"Take care, Baz."

"Sure, Lucien."

She is already moving away, breaking into a jog, cutting right up an alley that leads in the general direction of Agua.

The alley widens into a lane, divides, twists left, and then there's the sound of beating and banging and yelling again. Whistles blow and suddenly a flock of people is running toward her: a young mother holding a baby, an older woman, a man limping, then a scattering of children. They're all shouting, excited, frightened. One boy is holding a bunched-up T-shirt over his eye. "Police!"

She grabs the one who seems hurt. "Can I get through up here?"

"No! No one get through. They snatchin anyone. You go that way, the man gonna snatch you. See what he done me?" The little boy lifts the shirt from his face and she sees his eye already swelling and the dark of a bruise beginning to bloom. "Got me with his stick." He's almost proud. "Let go my arm now."

"What they wantin?"

"Hey, you let go!" The child suddenly twists like an eel and is away.

Baz jogs up to the next corner and almost runs smack into the back of a uniform with shoulders so wide he's halfway blocking her lane. He's got a long stick in one hand, the tip resting on the ground. His attention is on something happening way to his right. She presses herself back into a doorway.

There's another *crack*, and the ping and whine of bullet skidding off stone, and the uniform steps back real smart. A line of blue holding Perspex shields comes running past him, and behind them more blue, with snub-nose guns. One stops and fires; there's a *crump* and more yelling and a bitter smell. Gas? Maybe they're going to gas the Barrio, flush out everyone, all the rats too.

She backs away.

Tries another route. Gets blocked again. The place has gone crazy, like someone has just got a hold of the Barrio and tipped it into a pan and is shaking it and frying it, and no wonder Baz hardly knows which is up, let alone which way is out.

She tries the rooftops next. Makes it almost to thirty meters from Agua. She can see the back of the old buildings on the south side of the square, a wall blocking the Barrio in against the river, but she can't go any farther. A policeman spots her, and a moment later a bullet pings through a nest of tin chimneys that she's just standing beside and she flings herself facedown and wriggles back from the edge as fast as she can.

Something hard and sharp gouges into the top of her leg and for a moment she thinks she might have been hit, maybe just a splinter kicked up by the bullet. She rolls onto her side to investigate.

It's nothing. Not a scratch, just the key she had stuffed in her jeans pocket and then forgotten about in the fuzz of all this running and yelling and shooting. She pulls it out, thinking to slip it into her back pocket, and as she does so a second smaller key drops out onto the roof. Demi's key, the one for the motorcycle, and it gives her the start of an idea.

Gripping both keys in her right hand she crouches low, runs full tilt for the edge of the roof and jumps. The space between the buildings is not so far and she makes the leap easily and, with hardly a break in her pace, swings right, jumps again, ducks under a washing line, over a makeshift rainwater tank. Then she squats, taking a breath. Then runs again. Over onto another roof and another, all the time heading back to Lucien's courtyard. She skirts a high wall, all that's left of an old factory that stood there one time. She never wondered what was made there—what's the point in wondering? In the Barrio it is called Moro's Wall on account of the bodies found there, people who managed to step on the wrong side of the Barrio's boss.

She looks back. Nothing. Looks down: two men running quickly. Young, from the laundry. She slips over the edge, hangs for a moment, then drops, landing lightly on her feet. "Go home," one of the men says. "Go home before someone shoot your head off."

There's the loud *whoomph* of an explosion, a thick, burning gasoline smell. About thirty meters away, over toward Agua, a black cloud plumes into the air. The men run off.

Home? There's no home in the Barrio for her anymore. She hopes that Lucien is at the well. He might be able to help. It's a thin hope but she holds it tight as she sprints down the last lane to his courtyard.

Chapter Twenty-four

LUCIEN IS SITTING on his bench over in the shadow by the wall. In the distance Baz can hear the snap and crackle of gunfire and glass shattering, but for the moment anyway it doesn't seem to be coming closer. She sloshes water on her face and then joins him. He moves up a little to make room for her. "Lucien," she says, "you know anything about motorcycle?"

"Some."

Something in his voice makes her turn and look at him, shakes her out of her own worries. "You find Mama OK?"

"Didn't find nothin."

"Nothin! What you mean, Lucien? What happen? Mama all right. Nobody mess with her."

"No one see nothing. Kitchen burn right down. Mama gone. Everythin gone. All her cup, her kitchen thing. People see nothin," he says woodenly, "because they the ones doin all the takin, helpin themselves from another person's trouble."

Baz squeezes her eyes tight. She brought the trouble right to Mama, took it into her kitchen. It takes her half a moment before she can bring herself to say, "What you think happen to her, Lucien?"

"The man burn her down along with her kitchen," he says. "Or maybe he take her away, put her on the Mountain."

Baz touches his arm. "Mama 'bout the only good thing in the Barrio. She special good to you. Almost family."

"Almost."

"Maybe she's OK, Lucien. Maybe we find her when this over. Mama like a rock. Like she hold the whole place up on her shoulder, she so strong."

There's another loud *crump*, more shouting. She sees people running across the alley that leads down into Lucien's square, some clutching bags, one man hefting a TV. All over the Barrio people are beginning to stream away from their homes, running this way and that, trying to find a way out.

Lucien doesn't seem to notice. "I seen people big and strong like Mama," he says, "and they whittle down to nothin on the Mountain. Mama not so strong." He straightens himself. "What happen to you, hey? I thought you gone for Demi."

"Way into Agua all block by uniform. Just catchin my breath; gonna run up the river an' come in through Basquat. Take me a couple of hour."

"Where you got your name."

"Demi tell you that?"

"He tol' me."

The background noise is louder, a throaty roaring tangled up with the screech of metal tearing and grinding. "Bulldozers," says Lucien, "about as big as a house. I seen them lining up in Agua. Reckon they going to flatten down the Barrio."

She doesn't doubt him. "Come with me," she says suddenly. "Help me get Demi and we leave this whole place, go upcountry." She doesn't want to leave him behind. She's brought enough trouble into the Barrio and she doesn't want it to touch Lucien too and she knows, maybe she's always known, how Lucien sees her. Maybe he left a little sister behind back on the Mountain, someone like her. Lucien looks at her, blinking with surprise. "Come with us, Lucien. Nothin here for you."

"How you gonna get anywhere?" he says slowly. "Big country, Baz. You goin to walk to some other city, find some other Barrio like this one? Every place got a dirt town where all the thief and rubbish end up. We the rubbish, Baz. Police gonna sweep us up wherever we go."

"Tha's just fool talk!" She pulls the motorcycle key out of her pocket. "You say you know about motorcycle. You reckon you can ride one?"

"Sure. I ride one one time. Why, you got one hidden away some place? Demi steal one out o' some rich man's pocket—"

She interrupts him. "We just got one, Lucien, OK? Take you to it if you want to come with me. You could ride all the way into town, help me get Demi." She makes it sound easy, like all they got to do is pick him up from school or something, but she wants to go right now.

Lucien's not like her. Every day spent here by this well of dirty water; life's slow for Lucien. Ideas work across his frowning brow as he takes in what she's saying, what it means in real terms. "I hear one of Señor Moro's men, he lost his motorcycle just a couple of day ago."

"I hear that too."

"I hear there's a reward for anyone letting on they know where that bike ended up."

"You lookin for reward, Lucien?"

"Everyone lookin, Baz. Me, I'm just thinkin maybe that man see someone riding his bike in the city, he not gonna be happy."

"Lucien! Who care if that man never sleep again? You coming on out of here?"

"Wait." He ducks down into his little lean-to kennel and rustles about in there for half a moment before reemerging with a small cotton sack slung over one shoulder. He nods at Baz and without a word she turns and begins to run, Lucien following hard on her heels.

She runs fast, only slowing when a knot of people cluster across an alley, everyone excited, angry, worrying. Two young people pressing by gather little interest. "They not comin farther," Baz hears one person say. "They will pull the whole place down," says another. "Only a fool stay put when house come tumblin down."

Twenty minutes later they reach the baked black shoreline at the bend opposite her rusting boat. The sun is fully up and the day is starting to burn. "Wait, Lucien." She scrabbles under the hull of the upturned boat and pulls out one of the bottles of drinking water she has cached there. She gives it to him first and then takes two careful mouthfuls herself. She is thinking: to go all the way up to the bridge where they hid the motorcycle is going to take maybe two hours, and then what if the bike is gone? She will be stuck way out beyond the edge of the city and then by the time she makes it back to the hospital it will be late evening and her chance of getting in to Demi, if he is still there, will be gone. The time she arranged was three in the afternoon. There is only one option. She goes straight to the hospital and if the bike is where they left it, Lucien follows.

"Lucien, here." He is sitting a little way away from her, in the shade, his knees hooked up under his chin, staring out across the mud. He turns and looks at her. She has her hand held toward him.

"What that you got?"

"Dollars."

"I see that."

"You going to need gasoline maybe." He comes over and picks up the twenties.

"You got more than a full tank here."

She shrugs. "Take the key too." Then she tells him her plan:

that he collects the bike from where she and Demi hid it under the bridge and rides it down to the hospital, and that if all goes well, they will meet him somewhere close by there. She pulls out the phone and checks its number. "You call this number. If somebody else answer then you know it didn't go right and you free to do what you choose, OK?"

He is looking at her seriously. "You give me this key and this money, Baz. Nothing stoppin me just walking away. What happen? You trust me or something? Didn't Fay teach you nothin?"

She meets his gaze. They all thought him strange. The children tried to bait him sometimes, the way dogs worry an old dog or one that's sickening; even Baz never lingered down by the bad-water well. "Fay not so smart," she says at length, but what she's thinking is that it was Lucien who told her that when someone gives you their hand to take, you don't let it go. Fay seems happy to let any of them go when it suits her. "I trust you, Lucien."

He gives a slow smile then wipes his face with his damp shirtsleeve. "Under the bridge, hey?" She nods. "OK. I'll see you in the city, Baz. Be careful now." And he turns and runs. He's all long legs and skin and bone, his thin shadow wavering out across the flat glossy mud.

She stands. "Lucien," she calls after him. He pauses and looks back. "If anything go wrong, this where we gonna come."

He lifts a hand and then begins to run again.

She takes another mouthful of the warm water. Oily smoke hangs low over the Barrio but the sun is fierce on the back of her neck. It must be near ten now; she has five hours, but getting out of the Barrio and crossing the city will be dangerous; nowhere is safe. And if she doesn't make it in time, Demi will die in prison; that's for sure. Eduardo's promise is nothing. He won't let Demi or her live; they know too much. And it will be too easy: one of Eduardo's men, maybe that driver, Domino, will slip past the guard and that will be it . . .

She looks at the phone, Miguel's phone that she has gripped in her hand. She knows one person who might help. A woman with money, a woman with the power to say, "Do this," and it'll get done.

"Try it," she tells herself. "You don't ask, you don't get nothing." She pulls Señora Dolucca's card from her hip pocket.

Almost feverishly she taps in the number, the only phone number other than Fay's that Baz has ever called. Then she stands, rigid, the phone pressed hard against her ear.

It rings and rings and then someone picks up and a man's voice answers, a young man; a voice, she realizes with a sinking feeling, that she recognizes, but it's a colder voice, much colder, than she ever recalls.

Chapter Twenty-five

HIS VOICE STINGS.

"Miguel, you piece of maggot spit, why're you calling this number? I told you, you never call this number."

She holds her breath.

"Miguel," he snaps. "You there? You gone dumb or something . . . ?"

How could he tell this was Miguel's phone? She was calling the house, not a cell phone. These rich people, she thinks, they got everything keep them safe.

What can she do? Turn off the phone. Throw it down and stamp on it. This is what she would like to do—break his voice in little pieces, as if she is stamping on him. She doesn't do this though; instead she holds herself steady and she takes a chance. "You are mistaken, señor," she says, her voice neutral, polite, imitating how she thinks those cool frosty women serving in the jewel shops would speak. "I am phoning from Capricia," she says, naming the store where Demi stole her ring. It would make her suspicious, make her take the phone. "Can I speak to Señora Dolucca, please? It is important."

Silence. Then: "Who is this?"

"My name is Maria Mangales. I work at—"

"I know, you said, Capricia . . ."

Baz can hear a voice in the background. She is sure it is the Captain's wife. Then Eduardo, his voice muffled as if he has put his hand over the phone. "Not for you," he is saying.

Why is he there? Why did he pick up the phone? Half a minute later, she would have been the voice answering. Baz's throat is suddenly tight and she finds that she is blinking because one eye is watering. This does not happen to her, this tense feeling, not even when running from police. She sees Demi bundled out of his room, hustled down the corridor, the fat guard sitting in his office, the soap playing silently on his little TV. She takes a breath, steadies herself and repeats her message.

A door slams, and then at the end of the phone there is a little sigh of recognition. "I know who this is. It's Baz. The silent one. And you are in the Barrio. How is it in the Barrio, Baz? A little busy maybe." His voice is mocking. She doesn't answer. "Finding it hard to get off to work . . ." Then: "Oh, no. It is Demi you are worried about. Poor Demi. In that hospital, and you can't get to him. I am so sorry. You know, I think they will take him away today. He is so much better."

"Fay know you do this thing?" she spits the words. "All this bad thing!"

"Fay? My mother . . . ?" He gives a short contemptuous laugh. "She knows what I tell her."

She snaps off the phone. No help. Nothing. The Captain's wife will sit in her neat yellow dress, by her swimming pool, and she won't think anymore about Demi because she won't know. Baz rams the phone in her back pocket, takes a full bottle of water and sets off at a run. She takes a straight line away from the river—the sun, when she's not in shadow, burning down on the back of her head.

If she can make it to the market, she'll have crossed out of the Barrio and into the city.

She ducks and weaves by people waving their arms, shouting, hurrying, bundling their precious things together, but there's no one she recognizes and no one takes note of her, just another running child. She is west of her patch now, almost on the edge of the Barrio. She crosses waste ground and dry ditches; thorn and stumpy grass prick through her jeans. She doesn't stop.

Half an hour later she is behind the market at Basquat; her head is throbbing and her lungs are burning. She slumps down in the shade, leaning against a wall. She flips the top off the bottle, drinks three mouthfuls and then pours a little into her palm and smooths it across her face. She replaces the lid.

Two minutes. Then she will move again, round the market and out to the main street where she can find a tram to take her in. The market is busy, a different world to the Barrio.

The phone in her back pocket vibrates. She fumbles for it, hesitates, and then presses the green key and puts it to her ear.

"Hello?" The voice is uncertain, but familiar. "Is it you? The girl?"

Baz stays silent, listening.

"My son, Eduardo, pushed me out of the room. Are you all right? Did you want me?"

"Yes."

"It is you. Why did you ring? Are you all right?"

Baz holds the phone tight. "They will take my brother to the Castle today."

"Are you sure?"

"I don't know. I think . . . if he stay there, they will come for him."

"Who?"

"Men who will kill him."

Silence. And then: "Where are you?"

Baz stands. "I am coming to the hospital, but it has been hard. I'm not sure I get there in time . . . There have been many difficult things."

"Perhaps your brother would be safer in the Castle."

"Safer! Don't you know what happen in that place? No one come out. That place is only pain, is only death."

The market is noisy and Baz has to raise her voice. A woman bustling by gives her a sharp look. Baz ignores her. There is silence at the other end of the phone. "Hello, do you hear me?"

"Yes."

She takes a breath. "No one touch him if you there. Can you go to hospital? Can you stop them do this?"

There is silence at the other end of the phone. "I can't make promise," she says. She sounds unhappy. "My husband . . ."

"Your husband is Captain." And, Baz thinks, your boy—your boy is snake. But she does not say this.

"Yes, but he knows what I did yesterday. That I looked for this boy, for your brother. He was very angry."

Baz remembers the livid bruise around her eye when she took off her expensive dark glasses. He is a big man, the Captain. She has seen him on TV, thick shoulders and a dark, heavy face like a storm brewing; now he has brought his anger into the Barrio. Bad for the Barrio, but maybe good for his wife; maybe the burning and shooting and hunting down his enemies will make him feel calm again. "He believe his business partner cheat him. This is why he is angry. Not you."

"When he is angry," she says, "he is angry with whoever is near him."

"You will go to hospital?"

Señora Dolucca does not answer.

"Is Eduardo with you?" Baz pauses. Time is going. She must go. If she is too late, then she will think again, but why bother with this woman? She has her house; she has the ring. Maybe she thinks she has done enough. She has kept her deal. Baz understands. "Good-bye," she says, and is about to stab the off button when Señora Dolucca speaks again, her voice brisker.

"He left the house before I made this call. I did not want him to hear me. I will go now. I will do what I can."

The words seem to wash over Baz with a warmth that flows down into her chest and for a moment she almost forgets to breathe, almost forgets to thank this woman who will do this for them when she owes them nothing. "Thank you," she says, but the phone line has gone dead.

I will go now.

I will do what I can.

"Here. Take this. It is sweet." A woman in country clothes carves a slice of melon and leans across her stall, offering a slab to Baz as she weaves by.

Baz sinks her teeth into the soft green flesh. She hasn't eaten anything since early the previous evening. The juice runs down her chin. She licks it and smiles at the woman.

"Why you live in the city?" says the woman. "You come from the north, eh? Go home, find your village. Go to your village, make some boy happy."

Baz wipes her mouth and smiles again. "Maybe," she says. Then she thanks the woman and slips away through the market, breaking into a jog when she reaches the main street, and then running faster when she hears the tram coming up behind her, racing it to the stop, catching the back rail and swinging up onto the step, just as it's pulling away, grinning because this is the best part of living in the city, riding free, the warm air against your face, winning, not losing, the race. It is a good omen.

Chapter Twenty-six

BAZ JUMPS DOWN from the tram and hurries over to the shady side of the street. A few people are clustered around a shop where the whole window is stacked with TVs. As she passes by she sees images of the crumbling Barrio. A reporter standing beside the fountain with a line of police buses behind mouthing silently into her microphone. The camera pans away to the skyline over the Barrio: smoke and flame. Then a policeman, his visor tucked up, his expression relaxed, nodding and saying something.

She walks quickly down the street, avoiding eye contact, cross with herself for not cleaning up when she was at the market. No one sees you if you're clean.

She finds a water fountain and washes her face. Then uses some of Señora Dolucca's money to buy a clean shirt: white, simple, like children who go to the smart schools wear. The assistant nods with approval when Baz tries it on. Back on the street she drops the dirty T-shirt into a bin and then makes straight for the hospital.

It is three p.m. She reckons that if Señora Dolucca is there, chatting to the guard, it should be simple enough to ease Demi down the corridor to the gate at the back, down the stairs and out. Reflexively she checks the key is still in her pocket. All they need is a little piece of luck and five minutes. Five minutes out on the street, and even with Demi moving slow because of his wound, they can disappear. And if Lucien finds the bike and brings it to them, there will be nothing to stop them, nothing to stop them in the whole wide world. She has heard that expression before. Mama Bali used it one time, and Baz thought it meant the streets outside the Barrio. That was when she was little; now it means freedom; it means "away"; it means a new life.

* * *

The guard at the entrance is the same man who was on duty when she came with Señora Dolucca. He gives her a nod of recognition and flips up the barrier and she walks briskly past into the main building, gets a visitor tag and is shown through into the secure wing. Then she is allowed to go on her own down the dull green corridor at the end of which is the fat guard's office. Obviously not much has been happening, because through the window she can see he's taking his siesta. His head is flat on the table, his face turned away from her toward the little TV, which is still playing. She raps on the window but he doesn't stir. She tries the gate, not expecting it to be unlocked, but to her surprise it swings open and she slips through.

We will go now, she thinks. Everything so easy like this happen only one time. When you get one-time chance this good, you take it. You fool-girl if you don't take it and run.

She quickens her step, almost running to reach Demi's room. The door is shut and she hesitates for a fraction, wondering maybe if she should knock, wondering if he and Señora Dolucca are talking. She is tempted to put her ear to the door, hear what they are saying. She doesn't though; it would be the sort of thing Miguel would do, not her, not Demi, not even poor noisy Raoul. She turns the handle and pushes it open.

The curtains are pulled back and bright light is flooding through the window. She is aware of a voice, of Demi, sitting up in bed, and beside him the police captain's wife. Neither of them is speaking though. The voice belongs to the figure sitting over the other side of the small room, his back to the window. She blinks because the light is bright and for a moment she can't quite see. And then recognition hits her like a hard slap from Fay.

Eduardo!

She should run, but she can't. She feels as if a thin blade has pierced her and pinned her to this narrow space between the half-open door and the room.

"Come in," Eduardo says. "We were expecting you, weren't we, Mother? Come in and shut the door."

There is a horrible, creepy stillness in the room; only the ceiling fan is slowly turning. Demi's face shows nothing—his eyes flick to the door where Baz stands and then back to the figure in the chair. Señora Dolucca looks ugly, her cheeks sucked in, her mouth shut so tight her bright lips are a narrow slash of red. As for Eduardo, he is relaxed, one elegant leg crossed over the other knee, his expensive blue shirt open at the neck, a flat silver automatic pistol resting in his lap, a cell phone in his left hand. "Come in . . . Baz." It is as if he has to search momentarily for her name.

She takes a step forward and the door swings to behind her, clicking shut.

"Good." He flips his cell phone open and presses call. He is wearing thin leather gloves and she wonders why. Who would wear gloves in this heat? "Come up," he says into the phone. "We are ready." He listens for a moment. "Yes." He snaps the phone shut. "Now," he says, "isn't this good, Mother? You said how much you liked the girl and this boy, and now here we are, all safe and together."

"You can't do this, Eduardo," begins Señora Dolucca weakly. "Your father—"

"My father! My father, the Captain," he says, and snaps his gloved fingers dismissively.

Señora Dolucca shrinks, her head drops. She avoids looking at Baz, who is staring at her, disbelieving. This woman of power who would help her rescue Demi seems nothing now.

Eduardo leans back in his chair. "Maybe, 'Mother,' I will leave you your house, but from now on you will do what I say." His voice softens. "And my father will do what I say. Very soon he will know that he *must* do what I say." He smiles. "You see, to know everything is to have power, and one thing I know is that everybody is a thief. It is simple: some are smart and some are greedy. Your husband, my 'father,' is greedy. I, 'Mother,' am smart, which is why I am sitting here. All you need is to know things. I know this half man who calls himself Demi is a good thief, so I'll keep him." He turns his attention to Baz. "You—I don't know about you. You may be trouble for me. But I think not. You like Demi, and Demi is safe now, aren't you, Demi?" Demi doesn't respond, but this doesn't stop Eduardo: he merely smiles and continues. "I take him out of here, you come too, and nobody is going to stop me. We are safe."

Baz feels her throat tighten, a burning behind her eyes. "You can't make us do anything! We just shout one time and guards come. What you do then?" says Baz. "Tell him, Demi. He nothing to us. Better the uniform man take us than this one. This one poison." She feels rage building, like a flood behind a dam. She has the key. They could have escaped but for him, sitting there, so smug, so clean, and suddenly she is raging as she has never, never in her life, done before, and all the hard words she has ever heard in the Barrio stream from her, foul as river filth.

"Baz, you make it worse!"

Someone laughs. Eduardo.

Someone else takes her hand, grips it tight, but the rage is like a storm and she cannot stop.

And then the door suddenly snaps open behind her and cracks her in the small of her back, knocks her to her knees, winding her, and the flood of hatred dies as she gasps for air and trembles, shocked and hurt. For a moment all she is aware of is feet: Señora Dolucca's yellow high heels, Eduardo's white loafers. A rough hand grips the back of her neck, hurting her, pushing her face to the floor. She forces herself to go still.

"I did try to help," says the woman. "Eduardo was here before me. What could I do?"

Baz doesn't care; she just wonders why the guard hasn't come running from his office.

"You can let her up, Domino," says Eduardo.

The pressure on the back of her neck eases and the man shifts his grip, pulling her up.

"And now you see what they are really like, 'Mother.'" He makes "Mother" sound a like a sneer, a joke. "They are thieves, *my* thieves. I own them now. Don't I, Demi?" He stands up, folding the pistol into a handkerchief and slipping it into his jacket pocket. Then he takes off his gloves. "Get up, Demi. You're not hurt so bad." He tosses Demi his clothes.

Baz suddenly squirms away from the hand holding her neck and darts over to the bed to be beside Demi. Eduardo's man, the wooden-faced Domino, makes to grab her back, but Eduardo holds up his hand, stopping him. "Leave her. She's safe."

"Safe"—Fay's word.

"What this, Demi? What he sayin?"

Demi shrugs and, wincing slightly, pulls on jeans and a T-shirt and slips his feet into sneakers.

"Got no choice, Baz. Got to work for this one now. He got my number."

Baz has never heard him like this, defeated. Is this it then? she wonders. Is it over? They take this life, become like anyone else in the Barrio, not different, not special like Mama Bali or Lucien.

"Enough," says Eduardo. "Let's go. Domino, keep a hand on them. Mother, you come with me."

Eduardo leaves the room first with Señora Dolucca, mother and son on a hospital visit. Baz wonders why he wrapped the pistol in a handkerchief. Perhaps he does not like the oil on his expensive jacket.

Domino motions Baz and Demi to go in front of him. "You don't run or nothin," he growls. "You try somethin, I break you spine—that what I do."

What can they do if Demi has given in? There's no strut in him now, no chest puffed out, no street king, just small half man, not much better than a hurt dog. Baz keeps close to him, shoulders almost touching.

They walk the corridor, past the guard's office. The guard is there, unmoving, in exactly the same position as before, but this time she sees the dark wetness down from his hair, the blood-soaked collar. "Demi, you see?"

Domino gives her a warning prod and she winces, her back sore from where the door slammed into it. Better sore than dead. The corridor and stairs echo to the sound of Señora Dolucca's heels and the faint scuffle of Demi dragging his feet. Doctors and nurses hurry past them, but no one pays attention to Eduardo's silent group: a family, they probably think, so grim-faced they must have been visiting a dying relative.

That guard, thinks Baz, was just a fat man who liked his pastry, liked his TV show. Who would do this thing to him?

Eduardo tilts his golden head toward his mother, murmurs something in her ear, and Baz knows that of course it was him.

It would mean nothing to Eduardo to snuff out a life like that, but as to why he should do such a thing, she can't think. This fat man would have unlocked the gate for the police captain's son and the police captain's wife. Perhaps he killed him just because he could, or maybe so that Señora Dolucca could see what this son she brought into her home could do, and so Demi could see. Maybe.

They walk into the entrance lobby and Eduardo takes Señora Dolucca's arm, holds her close as if she needs support; Domino herds Baz and Demi close behind them. Eduardo hands over all the passes together. The duty guard at reception is so bored he barely glances at them.

We are invisible now, thinks Baz.

The hour hand of the clock at the entrance is just on three, exactly when Baz had planned to slip past the guard, unlock the iron gate and escape with Demi, and now here they are, walking out the front door. Except they're not free; they've just stepped out of one bad place and into another.

The heat outside is so thick it's an effort to breathe. The guard at the outer entrance stays in the cool of his little building. Through his window Baz sees him touch the brim of his cap to Señora Dolucca before raising the barrier. They walk out onto the street. A tram hisses by, cars, a bicycle. Over on the far side of the street men sit in the café where Baz waited the previous day, the news vendor is on his stool on the shady side of his pitch. Ordinary life. Nobody knows that here, walking on this sidewalk, is a smart young man with a gun folded neatly into a handkerchief; here is the wife of the city's captain of police, and she is terrified; here is a broken thief with a bullet wound in his arm.

Eduardo's car is a little down the street, half pulled up onto the pavement. A man sits at the wheel. He must see them in his wing mirror because the two doors on the pavement side flip open. Eduardo quickens his pace, and although Domino curses Demi and pushes him, a gap widens between Eduardo and Señora Dolucca and them. Could we run? thinks Baz. If a tram passes, could we run and swing up on the back? Could we do this before Domino can catch us or pull a gun? He would have a gun too; a man like him would have a gun, a knife, and hands that can kill. But still, maybe they could run. She sneaks a look at Demi, catches his eye. Can they?

He understands the look. A tiny shake of his head and one word, not spoken but she knows what it is: "Go."

She looks away. How can she—on her own? She takes his hand in hers. What will happen will happen to them both. This is it.

Three paces to the car, Eduardo guiding Señora Dolucca in, his head turned away from them. "Let go his hand. What are you? Babies?" His voice scornful, another prod and Demi stumbles slightly. Instinctively Baz turns to steady him and sees a car swerving away into the middle of the street and, in the opposite direction, a motorcycle careening across from the far side of the street, against the traffic, its engine revved up to a howl.

Chapter Twenty-seven

HE'S HUNCHED FORWARD over the handlebars, his face set in concentration. A man darting across the road clutching a bag of vegetables gets in his way. Lucien brakes hard and his back wheel skids wildly to the right and then back. The man jumps out of the way, curses angrily, shakes his fist, but Lucien is already zigzagging through the traffic, his front wheel slamming into the curb, the engine howling.

Baz tugs Demi back as Domino spins, dropping to one knee, pulling a gun, but he's too late. Lucien swings his body to the right and the bike slews round like a jackknife, slamming straight into Domino, banging him backward into the hospital's outer wall where he lies a crumpled mess, his right arm at a strange angle.

Lucien wrestles the bike upright while Baz hustles Demi onto the back. She glimpses Eduardo half in, half out of the car, turned looking back at them, disbelief on his face, his driver opening his door, his arm stretching out across the roof, pointing in their direction. There's a crack and whine, but she's already squeezing up behind Demi, grabbing him tight round his waist as Lucien twists the bike away, bumps down into the road and with one juddering wobble they're away, accelerating. Maybe there's another shot, maybe not; she doesn't know. She has her eyes shut tight, her face pressed into Demi's back. If the bullet comes it will hit her, and this is how she will die.

But the bullet doesn't come, and though Eduardo will follow them, or try to, his car is facing in the opposite direction and it'll take him valuable seconds to pull out and round. They have a good start, made better by the way Lucien pushes the bike in between cars, bursting a set of lights, randomly turning right, then left, breaking away from the main roads.

After five minutes he pulls the bike in behind a gas station down in a poor quarter on the west side. For half a moment the three of them sit on the motionless bike, the heat rising up from the hard ground, thickening around them now that they're still. There's the sound of someone beating on a panel on the far side of the gas station where there's maybe a makeshift garage, but here there's nothing but broken and rusted-up bits of cars and a pyramid of old tires.

Baz is the first to move, sliding off the back of the bike. She feels dizzy, unsteady on her feet, a little high, like one of the men from the smoky dens down in the Barrio. Too much, too quick—but all good, all safe. Somewhere in the distance a siren wails, but way off. A helicopter scats overhead, zigging north, not interested in three small figures way down below. Maybe they are invisible.

Out of habit she checks the blind side of the building; always know what's round the corner, always know you got a back door. One old man working in a makeshift garage like she thought. She waves to the boys to tell them they're safe and then comes back to them, stopping by Lucien and touching his arm and gazing into his face so intently that he turns his head sideways to her. "Lucien," she says, "you save us big time. Thank you, Lucien. Me and Demi owe you."

"You give me the key, Baz; you give me money for gas. Course I came." He shrugs and twists round on the bike. "Hey, Demi— you don't look so good."

Demi is hunched over, checking his arm. "Me?" he says. "Demi always look good—what you sayin, Lucien?" he says, straightening up, some of the lost swagger coming back into his voice.

"Just you drive this bike like some old granny woman, give me more hurt than if I get kick by a mule."

"This boy twist your head off with his bad talk," says Baz, exasperated and happy in just about equal measures. "You thank Lucien, Demi, or I take you back inside, back to the Castle myself!"

"Whoa! Who this rag girl tellin me? You forgettin, I got the hands, an' I got the . . ."

"Demi! You the one got taken; Lucien an' me haul you out o' trouble. Quit foolin." She eyes him critically. "You reckon your arm gonna be OK?"

Demi grins. "You got big real quick, Baz. Actin' like Mama Bali now . . ."

Lucien exchanges a look with Baz, then wipes his face with his shirttail. "What now, Baz? Reckon we got to move; uniform gonna be lookin for this machine."

Demi's grin fades. "They lookin for more than some old bike. They kill that guard, and that gold boy, that Fay-rat, pin it on me." He tells them how Eduardo came bursting into his room hustling his adoptive mother, shoving her so she fell awkwardly across the end of the bed, shouting at her, shouting at him. "Thought he gone wild-crazy. Maybe some drug or other. He drop the gun, you know, right by me." He looks at both of them and shrugs. "I took it up. Thought I could walk right out o' that place like some swagger-man but when I point the gun at him, this Eduardo just become another person, worser shady man than you dream, you know. He laugh at me, tell me to pull the trigger. 'Go on,' he say. 'Put you finger on the trigger, boy. Kill the Captain son, be hero for the Barrio.' The woman cryin and him tauntin . . . I pull that trigger, reckon to hit him in the leg— payback for setting us up, getting me snapped by the uniform."

"And? What you sayin?" says Lucien.

But Baz knows, has it figured. This is why Eduardo had taken such care with that little pistol, why he wrapped it up.

"Gun just clicked. Nothin. He walk right up and take it out o' my hand. 'Thank you,' he say. 'You just sign you life to me.'"

"He got your prints on the gun," says Baz.

"Got my prints and he reckon he got my soul. 'Safe,' he sneers. That just like Fay. You hear him in there, Baz, just like Fay all the time: safe, safe. Means you step out of line one time, you get handed to the bad man, take you to the Mountain. He goin to give that gun into the police anytime, and then laugh when they come lookin for me."

"Got to catch you first," says Baz. "This is what I say we do."

As they stand around the bike Baz quickly outlines what she wants: sell the bike and head straight for Norte and take a train to one of the towns in the north; start again, start fresh. Even if they wanted to, she says, there's no going back. The Barrio is being leveled, Fay has forgotten them, and now that the devil-boy is set to run the city, they have no choice but to run.

Lucien nods. "You right, Baz. You an' Demi better go now. I take you there, ride you up on the bike even, find a place up there to sell it. Maybe I follow later."

"No way!"

"No one lookin for me," he explains, his eyes fixed on Baz only. "I got to find out for sure what happen to Mama. If she dead, I want to see her buried right."

Demi is looking from one to the other. "What happen?"

"They burn her out," Baz says. "Cos of that bad-luck ring, someone know she helpin me."

"That someone Fay, maybe?" asks Demi.

"Maybe."

"Well"—he hooks his thumbs into his jeans pockets—"I goin back too, Baz. You do what you want but I'm takin some of what Fay owes me for all the time I bring her good things."

"I took the ring."

"An' you gave it away, girl! Most crazy thing you ever done." He holds up his hand to stop her. "I know why. It's OK, but I tell you, everythin change now. Maybe we got no place here, but I'm not leaving with just the skin on my back. You go ahead if you want, but me, I'm headin for the den, take what's mine. Lucien, you gimme a ride?"

Baz studies the two of them: stubborn as rock. She tries to argue with Demi, shows him the money Señora Dolucca gave her, but he won't listen. And she realizes that in fact he is not so different to Lucien. Whatever he says, it's not really the money pulling him back; he probably doesn't even know it himself, but Baz knows: what Demi really wants is to see Fay one more time, just like Lucien's got to make a good-bye to Mama Bali.

The trouble is the Barrio has to be the one place Eduardo is going to be looking for them. And yet what choice does she have? Head north on her own? Of course not. She's got no more choice than they have; she has to go along with them. At least she can watch his back, maybe stop him running blind into the wolf's open mouth. The Barrio's going to be nothing but sharp teeth.

She sighs and agrees, but insists they get rid of the bike. Demi's cross, but she's right—the three of them on that bike, they wouldn't get through Agua before someone recognized the bike or them. They wheel it round and offer it to the garage owner. He takes one look at them and offers a fifty-dollar bill. "Take it or leave it," he says, "but I'd say that bike of yours is hotter than an angry judge."

They take the money and then make their way back across the city by tram, burning a little time to make sure they don't hit the Barrio before the dark falls.

*   *   *

There's a police presence down in Agua: uniforms outside Señor Moro's bar; heavy-looking men, in combat gear, helmets and automatic rifles. There are more over by the fountain, where four giant bulldozers are lined up. But people are moving around, avoiding Moro's but coming in and out of the other bars. Some groups are gathered down by the main way into the Barrio itself; it looks to Baz as if one whole building at the corner has come right down. "You see that?" she says, gripping Demi's arm. "D'you see what they doin? Like they eatin it up piece by piece maybe."

They skirt the crowd, even though it doesn't seem as if the police are actively stopping anyone from coming or going. Perhaps their battles are done, all the shady men cleaned away; perhaps they have just backed off for the night. The Barrio in daylight is one thing; nighttime is another matter, even for city police tooled up for war.

They slip down the skinny lane, the one Demi and Baz usually use, that runs like a vein deep down into the Barrio, and then split from Lucien when they get to the corner where Mama Bali's used to stand. "Norte," says Baz, "tomorrow—all right, Lucien? You comin with us. Half nine at Norte. We catch the morning train for Tianna." She takes his rough hand in hers. "You hear me?"

Lucien makes his shy smile. "Hear you, Baz. Norte, morning train for Tianna."

"Out on the concourse. We get your ticket. OK?"

"OK." He raises his hand and gives a clenched-fist salute and heads off.

Baz and Demi make toward the den. "What! What you sayin to this boy? You buyin him tickets tomorrow? You fallin for Lucien? I thought you only got eyes for me. I get some bad luck and you run out on me, you not much of anythin, girl."

"Demi, you got worse mouth than a squealin pig."

"Where you see pig?"

"Seen him in the market before they hang him up by his tail. Maybe that happen to you one time, you keep squealin like you do."

It's their old way, trading insults; Demi playing big, she cutting him down to size—but this is different, a whispered routine, covering what they really feel as they move quickly and silently through the labyrinth. Around them the Barrio breathes. An angry orange light flickers up in the sky to their right: another building burning down. Heavy music judders in the thick air. Dark figures hurry by them; each time they hear someone coming they press themselves into any gap or crack that'll bury them in darkness, holding their breath, every sense alert, eyes straining into the darkness, tense and frightened.

And resigned—at least that's what Baz feels. They were so close to being free and now they might as well have gone right up to the Castle, banged on the giant doors and yelled at the hard man to lock them up and throw away the key. Maybe that would have been better than this, stealing their way into the Barrio. Who will be waiting for them at the den? Fay. Fay will know they have escaped. Fay will expect Demi to come back. Fay's had Demi on a leash for so long she won't be able to imagine Demi thinking for himself.

She'll be there, waiting, planning, thinking that she's safe with her angel-boy and his clever schemes. She's blind though, thinks Baz, love-blind; she hasn't seen what he's really like, hasn't heard that hard laugh when Baz said Fay's name to him. She pushes the thought to one side. None of that matters. Now she just hopes the bulldozers keep away long enough for her and Demi to do their thing and then run free.

They are down on their bellies, working their way slowly along the old ditch near the den, when they spot the first of the gang: Giaccomo, up by the plank that crosses the ditch. He's obviously meant to be tucked in against the wall of the building behind, but Giaccomo was never good at being hidden, not unless Miguel was there to tell him what to do. So the fact that they can see him so easily means he's on his own. He's on lookout though, no other reason for him to be standing out there at this time. Baz glimpses a glow of light in his hand. Fay's given him a cell phone. Fay's getting generous in her old age, generous or just nervy maybe. She always said cell phones were too easy to trace, and she never wanted anything tracing back to her. Preferred doing things face-to-face. "You can tell when a body's lying to you when you see their face," she always said. Baz wonders how many times Fay lied to her and Demi.

She touches Demi's good arm, runs her finger under her throat. "Not this way." And they both squirm back a little. There's an old drain under the building where Giacco is standing that connects to the ditch right by the entrance to the old warehouse, Fay's place. Carried floodwater and sewage one time, but it's been dry since before Baz, Demi and Fay came into the Barrio. She and Demi crawled the drain a hundred times when they were smaller, used it for a dare sometimes with new children coming into the gang, but not for years now. She doesn't even think Miguel or the others would know about it.

"Tunnel," she whispers into his ear and he nods, knowing instantly what she means. "You goin to manage with your hurt arm?"

"Quit fussin, Baz," he hisses.

"OK." But she can tell that that wound is giving him pain.

They ease back about ten yards, and then quietly and quickly Baz scoops away rubbish till the entrance is exposed. Black, round, like a mouth, snake-mouth. She half thinks she should just let Demi go on his own; he's the one so keen to take what he says Fay owes him. But what good's money if you're buried down here with all the dirt? What good's money if you got Fay and some shady man watching you as your stealing fingers dip into that space in the wall and pull out Fay's treasure?

But what would she do belly down in this ditch, waiting? What would she do if she heard the yell of him getting caught, getting beaten? She would have to go right in there and get caught herself. She takes a breath and sizes up the hole. She reckons they should still be able to squeeze down it, like paste from a tube maybe, but they could do it. Sure thing—no one would expect them coming up out of the ground right by the front door.

She glances back at Demi—the whites of his eyes glint at her in the darkness. He pats her leg and she takes a breath and eases herself into the mouth of the drain, arms stretched out in front of her, trying not to think of spiders or snakes or rats. There are rats big as dogs down in the Barrio. Her mouth is closed tight. There's dirt down her neck, dirt coating her face, on her lips, clogging her nose, making it hard to breathe the stinking air.

The sides of the drain are gritty as sandpaper and as she inches forward she feels her new clean shirt beginning to shred.

They should be at Norte getting themselves tickets, but here they are in a drain under the Barrio, and the Barrio's tumbling down around them. And, she thinks crossly, all Demi wants to do is go thievin!

Her jaw is tight, the tips of her fingers raw, her eyes clamped shut. And she is angry now, but anger is good; she grips it tight, lets it fill her mind, leaving no room to picture what's up ahead, no room to picture those dog-big rats waiting for her. She just keeps scraping. They must be halfway now. There is no going back. Not even a worm could wriggle backward along this drain.

Something grips her ankle and she almost screams before realizing it's Demi. "Here, Baz?" He stifles a cough.

With agonizing slowness she works herself round so that she's lying on her back and she tracks the top of the drain with her fingers, feeling for the flat surface of the cover. "No. I got nothing."

There's rasping and scuffling and a stifled groan as Demi shifts himself round too.

She waits, trying to steady her breathing, slow it down, stop that panic building. She hears him fumbling, the hiss and trickle of more dirt pouring in and then a scratching of metal sliding back and a waft of air. Demi is still for a moment. She knows what he's thinking: is it clear? She jigs her foot at him, a signal to get moving. Why wait? If they don't move they're dead anyway. They're better caught than tombed down in a drain with nothing but rats and bugs for company.

She hears him slither out and then instantly she feels his hand round her legs, tugging her backward until she too can wriggle up through the hatchway. In one movement she rolls to her feet, crouching, scanning back up the alley. There'll be someone at the corner, someone up on the roof, maybe someone down by the river; rat's eyes looking out for them. Looking *out*, not looking right down by the door into Fay's building.

Wordlessly, working as one, they slip shadowlike into the ghostly empty space of the ground floor of the warehouse, pause again to listen and look. No one on the stairwell. They hurry down to the cellar, feel their way through the inky blackness to Fay's hiding place, finger their way to the loose brick and slide it free.

Easy. It's so easy, thinks Baz. Nothing come this easy. Nothing. Even when we workin a mark, huntin a fat little purse . . .

Every second that goes by, Baz expects the sound of feet coming down behind them, the flicker of a flashlight, voices, Fay.

"Heavy," breathes Demi. "Like she got everythin we done lock up in this little box."

"You happy? Want to stand here dreamin all night or you ready to go?"

"I'm thinkin," says Demi.

Baz edges back to the stairs and then stops, waiting. Why can't they just go? What's he doing? What's happened to him? He doesn't need to think; Demi moves, quick, so quick nobody can tell he's there, what he's doing. His hands do his thinking for him, so what is he doing now?

Way up at the top of the building she hears a door open and close.

"I'm thinkin we gotta tell Fay what we doin now." Demi's voice is so quiet it's almost like he's talking to himself.

"You crazy?" she hisses. This is it. She knew he would do something like this, but it doesn't stop her trying to hammer some sense into him. "You think she let us walk away now?"

"Want her to know I'm not thieving from her," he says, "only taking what's ours. We got a right to do that." Baz can't see him at all now; he's lost in the darkness. A voice without a body.

"Got what you want right in your hand," she says desperately. "Just take some of what she got; leave the rest. Show you'self to her and you gonna lose your head." She senses him moving toward her, feels his breath on her face.

"Got to, Baz. She—"

"She different now. We don't mean a thing to her. You seen it, Demi. Wake from your dreaming."

"Not different to me."

And that's it. He slips by her, a solid shadow in the blackness, suddenly taking shape as he moves up the stairway away from her.

Chapter Twenty-eight

HE DIDN'T ASK HER to come with him! Didn't ask her to wait!

Every instinct in her body is telling her to get out of there, to go now, while she has the chance, but she doesn't move. She feels him moving up the building, soundless even with the hurt in his arm making him struggle.

Suddenly all the anger and raging drains out of her. People can't let people go, even when maybe they should. She takes the stairs two at a time, catches him in the bare cement-floored space outside the den.

They look at each other. "Wipe your face, Baz," he says, not in the old Demi voice but soft.

She takes the sleeve of her shirt and tries to scuff away the dirt and wet from her eyes. She wants to tell him he doesn't look so good either, but she doesn't trust her voice. He pushes open the door.

It's less than two days since they walked out of the den to do the job Fay wanted them to do, but it feels much longer; it feels somehow as if the room should be different. It's not, of course; maybe a little messier, that's all. A bulb on a long flex dangles from the ceiling, the table in the center is scattered with dirty plates and glasses. The boys' sleep mats are scuffled up with their scraps of clothing, the ledges under the big windows bare except for the one where Demi had his space; no one has touched his things, his mat is rolled neatly, an old pair of sneakers he hadn't been able to bring himself to throw away tucked on top. Demi's window looks out across the dead river, and the grimy glass shows nothing but night. The window on the other side of the room is speckled with the lights of the city and the orange glare of fire burning somewhere in the Barrio. The stove to the left is open and cold; the door to Fay's makeshift room over in the right-hand corner is open too. The room is warm and sour with the tang of old clothes and smoke.

Fay's alone, sitting in her usual chair at the end of the table, a pitcher of wine at her elbow, her cell phone by the glass she's drinking from, a tin saucer piled with cigarillo butts. Her face, apart from black shadows under eyes, is death pale, her hair a wild wiry tangle of orange, her cream jacket stained and creased; she looks like she hasn't slept for a week. She doesn't move, doesn't blink when they come in and stand in the doorway, just stares across at them as if they're not real.

Demi is the first to speak. "Hey, Fay," he says, "brought you something."

Her eyes flick down to the thick box he's holding and widen slightly as she takes in what it is. Baz expects her to scream and rage at them, but instead her mouth turns down into what's almost a smile. She shakes her head. "How you get in here? I put the boys all out lookin for you. I told them where to be, told every one of them. What you do to them, Demi?"

"You don't think we smart enough to get by someone dumb as Giaccomo?"

"Thought you'd be smart enough to keep away from here. What were you thinking, Baz? Your idea to come home? No." She shakes her head. "Don't reckon it was you—you got an understanding of what's safe. Demi don't got that, do you, Demi?" She slops some wine from the pitcher into her glass. Her hand, Baz notices, is unsteady, but her voice is clear. Fay can talk sharp as a blade even when she can hardly stand from the wine.

"What you mean, Fay? We not welcome here? And this"—he holds up the box—"you don't care 'bout this, all this precious thing we brought you? You just keep it stuff away, so we can't touch none of it."

Fay shrugs. "Put the boys out there to warn you away, Demi, but there are only three of them now and none of them good. Got nobody good since you gone and Miguel's gone too, gone to Eduardo." The phone vibrates, jigging sideways on the table until Fay catches it and checks the message, puts it down again. "Eduardo's the new man, Demi; everything belong to him now. The new Señor. He got all the shady man in his pocket. Moro is meat for rats. Police found him, facedown in the dirt where he belong. Now Eduardo's comin here for you."

"You told him?"

"Told him nothing; that boy think for himself. He got this place wrapped. You good, but you not invisible."

"He so smart, how come the police tearing everything down?" says Baz.

"Tear this down and what you got? Shiny office, shiny new building. River going to run; everyone saying that now. Barrio going to be like some rich man's dream, and who got that dream in his pocket? You want to know?"

"Your boy," says Demi.

"My boy goin to sit on so many dollar, he going to be king of the mountain."

"And he goin to give you protection?" says Demi bitterly. "Like Señor Moro?"

"This different." She takes a deep swallow of wine. "This family."

An image comes into Baz's head of Raoul, his smile an old

ghost, his body leaning against the wire. Raoul was family. And she remembers something else. She remembers what Señora Dolucca told her about her husband and the street girls. "And the Captain—he family too? He give you protection?"

She frowns, puzzled. "What you sayin?"

"The Captain, he give you protection when you first come to the city."

"You, Baz. You always knowin more than you say. But you wrong in this thing; the Captain don't ever give, the Captain take. That Captain when he just a uniform, working the streets, he take me, take me when I don't know how the city work, take me, and when the child come, he take the child . . ."

"The Captain Eduardo's real father!"

"The Captain real all right. Maybe blood family don't mean so much, Baz . . ."

"Your boy no concern to us, Fay," says Demi, his voice hard, all business, or trying to be. "We come to make a share out of what's our due, eh." He holds up the box. "Three-way seem fair. What you say?"

Fay shrugs and gives her almost-smile again. "Go ahead, Demi. You open that old thing."

"Your pension," says Demi. "Take us out of here. Remember that?" He flips up the lid, looks down, and then his eyes go wide like he's been stung by a wasp. "What this?" He tips the box up. Nothing falls out but some loose change and a couple of small plastic bags of white stuff. "Baz!"

"Me? I took that ring only, and some dollar to get you free."

Fay grunts. "Everyone dip a hand in the honeypot. You think I leave it there for the world come dip his hand too? Forget it, Demi. That box of mine always small time, and we the smallest fry in the river now." She suddenly picks up the glass and takes a slug. "Small fry get eaten unless they change, or unless they real quick and know how to keep out of trouble."

"River's dead," says Baz. "Nobody goin' to build nothin' beside that stretch of mud."

Fay shoves back the chair and, a little unsteadily, gets to her feet. "You both dead unless you get gone; dead or rag an' bone on the Mountain. You want that? Hey? You want that? Cos he downstairs. You want to look, you look an' see." She points to the city-side window. Demi glances at her and Baz runs over to look.

By craning out they can peer down into the alley that runs past the building and down to the river. There must be five, six, maybe seven figures down there, a couple with flashlights, they're already beginning to move into the building. "They comin, Demi!"

Fay's over the other side of the room, struggling with a coil of rope. "No time for the roof; you go by the window. This one. Baz, the door!"

Always have a way out, that's what she told them.

Baz runs to the door, closes it and runs the bolt across. Demi tosses down the box, forces open the river-side window, knots the rope and throws it out. It's a bigger drop than from the Dolucca house.

Demi reads her mind. "Think lucky, Baz—at least we don't got police car cruisin down there."

No, they got different sharks looking for them.

She scrambles up onto the sill, but before swinging her legs out she turns back, looks at Fay standing there, so close, anxious. Fay never had this look, not even when Señor Moro came calling. Baz wants to say something but it's too hard. Demi too seems more little than big, no swagger, no proud talk. He's looking at Fay like a hurt dog, but Fay's looking at Baz.

"Go, Baz!" says Fay. "Get out o' this place."

Baz hears feet on the stairs, a rattling at the door, and she's over the sill, gripping the rope tight, clamping it with her thighs and skinnying down. A moment later Demi follows, sliding, burning his hands, almost knocking into her. She drops the last six feet, landing soft, crouching into the shadow. Demi hits the ground a second after, grunts in pain. The rope snakes down on top of them.

Baz, looking up, glimpses Fay's white face at the window, then she's gone. There used to be times when Baz was heading out to the boat and she would look back at that window high up in the old derelict building and there would be that light glowing. It always made her think of soft gold.

She turns away and, without saying anything to Demi, starts along the bank, heading up to the bend, instinctively making for the boat, her safe place. How long do they have before the men come looking, clattering down the stairs in their Italian shoes, running fast? Minutes. She quickens her pace. Fay will tell them . . . Pickpack, Raoul, boys whose faces she can't remember anymore, all gone when Fay told because they brought her trouble, and she and Demi have brought her big trouble now, brought it right up to her door, laid it at her feet, and it's not going to disappear like the ice Demi thought so precious and that melted away to nothing.

Maybe this time is different. She looked different; she helped them get away.

Their feet sound noisy, scuffing through pebbles and trash, and all the time the Barrio murmurs.

She slows, suddenly aware that Demi's not beside her but lagging behind, clutching his hurt arm.

"You OK?"

He doesn't answer, just doggedly tries to keep pace with her, but she can hear he's breathing hard, like a nerve's getting scratched with every step he takes.

If the men come now they don't have a chance.

"You got to hurry, Demi!"

"What you think I doin?"

And then from somewhere behind them comes a thin, high scream. It could be a child, it could be a woman. Sometimes you hear this in the Barrio and you mind your business, but Demi freezes, then makes as if to start back. "It's not Fay, Demi!" Baz grips his arm, shakes him. "No one hurting Fay. What you thinkin? Eduardo not going to touch her. She his mother, his real mother. Come on." She tugs him and tugs him again, but it's only when a figure appears at the window and a flashlight begins stabbing randomly down along the shore that he moves, jolting along after her.

They have barely covered another ten yards when there's a shout from the window and when Baz glances back she sees the light's beam working methodically, slowly, carefully, digging into the pools of black tucked in among the piles of scrap and rubble, the rotting upturned hulls of boats. They go as fast as they can, as Demi can, a half walk, half run. They make it to the bend. Another few seconds and they will be out of range, but the beam is almost on them. She grabs him, pulls him sideways, gets her fingers under the edge of the hull where she caches her water and yanks it up. "Get in, Demi," she says quickly. "I'll lead them a dance; you too slow."

"OK, just this one time, you go, girl. Next time me."

"Sure."

He squirms under the tilted-up hull, she shoveling him from behind. "Don't you move, you hear. Lie still till I get you."

"I can't breathe." His voice a muffled complaint.

"You won't breathe if they catch you." She lets the hull drop and then sprints back out into the open. Immediately the light finds her.

"That's one!"

She runs like she's trying to shake the light, swerving, cutting right, left, zigzagging as if she's lost something. She wants them to get a little closer, to feel as if they can catch her without any trouble, without having to think too much.

The men are shouting, calling, their hard shoes scuffing the muck, someone cursing the mud, maybe his nice Italian shoes getting spoiled.

Not yet, she tells herself. They got to be close, breathing down her neck, stretching to grab her. So she stops, looks back as if startled, letting herself be blinded in the glare, so that they can see clearly, see she's nothing, frightened, easy meat.

"You! Stay there. You not running anywhere!"

She closes her eyes tight, slowly counting: one, two, three, getting rid of the blindness from the light, giving them time to get a little closer.

One of the men yells suddenly, "This the bitch-girl stole my bike!"

Baz spins away, opens her eyes into the darkness, letting her pupils dilate. Now she can see. There's the hulk, way out across the mud. She glances left and right, gets her bearings and runs down to the edge of the hard mud and begins to angle her way out into the river, still hurrying, trying to make it look easy, look safe. She looks back, holding her hand up to shield her eyes from the light this time. She turns, quickens her pace a little just so they think it's safe, makes it to the buoy and clings on to it as if out of breath, frightened.

Four of them come straight out for the shore in a line, running fast and then suddenly slower as the mud softens, up to their ankles in the sludge. Just a little more and they'll go deep, just like Demi did; but she won't stir to help them. She watches, calculating the distance, her heartbeat slowing.

"You come here! I swear I'll tear you in pieces!"

He's the angry one, young, narrow-faced, pushing on ahead of the others. He's the man Demi and she tumbled from his bike, the guard from the Mountain that they left tied up like a piece of pork belly. He wants to beat her, make her pay for the trouble they caused him. He would have lost face for that. Nobody likes to lose face, not these men; they would rather kill you and leave you for the dogs and rats to pick at.

Come, she says to herself, just a little closer.

And they're all plowing on, wading deeper, up to their knees, the angry man ahead of them five paces. She can see the shine of sweat on his face, the mud glistening on his jacket, how it's slick round his thighs. "Hey!" he shouts, and there's a tight note of worry in his voice now. "I can't move."

The other three ignore him but they're struggling too, yelling at her, at each other, one of them fumbling with a cell phone, one waving a gun, letting off a round that zings past Baz.

"Daro!" one of them yells, "What, you crazy? Quit that 'fore you kill us all, eh!" But Daro, the man with the gun, loses his balance and, flailing his arms like a windmill, lets off another round before tipping over into the mud. The other two keep coming. "Why you stop, Rico?"

Rico, the narrow-faced one, doesn't answer. He has his gun out, pointing it at Baz, his arm wavering. The mud up to his waist now. His mouth twisting and working because he's scared now, spitting out the words to her: "You make us do this, you filth. You trap us out here. I swear I kill you," but he doesn't shoot. "I swear unless you get something . . ." He begins to tilt forward, tries to lean back but can't. He drops the gun, frantically scrabbles for it, tilts forward more. The gun slips under the surface. "Jesus, Mary . . ." No bluster now.

If he keeps still, she reckons, he can keep his face out of the mud for maybe five minutes. She steps away from the shelter of the buoy. "You got friends," she says. "Maybe they help you."

"You could get rope, get something . . ."

"You keep still or mud'll choke you up."

"What are you?" He's breathing's ragged, panicky, but he's stopped moving, his chin's tilted up, his neck rigid. "You got no feelin . . . Jesus!"

She thinks about it. Feeling? What feeling they show for Raoul or any child they keep pen-up on the mountain? She can move now; they're all stuck: three of them in a ragged line, up to their waists, silent, caught in their own struggle to get free from the mud, like a row of pegs on Mama Bali's washing line, tilted this way and that. The one called Daro is almost gone.

"I got no feelin for you," she says.

She saw up to seven when she looked down from the den, so more are going to come anytime now and see what's happening. Three, one of them Eduardo. Maybe they'll come running to save these four. Maybe not. Baz doesn't intend to wait and see. She takes a last look out to the boat. No one ever found the way out to it, not even Demi. And in that dream she had, the water came and the boat floated free . . . For half a second she's tempted to go on out, hide away out there, nothing touching her, but it's fool-thinking, child-thinking, dreaming.

Dreaming's no good; dreaming doesn't get you safe. "Keep still," she says to Rico. "Mud swallow you fast when you wriggle."

He has his head twisted back to the shore, maybe trying not to see how close his face is to the mud. He doesn't answer. These men are not used to being told things by children, being told anything by anyone other than their boss. They hunt. They do. They make people frightened. Not anymore perhaps.

She runs back lightly, leaving the men behind, ignoring the cursing of the two behind Rico. There's only one thing to do now: disappear. Vanish into the night: leave the Barrio, leave the city, go far, far away where no one will know who they are.

She sees the stab of the flashlight just as she reaches the upturned boat; they're coming.

She lifts the hull and Demi's all curled up, like a tidy dog. He twists his head and then grips the hand she offers him. "You always pulling me up, Baz."

"You got no weight."

He puts his arm round her shoulder, she an arm round his waist, and leaving the river behind them they thread their way quickly, taking the route Baz used earlier, the one that will bring them up near the market.

After twenty minutes they take a rest. The river is a long way behind them and the Barrio is about as still as it ever gets. Baz reckons it must be well after midnight now and she's aching with tiredness. She wonders about Lucien. She wonders if they can really wait for him at Norte. Do they dare do that? Will Eduardo take that much trouble to hunt them down? Why should he want to?

Finally they reach the market and make themselves a nest

under one of the stalls, strips of plastic, paper, cardboard. She scavenges some squashed brown bananas and then slumps down beside Demi. The fruit is so soft it's almost liquid and does little to still the hunger, but she's been hungry before. They'll eat tomorrow. "Plate of sausage so piled high, dog couldn't jump over it," she murmurs.

"Fat-man pastry, Baz. All I gonna eat when I rich is fat-man pastry."

"I never going to work with a fat man, Demi. Fat man get stuck running down alley, get stuck going through door. You wanna be fat, you find new partner." She curls up next to him, tucks her arm up under her head and closes her eyes. It feels safe, the night's warm, trouble seems a long way away.

There's a long silence and Baz has almost drifted into sleep when Demi says, "She try to give me money, Baz. She didn't fuss 'bout the box, she just try to push a whole lot of dollar in my hand. Just when I'm going out the window, that what she do." His voice seems a long way away.

"Tha's good, Demi," she manages. "We need dollar for the train."

But she doesn't hear him say, "Tha's not it, Baz; tha's not what I'm tellin you," because she's already asleep.

Chapter Twenty-nine

DARKNESS. Devil-black darkness. So thick and black, Baz can see nothing. So thick that for a moment she wonders whether she's dead and buried, stuck in a poor-man coffin deep under the Barrio, except there's something soft and warm under her head, and though she's as blind as an old rat, she knows it's Demi's shoulder. She knows where they are. She shifts her head and closes her eyes again.

Then she hears the voices.

Voices and footsteps. The scrape of wooden boxes being dragged sideways, rubbish kicked. "What you got?"

"Nothing."

A dusky breeze shuffles the plastic cover of the stall they're nestled under. Dust swirls in, gritting her face. Demi's hand tightens on her arm.

Police? Men from the river? Eduardo's men?

A man talking quietly. Then silence. Then talking again. Cell phone. "No. Nothing . . . Yes. We do that." Click. The cell phone being snapped shut.

"*Vamos.*" A voice as dry as old leather.

She holds her breath. Demi's the same—tight as a trap but they're the ones trapped. The whole city feels like a trap now to Baz, so many streets crisscrossed with more streets and squares and little alleys. One time she and Demi could go anywhere, walk free as kings, and even when a mark got wise and they had to run, running was easy; every corner was a friend, every alley safe, every tram a ride home to the Barrio. Now she pictures all those streets hanging over her like a net. And on every one a shady man watching or a policeman checking or a camera spying. She wishes she was small again, so small not even a dog would pay her any attention as she went by.

They hear the men moving away. They wait, alert for any flicker of sound, until they're sure it's safe.

Demi moves first, rolling onto his side, lifting the edge of the plastic, then snaking out on his belly. Baz follows and crouches beside him.

It's dark still but already softening to the gray of dawn. The market is spread around them, a scattering of empty stalls like shadowy islands, but there's no sign of the men anymore. Maybe they had been scouring the Barrio all night and just had enough. Maybe they were trying to figure out where she and Demi would run to. Fay could tell. With money in their pockets, she would know they would try to leave the city, head for Norte, go someplace with pools and the soft life. Yes, Fay would know this, but Baz didn't think she would tell, not unless she had no choice.

Lucien could tell too. If anyone recognized that it was him riding the bike at the hospital they would tear his skinny arms off, but she didn't think Lucien would tell them anything. Never.

"We're OK, I reckon," Demi murmurs, stretching his arms and then wincing. "You small but you got heavy head, Baz," he says.

"You just nothing but bone, Demi. My neck all crimped up, cos your shoulder worst thing I ever lay my head on."

He sniffs dismissively, then pulls out a pouch he has tucked into the waistband of his jeans, checks inside it.

"What that?"

"Told you. Fay give a roll of dollar 'fore I scat out the window. Just press it on me. Didn't mind about the ring either, you taking it. Thought she skin us for that. Kept sayin none of that matter, Baz. She just hustle me out."

"Fay got new business," Baz says. "Maybe all we done just small in her mind now."

Demi tucks the pouch back. "Maybe, but she give us a big lot o' dollar . . ." He squares his shoulders, sniffs, spits, toughest street boy in the city.

If Baz had been looking at him, not thinking her own thoughts about Fay, she would have seen through the tough-guy act, seen how much Demi needed to believe that Fay cared for them. Instead she says, "She got her reasons; Fay always got a reason for what she do."

"Oh, maybe you don't know so much, girl."

Baz shrugs. "Maybe." She looks toward the Barrio, where an oily finger of smoke is hooking up into the sky.

"OK." He's jigging on his toes. "We got to go. People comin in to set up. We go, Baz, make that early train. What do you say?"

"OK. Catch the tram from Agua?"

"Agua quickest way, but we keep our heads down. They see us, they gonna kill us. No question, know what I mean. Least thing they do is bury us head down in the mud you got them stuck in. Tell you that for nothin."

"Demi, you always full of nothin."

They leave the market as the first of the farmers and stall-holders begin to pull in, some wheeling carts and barrows, others in battered three-wheeler vans. None of them pays attention to a pair of dirt-scuffed strays, no more strange than hungry dogs, and the city's riddled with stray dogs.

They walk, Demi still protecting his bad arm, but it's not so far and he doesn't complain. They stop only to buy bread and coffee, Demi taking a risk, breaking a fifty dollar bill in an early-morning bar, but the owner is still too groggy from the previous night's rum to do more than hold the bill up to the light and see that it's the real thing and grumble a little that it's going to clean him out of change before the day's even started. After they've eaten they make their way down to Agua.

Demi turns toward the tram stop, but Baz catches his arm. "Look," she says, pointing across the square to the main way into the Barrio. "A whole lot waitin to happen there."

*   *   *

The police are there, of course, but they all look relaxed, easy, as if the battle is over, the war won. They stand in small groups, drinking coffee, biting on sweet rolls, smoking, Perspex visors tipped back, talking, sometimes wandering over to the barrier they strung up to keep out the city folk who've come down to watch the Barrio get its teeth knocked out. It's a thin crowd, just the early-comers with nothing on their minds but a chance to see someone else get a little misery.

Baz and Demi join the edge; Demi, despite his agitating to leave right away, is drawn forward as if by a magnet, easing between the shoulders of bystanders until he is up at the front. Baz follows him. She's hoping that Lucien is already out of the Barrio. She checks the time with Demi; it's a little before nine. If he gets caught up in whatever action the police are planning, he won't make their train. What will they do then? She stands on tiptoe, straining to see, and then shifts through the scattered crowd till she finds a gap. There's nothing though, nothing but police, police and the men in shiny suits, the new shady men. There they are, on the wrong side of the barrier, mixing with the uniform like they are one and the same. She sees a man from way back, one of Moro's lieutenants, a craggy-faced Indian who always liked to dress himself in fancy red silk shirts, she sees him up by one of the giant bulldozers, hand on the foot step, looking up at the burly driver, another Indian, built big as his machine, swapping news like they grew up together.

"Something happen here," says Demi. "Someone make a deal and everything got change around." His face is pulled up tight and there's sweat on his brow. Demi doesn't sweat easy, not like the big boys. But he's sweating now and his voice is stretched tight and hard. "Eduardo made some deal."

"Something happen," Baz agrees, though she can't really imagine the kind of deal Demi is thinking of. But there's no crackle of gunfire, just the deep, warm thrum of the bulldozers gearing up and rolling out and then the satisfying *crump* of walls crumbling, and dust floating up into the early-morning air, catching the sun, making the smoke glow.

A bystander sips loudly from his paper cup of coffee. "Only clearing a block at a time. Gonna throw up some big buildings. All glass, like Chicago. That's what they say. New city right down here. Who'd have thought it?" Eduardo, thinks Baz, because that is what Fay had told them. He tears the end of a croissant and stuffs it in his mouth. Someone else says, "Heard that too."

The first of a trickle of Barrio refugees start to come out through the police lines and into the square. Maybe this is the last chance for people to leave. There are Chinese hauling boxes and bundles, old men in high collars, bent over sticks; they must have knocked down the laundry and the gambling den. There are ragged families carrying nothing more than stuffed plastic bags or straw baskets, children clinging to their mothers, no one crying, no one looking up. She knows some of these people but they are not her business. There's no sign of Lucien.

"Better for everyone if those bulldozers just shoveled all that rubble on top of them. One less problem, eh? One less thief in the city," declares the man shoveling the last chunk of croissant into his mouth.

"A body got to live," Demi says to him.

The man eyes him coldly. "A body got to live if he pay his tax and he keep his hands out of my pocket."

"Boy's right," says a young guy. "You lose *your* home you don't feel so good, I bet."

"Yeah," the man growls, "well, me, I paid for my home. This one looks like he belong in there with them, eh. You Barrio-rat, boy? Eh? I got my hand on my wallet—I advise you do the same." He spits and turns away.

The young man looks curiously at Demi. "Looks to me like the city got plenty of fat rats it need to get rid of before it need to worry 'bout poor folk in the Barrio. Fat cats too," he says as a black Mercedes with darkened windows rolls up. Suddenly all the uniformed men are a little more alert, straightening up, stubbing out their cigarettes, looking toward the stocky man getting out of the back of the car. The Captain. Shiny knee boots of black leather, a green uniform, and square dark glasses masking his face. His lieutenants snap him salutes; he nods and then he stares down into the Barrio while a man in a suit tells him things, watching the bulldozers do their work.

Baz turns round to catch Demi's eye but he's slipped away. She doesn't move. He won't go without her; he's just seen something, like a dog checking this, checking that. A moment later he reappears.

"What you got monkey face for, Demi?"

"That man so worry he goin to lose his purse, I help him out a little." He holds up a fist of crumpled notes and then wedges it into his hip pocket. "Come on, Baz, we gotta go now."

"He goin to think it you!"

"I see him step on the tram. What he gonna do?"

"When he find he can't pay, he goin to jump down, that what he goin to do. He goin to come runnin this way. I swear mad fly bite you, cos you got no sense at all. Boy, sometimes you make Giaccomo look like he the one with brains!"

"What you fussin? All that man find if he come lookin is me gone. Come on, Baz, please . . ."

The "please" takes her by surprise, but at that moment her attention is caught by the Captain bending down and speaking to someone still inside the black Mercedes, someone not wearing a uniform but neat blue jeans. Someone young then? She can't see more than that because the figure in the car is shielded by the darkened glass of the window. It doesn't matter; she knows who it is. Eduardo. Working with his "adopted father" now? The man he robbed, the man he sneered at; but now he is sitting in his car, making use of him, like he made use of Señora Dolucca, of Fay too. He very clever, she thinks, too clever for her and Demi.

"Baz! You dreamin? We gotta move. Lucien gonna be waitin. This place too hot, Baz." He tugs her hand, anxious to leave.

"OK, OK."

She hears the jangle of a bell and the familiar squeal of a tram pulling into the square and they run, catching the tail of the tram just as it is pulling away.

"What happen? For a minute back there you look like you almost for stayin," he says, dropping into the seat beside her.

"If I stay, who goin to pull you out of trouble all the time?"

He does one of his exaggerated shrugs, his shoulders almost touching his ears. "Find someone."

"Oh yeah. Well, you got no need, Demi."

He turns and looks out of the window. After a moment he says, "Don't want to look for no one else, Baz, hey," and he puts his hand out palm up, and she lightly smacks hers down onto it, and for a second his fingers tighten around hers before letting go.

"How far north we goin to go, Demi?" she asks.

"All the way the train take us."

She closes her eyes as the city streams by outside the tram window. Safe. They have dollars, enough for the train, enough maybe to start up somewhere new, find a place. It can't be so hard. Nothing can be as hard as the Barrio, nor as terrible as the Mountain.

Chapter Thirty

BUT THE BARRIO, with its tangle of alleys and lanes, is already half dead. Only a handful of the bigger buildings remain, jutting up from the rubble and dirt. Stark and naked they look, as if surprised by this new wilderness.

There, right in the middle of this new space, is an old church with a high domed roof, Baz and Demi's safe place, their island in a peaked and tilting sea.

Over by the dry river are the old, derelict warehouses, bleached to the color of bone. Maybe Fay is there, looking from her window back up to the city, wondering about Baz and Demi, wondering whether she should have let them go, wondering if the golden son who found his way back to her is the past and the future she wants.

And Eduardo, the new Señor, is sitting in the back of that black police car, parked up at Agua, maybe looking out of the darkened window over all that he has achieved. Or maybe his mind is on Baz and Demi, angry that two of his mother's thieves have escaped, and there are now two mouths that can talk too much. The new Señor, like his mother, will do anything to be safe. Maybe he is angrier still that they bloodied his nose, and in public: one of his men is in intensive care, smashed by the motorcycle; three had to be rescued from the stinking mud; one is dead, sucked into the river. Maybe the new Señor is coldly considering a suitable fate for Baz and Demi. A new Señor cannot lose face, and this Señor has waited so long, planned so carefully, that surely no rats squealing out of the Barrio will be allowed to escape.

The new Señor will have eyes throughout the city.

On the tram heading for Norte the bell clangs and the driver calls another stop; Baz and Demi stay seated. The tram fills up. Everyone going about business, plugged into music, clutching bags, reading the day's paper. A man complains that the tram's too full and he paid for a seat and maybe children should get up. Demi ignores him. Baz glimpses a front-page headline: "MISSING!" Headlines always shouting about something or other. She misses Raoul. She misses the time when she and Demi and Fay were just three and they seemed family almost; she hopes and hopes that when they get to the station they'll see Lucien. She doesn't say this to Demi. Another stop. The center. They push down the aisle and step off, cross the road to pick up the tram that'll take them up to Norte.

This is the smarter part of town and Baz is conscious that they're grubby. She takes Demi's hand, gripping it tight when, instinctively, he tries to pull it free. "What you playin?" he hisses. "You goin soft?"

"Thief don't hold hand," she says. "Try look like you carin for me. Nobody mind children if they lookin sweet."

He grunts. "You somethin, Baz. Times I think you almost got smart."

They board the new tram, politely put up with the driver telling them to wait till everyone else has bought their ticket, ignore him telling him that there's no free ride on his tram, and hand him the right change for their journey. He punches out their tickets. "Anyone lose their purse on this bus and I'll drag you to the Castle myself," he says deliberately loud so everyone around can hear. Baz makes as if she's about to cry and a woman snaps at the driver, telling him to let poor children alone. Life is hard enough, she says, without men like him making people's lives a misery.

She smiles at Baz, and Baz wipes her hand over her eyes and smiles shyly at the woman and then she and Demi move to the back of the car, stand out on the little platform at the back. "Maybe you get a job acting, be on that soap Fay like so much."

"You the actor," she says. "Act big-head all the time."

Demi grins. "Big head for big ideas."

Ten minutes later they swing down and climb the steps up to the station and head straight for the ticket office. There, in the middle of the huge room, the crowd swilling around him, is Lucien, thin and scraggy in a threadbare jacket.

"Demi, look who you see!" She's about to push her way straight to him, she's so happy, but there's a look in his face she's never seen before. He should be smiling, relieved to see them, but he's not. He stares right through Baz as if she doesn't exist. "Somethin not right," she says.

Instantly Demi drops down to one knee, pretending to tie a shoe. Baz ducks down too. For a moment they are enclosed in a sea of legs. "I don't see uniform, don't see APA. No one lookin for us here, Baz. We done nothing."

They haven't. Haven't picked a pocket, swaddled a fat purse, but that doesn't mean they're safe, she knows that. He knows it too. "Talk to him," he says. "You can get close, no one see you. Find out why he got a face like a shaky ghost."

"And you get ticket for Tianna." Tianna is the next city up the coast, takes only four hours to get there. They could stay there, make plans, move on a little later.

"Tianna. OK."

"Wait for us out by the barriers, eh?"

He nods and skinnies through the legs and then eases himself into the queue for one of the ticket windows. Baz twists away and works her way back to the entrance, where she runs down the steps, sprints along the street, checking that no one's shadowing, and then comes in through the side door. Lucien's still standing just where he was before, like someone nailed his feet to the floor. She scans for cameras. None. But someone is watching Lucien, else he'd have moved, would have followed one of them. She scans again, slowly this time, checking faces, uniform, suits . . . suits! Over by the window, flicking the pages of the city paper, a suit—but not one she recognizes. One of Eduardo's men, she decides. If she doesn't know him, he won't know her—unless he sees her talking to Lucien.

She eases herself through the crowd, winding her way around till she's inches behind Lucien and hidden from the watching man. People thread and weave around them. She tugs the sleeve of his old jacket and grips his thin wrist. "Lucien." She feels him tense.

"Baz!" He ducks his head. "They got eyes on me, Baz." He hardly moves his lips, but his voice has a shake in it.

"We seen him."

"I swear I didn't tell."

She turns a little away. Still clear. Still just the one. "Don't feel fret for me an' Demi; we keepin safe."

"Just come here like you told me, Baz. Swear it. I come here, but I seen one of Fay's boys. Maybe I get followed, because the man come stepping at me soon as I get here."

Miguel. Rat Miguel! He's the one. Who else? None of the

others as good as him. And then he phones Eduardo, and Eduardo sends a suit to set a little trap, spin a little web.

"Man told me to stand here, not move, say he kill me if I move before you come. Say I got to hug you when you come in so he know it's you. Want me to give you away. He's hard, Baz. He's a killin man. You think Fay tell the boy to follow me?"

"No, Fay not the one." Her eyes keep flicking around the lobby, checking to see if there's more than one of them, hoping Demi has the tickets. They're so close. That train is just sitting out there waiting to take them away. If Eduardo just got this one suit and thinks that's enough to stop her and Demi he's not as smart as all that, but they have to move quick or the train is going to be heading north without them; and Lucien has to give this man the slip.

"Listen, Lucien," she says. "Tell him you got to go to the men's room. Tell him you can't wait. Tell him you'll be right back. Then you meet Demi an' me out by the barrier for Tianna." It might work.

Sweat trickles down his skinny face. "They sayin you an' Demi kill someone."

"That fool talk! You believe that? Who you think we go killin, Lucien? Mad dog bite you or somethin?"

"Tellin you what they sayin, Baz. TV sayin Captain's wife gone missing. They sayin you and Demi must've killed her. Everyone sayin it. Papers sayin it. Sayin you an' Demi hard. Sayin Captain wife like a saint woman, visit Demi when he sick in the hospital, but you an' Demi steal her ring, kill her, kill the guard. Sayin thief-rat like you two some sort o' plague that the police got to wash out of the city. That what they sayin." The words come spilling out like static on the radio when a storm's about to break.

She grips his arm, pinching it tight without meaning, pressing the jacket into the sore. He winces, and she quickly lets go. "They got our pictures? They know who we are?" She has no time for worrying about Señora Dolucca. Not now. She feels a knot in the back of her neck, tight like a policeman's grip.

"No," he murmurs. "Didn't see no picture . . ."

The knot eases. "Then go. Go now, tell the man what I say, and remember—Tianna."

He gives a faint nod of his head and Baz slides away through the moving crowd, glancing back again when she's at the side door to the lobby, sees Lucien moving, the man folding his paper. Then she darts out into the street and sprints back to the main entrance. Now is their chance: if they get away now, they can lose themselves in Tianna. They can move on. And there'll be three of them. She'll grow her hair, wear a skirt. They'll be a family. They'll be safe. All they have to do is get to the train. That's all.

She forces herself to walk up the wide steps and into the station. Sure people hurry, but children like her running always means the same thing to the uniform, means that that child's trouble and they'll snatch her up, snap her up like a dog on a rat.

Baz scans the concourse, but she can't see Demi. OK, she tells herself, he's at the platform. All she has to do is find the platform. She forces herself to slow down, walks to the center of the concourse and looks up at the board. How many times has she been here with Demi and never once done this, never noticed how many names are up there in small white letters, flickering a little, making it hard to read, times clicking up, platforms blank and then suddenly with a number? There! Tianna. Platform seven. She has four minutes!

She walks quickly to the barrier. Travelers are streaming

both ways along the platform and there are hawkers and fruit sellers and men selling hot dishes of food in spindles of greasy paper, and others bent double with a load of ice-cold water trunked up on their back.

But there's no sign of Demi. He said he would be there at the barrier. She looks back to the entrance. Maybe he went back to find her. Maybe he got snatched by the man . . .

Demi's too quick. Nobody snatch him. And he said meet at the barrier.

But where is he?

She wishes she didn't look like a scruff-rat from the Barrio. She wishes she was clean. She wishes she and Demi and Lucien were right here, walking down the platform together, boarding the train, finding their seats, leaving the city.

She jumps up onto a luggage trolley, ignoring the grizzled worker in his yellow train-company vest swearing at her and telling her to get down. "That train going to leave on time?" she asks him.

"How do I know? Get off it before I call a policeman. You want that?"

She doesn't bother to answer, just jumps down and jogs along the edge of the concourse. No time to worry about what people think of a running child now. She checks the benches where whole families just in from the country are sharing food, staring around them, excited like this is the heart of the city, the end of their journey. She checks little stalls selling cheap nothings to people who don't know better: a man throwing bones, telling fortunes—any fortune you want to hear, he's got a gift for telling it. And a woman writing letters for people who want to tell their family they're safe. Who's safe in the city?

*   *   *

The big clock says she has two minutes, but with no ticket and no Demi she's going nowhere. She stops. She turns round. And she sees a scuffle over by a newsstand near the platform where she'd been standing only half a minute before: two boys in a fight, a man waving his hands, a policeman walking toward them, quickening his pace, breaking into a run, the shrill bite of a whistle. She knows it's Demi, and the other's Miguel, scrapping like dogs, and the uniform's wading in, whistle shrilling, his baton cracking down.

Without thinking, she runs flat out toward them, just side-stepping an old couple who stop right in front of her, drawn like her by the mess of boys fighting. Momentarily distracted, she doesn't see the small boy hurtling toward her, glancing left and right as he runs, and they collide, shoulders cracking together and losing their footing, tangling up on the floor of the concourse. Instantly she pulls herself up, clutching her banged shoulder but ready to move.

The boy, chin grazed and bloody from where he struck the ground, blinks and almost yelps her name: "Baz!"

It's Sol, the baby of the gang, snot-faced and frightened and wriggling to his feet. She grabs him before he can escape. "What you doin?" she hisses. If she were a snake she would bite him she feels such cold rage for him, for all of them.

"Fay tol' me come here. Want to check you an' Demi safe."

She doesn't believe him. "You come with Miguel!"

"No. Swear it, Baz. Miguel gone from Fay. Let me go, we gotta run, Baz." He suddenly twists free and is off. She half starts after him, then stops. Over where the fight had been, the uniform man is hauling Demi up off the ground with one hand, his fist twisted in the neck of Demi's T-shirt and Demi's head flopped forward like he's a dead monkey or something. And the uniform's got his right hand with the baton in it high up in the air and he's bringing it down. Why? Demi doesn't even look half alive! But then she sees it's not Demi he's hitting but Miguel, his arm up shielding his head, and yelping as the baton strikes; and then the policeman has let the stick drop so it swings from his wrist and he can grab the boy with his right hand, grab him tight round the neck.

Both of them snatched tight. Two boys for the white van. Two boys for the Castle.

This is it. There is nothing. Baz just watches, her feet like lead, her shoulder throbbing, her face numb. Two times. Demi's luck is all used up. Nobody gets lucky two times. Nobody going to talk him out of the Castle.

Chapter Thirty-one

"LUCK!" Fay used to say. "What you mean, girl? Nobody get lucky. You use your eye, you see, you take opportunity. That the way to live; nobody get rich and stay out of the Castle if they go lookin for luck. You get my meaning?"

Baz sees the uniform no more than five meters from where she's standing, with the two boys dangling from his fists like he's going to hang them up to dry, and she knows that this is no time for thinking and wondering. There's got to be more uniform coming; maybe there's already an APA agent right by her shoulder, ready to snatch her up too. But none of that matters.

She takes a breath and launches herself in a sprint and then a dive, hitting the back of the policeman's legs just behind the knees so he comes down like a big tree, half crushing Baz's head with his backside as he falls.

There's shouting and someone pulling her one way and someone else with a hold on her leg tugging her another way. She lashes out with her left foot, connects, there's cursing and then she's free and somehow Demi's up, his face a grimace of pain and there's blood running down his arm, but he's holding her hand and they're running for the platform. Glancing back over her shoulder she sees the scuffle's started again. She glimpses Miguel up on his feet, aiming a kick at the policeman, and then she sees a thin face in the crowd grinning at her, hands raised, making a *T* with his fingers and then instantly weaving his way out of the commotion—Lucien!

Just ahead of them, the train for Tianna whistles and begins to pull away.

"Train's gone, Demi!"

"Keep going, Baz!"

They run as fast as they can, lungs bursting, past the platform, down the concourse and swing onto platform four. There's a local train pulling out, but Demi isn't intending them to go for this one. He urges her along the platform and then jumps down onto the empty tracks. For a second she hesitates, looking back again, remembering the way the APA man shot the running boy the last time she and Demi came up to Norte, but there's no APA behind them, just a railway official waving his hands angrily and blowing his whistle. Demi is already half running, down the middle of the track.

Thinking that he's crazy but that now there's no going back, she jumps down too. At the end of the platform he skips across the live rail and points to the Tianna train about twenty meters down the track, pulled up while half a dozen goods wagons are being shunted up and coupled on.

"Hurry!"

How long have they got? Once the train begins to move, that will be it. There is no other way out for them. Please, thinks Baz, please. Just a little time . . .

They run, hopping and jigging across the rails, trying to match their strides to hit the sleepers, and then, just as they get to the train and Demi is up and pulling open the door of the very last carriage, the train jolts and begins to move. Baz is a heartbeat behind him, but already the train is picking up speed. She reaches for the edge of the door, misses her step, stumbles and then, as she falls, Demi's hand is gripping hers, his good arm hauling her up, holding her tight, making her safe.

*   *   *

There's a couple of flat-faced country women in front of them, who look at them but say nothing, just move their legs out of the way as Demi pulls the door to. A fussy man across the aisle grumbles at them and holds his briefcase tight against his chest. "You got no right coming on this train. We all paid for our tickets."

"Paid for ours too," says Demi. "Come on, Baz."

The train jolts into movement while the two of them work their way up the carriage and into the next one. The conductor stops them, but when he sees the tickets Demi pulls out of his hip pocket he waves them along. "Places farther up," he says, and a few minutes later Baz is slumped in a window seat, the edges of the city rolling by beside her, and Demi grinning. "What you ever do without me to do your thinkin for you, Baz?" he says.

"Live easy life," she says.

"You should have seen me, Baz. When that uniform hold me up he think I'm dead, and then"—he makes a blow-whistling noise and snakes his hand—"I'm more alive than the miracle man. So what you doin chargin into the uniform like you some bulldozing crazy elephant girl?"

"Rescuin you, Demi. Like I doin all the time."

He puffs out his chest. "No need. Take an army to catch me."

"Demi, when you gonna grow up some?"

He laughs, delighted with himself. "When we get to Tianna maybe."

"You see what happen to Lucien?"

His grin fades. "No, that rat Miguel was on me soon as I buy the tickets, sneaking at my elbow, trying to rob me of what we got." He pats the bulge in his jeans pocket.

"Miguel never come here to thief," she says. "He come here spyin. He eyes for Eduardo."

"Guess he got greedy when he saw my roll of dollar." Demi grins. "He goin to wish he kept his hand from my pocket. Cost him a tooth for sure."

"Cost him more than that if the uniform grab him by the collar."

Demi shrugs. "You right about him all the time, Baz. He just street rat. What happen to Lucien? You tell him where we goin?"

"I tell him."

"He catch us in Tianna, Baz. That boy fool me all my life. He look nothin but skin an' bone but he like a bull, know what I mean? The way he ride that bike . . ." Demi puffs out his cheeks and shakes his head. "Straight for the gun. He snatch us free, Baz."

"I know that, Demi." She smiles. It's rare for Demi to admire anyone but himself. And she remembers Lucien's signal, *T* for Tianna. He would find them and then they would be three.

Demi turns his head and looks out of the window.

She watches the telephone lines dipping by. "They all gone from us, Demi. All the people in the Barrio."

He nods. "Fay too." He's silent for a minute and then says, "Gave us all that dollar she got save up. I think she want us to live a life. That's what I think."

Baz doesn't know what to think, but she remembers what she always hoped—that Fay and Demi would always be there, that she would always be a sister for her. But she never was a sister. Maybe she did such a hard thing when she gave away her baby that's what twisted her up. Maybe Fay had been giving away children so long, one here, another there, that she lost all feeling. Didn't care anymore. And then he, her own child, came back and she started to feel again. Maybe Sol had been telling the truth. Maybe Fay really did want to know they were both safe.

Outside, the last of the city slips behind them and dusty fields begin to unroll. She feels an ache in her eyes and in her chest, as if something in her whole frame is shrinking. It's nothing she's quite felt before, not even when they left Raoul behind the wire up on the Mountain. This is a sadness for what might have been. She doesn't cry, never has, Demi neither, not even when Fay beat him. She rubs the heel of her hand in her eye. "Demi, you think anyone gonna come looking for us?"

He shakes his head. "They look all they want, but we goin to be different when we get to Tianna, Baz. Gonna be different people."

She looks at him, about to tell him that he sounds different already, but he has his eyes closed now, his forehead leaning against her shoulder, and so she says nothing.

A little while later a woman comes down the compartment and takes a seat across the aisle. She offers Baz some fruit, fat juicy plums, and says to her, "You want to take some for your brother when he wakes up?"

"My brother," she says. "Yes, he'd like that. Thank you." Then she too closes her eyes and lets the rattle of the train taking her north ease her into sleep.

Epilogue

The river began to run again about the time they pulled down the Barrio. Cold water flowing from the dam, swallowing the mud, swirling around the rusted hulk up by the bend in the river, pulling and tugging at it until it rose right up and swung round on its old mooring, like it was ready to head upstream—a ghost ship looking for its ghost captain.

But then in the rainy season there was a black storm, and a flood came, a huge wall of water bursting the river's bank. And the old wreck was gone, floated right out to the ocean, some people said.

Shiny new buildings all crisp with glass and steel grew up on the waterfront. Cool offices for the new businesses that flourished in what came to be called Dolucca Town, after the police captain's son, Eduardo Dolucca, brilliant businessman and landlord of the new dockland. Everything gleamed in Dolucca Town. Even in the high heat when the city burned, fountains played and water flowed down the streets, washing them clean. There was never any rubbish, never any dirt, never any poor folk anywhere. Funny thing though—every once in a while a small spray of flowers and a tin cup of water was left in the corner of the courtyard of the tallest building, Eduardo Dolucca's very own office block. Not that he ever saw these common country flowers. The doorman always picked them up and took them home for his wife, imagining that it must be someone from the old Barrio days coming back remembering an old friend. He was right. To remember is important, and Mama Bali was remembered.

Eduardo's father, the police captain, retired a very rich man, richer, it has to be said, than most policemen get to be, though lonely perhaps. For a while there were rumors that his wife and daughter had been killed about the time the Barrio burned, but they never found the bodies and no one was ever arrested. Most people believed that she and the little girl just ran away from him because he was a violent man. It wasn't long though before their disappearance became an old story and they were forgotten. No doubt the police captain found comfort in the success of his son.

The poor, the petty thieves and the pickpockets drifted across to the bad land over the river, where the air smelled sticky from the rubbish mountain, and a dirty new Barrio slowly emerged there. And a sharp-faced woman with a pale face and fiery red hair taught children to steal. She never looked across the river to where she had once lived and she never again spoke to the boy whom she had given away as a baby and who had promised her a paradise.

Thank you for reading this
Feiwel and Friends book.

The Friends who made

SHE THIEF

possible are:

Jean Feiwel, *publisher*

Liz Szabla, *editor-in-chief*

Rich Deas, *creative director*

Elizabeth Fithian, *marketing director*

Holly West, *assistant to the publisher*

Dave Barrett, *managing editor*

Nicole Liebowitz Moulaison, *production manager*

Jessica Tedder, *associate editor*

Caroline Sun, *publicist*

Allison Remcheck, *editorial assistant*

Ksenia Winnicki, *marketing assistant*

Find out more about our authors
and artists and our future publishing at
www.feiwelandfriends.com.

OUR BOOKS ARE
FRIENDS FOR LIFE